the best of AMAZING

Amazing Stories

THE BEST OF *Amazing*

selected by JOSEPH ROSS

1967
Doubleday & Company, Inc., Garden City, New York

To Anita
Who helped
and
Two boys named
Michael and Kenneth
Who tried to

FOREWORD

In 1959 a lecture by Englishman C. P. Snow—the distinguished scientist and novelist—so aroused the community of scholars in most Western countries, including our own, that ever since then we've been hearing lively discussion on the fundamental point he made: that in the Western world today we now have *two* cultures instead of one, two intellectual communities—the scientific and the literary—each of which is becoming so divorced from the other that our universities can turn out thousands of young scientists who know next to nothing about art and literature—and thousands of Humanities majors who boldly declare their ignorance of even the most elementary scientific principles. The result: a widening chasm between two cultures, a dangerous gulf into which we all might fall.

But that was almost a decade ago, and—in America at least—there have been attempts to do something about it (some of which Snow has viewed with cautious optimism). At the time, though, at least one group—all those who read and love the best in science fiction—probably wondered then and still wonders now what all the fuss is about—because in every really first-class science-fiction story (from John Beynon Harris' trenchant "The Lost Machine" to Frank Herbert's semantic "Try to Remember") haven't they found the very thing Lord Snow sees as missing in our Cold War world—a natural fusion of two cultures that should be one? For, if you think about it, what *is* a science-fiction story anyway if it's not a *literary* exploration of some *scientific* idea, an imaginative try at predicting what impact science can have on man, on society, on the very quality of life on this planet?

What's more, steady readers of science fiction—especially those who have been around a while—also know that as a literary genre science fiction has understood this all along, that it has been coming to terms with science for a very long time indeed, in its modern form at least as far back as April of 1926, when Hugo Gernsback brought out the first issue of *Amazing Stories*—the world's first all-science-fiction magazine. Before that, of course, there were the literary giants—Poe, Verne, and Wells—but it was Gernsback (as farseeing as ever) who, half a lifetime ago, helped bring to a focus the growing taste for fiction blended with science, for "scientifiction," as he called it at first.

And he did so with such remarkable tales as "The Runaway Skyscraper" (Murray Leinster's first science-fiction story) and David H. Keller's "The Worm," surely one of the profoundest —and most terrifying—"Kelleryarns" ever to come out of the pulps. But these were just the beginning, forerunners of many wonderful things to come—tales such as Isaac Asimov's first sale, "Marooned off Vesta" (along with its sequel, "Anniversary," written twenty years later). Then there was Nelson S. Bond's

"The Priestess Who Rebelled" (which he now prefers to call "Pilgrimage"), certainly his best work in this field—and his own personal favorite as well. More recently we've seen "Sunfire!," a superb example of how beautifully Edmond Hamilton has caught the modern style.

That's the kind of story you'll find in *The Best of Amazing*, the first anthology to be drawn exclusively from the pages of a magazine that has been appearing regularly for the past forty years. By rights, of course, it's a book that should have been assembled by Gernsback himself—even though his official connection with the magazine ended in 1929—but that wasn't the way it worked out. Still, no matter who occupies his editorial chair later on and no matter who culls stories from the back files now, we all inevitably do so in the shadow of the man who has so often been called—and rightly—the Father of Science Fiction.

So this one's for you, Mr. Gernsback. Though long delayed, let it serve as the tribute we all pay to the man who brought two cultures together—long before anyone coined that fashionable phrase.

JOSEPH ROSS

Nutley, New Jersey
March 1967

CONTENTS

Long before making his John Wyndham pseudonym more famous than his real name—for modern classics like *Re-Birth* (1955) and *Consider Her Ways* (1956)—John Beynon Harris had already won himself a respectable niche in the science-fiction pantheon of the thirties. Largely because of the following short, in which—for the first time—the story was told from a machine's point of view, in this case a robot in trouble—made on Mars but stranded on a very primitive world indeed—a place called Earth.

THE LOST MACHINE

John Beynon Harris

"Father, here, quickly," Joan's voice called down the long corridor.

Dr. Falkner, who was writing, checked himself in mid-sentence at the sound of his daughter's urgency.

"Father," she called again.

"Coming," he shouted as he hastily levered himself out of his easy chair.

"This way," he added for the benefit of his two companions.

Joan was standing at the open door of the laboratory.

"It's gone," she said.

"What do you mean?" he inquired brusquely as he brushed past her into the room. "Run away?"

"No, not that." Joan's dark curls fell forward as her head shook. "Look there."

He followed the line of her pointing finger to the corner of the room.

A pool of liquid metal was seeping into a widening circle. In the middle there rose an elongated, silvery mound which seemed to melt and run even as he looked. Speechlessly he watched the central mass flow out into the surrounding fluid, pushing the edges gradually further and further across the floor.

Then the mound was gone—nothing lay before him but a shapeless spread of glittering silver, like a miniature lake of mercury.

For some moments the doctor seemed unable to speak. At length he recovered himself sufficiently to ask hoarsely:

"That—that was it?"

Joan nodded.

"It was recognizable when I first saw it," she said.

Angrily he turned upon her.

"How did it happen? Who did it?" he demanded.

"I don't know," the girl answered, her voice trembling a little as she spoke. "As soon as I got back to the house I came here just to see that it was all right. It wasn't in the usual corner, and as I looked around I caught sight of it over here—melting. I shouted for you as soon as I realized what was happening."

One of the doctor's companions stepped from the background.

"This," he inquired, "is—was the machine you were telling us about?"

There was a touch of a sneer in his voice as he put the question and indicated the quivering liquid with the toe of one shoe.

"Yes," the doctor admitted slowly. "That was it."

"And, therefore, you can offer no proof of the talk you were handing out to us?" added the other man.

"We've got film records," Joan began tentatively. "They're pretty good. . . ."

The second man brushed her words aside.

"Oh, yes?" he asked sarcastically. "I've seen pictures of New York as it's going to look in a couple of hundred years, but that don't mean that anyone went there to take 'em. There's a whole lot of things that can be done with movies," he insinuated.

Joan flushed, but kept silent. The doctor paid no attention. His brief flash of anger had subsided to leave him gazing sadly at the remains before him.

"Who can have done it?" he repeated half to himself.

His daughter hesitated for a moment before she suggested: "An accident?"

"I wonder," murmured the doctor.

"No—no, not quite that," she amended. "I think it was—lonely," the last word came out with a defiant rush.

There was a pause.

"Well, can you beat that?" said one of the others at last. "Lonely—a lonely machine: that's a good one. And I suppose you're trying to feed us that it committed suicide, miss? Well, it wouldn't surprise me any; nothing would, after the story your father gave us."

He turned on his heel and added to his companion:

"Come on. I guess someone'll be turnin' this place into a sanitarium soon—we'd better not be here when it happens."

With a laugh the two went out leaving father and daughter to stare helplessly at the residue of a vanished machine.

At length Joan sighed and moved away. As she raised her eyes, she became aware of a pile of paper on the corner of a bench. She did not remember how it came to be there and crossed with idle curiosity to examine it.

The doctor was aroused from his reverie by the note of excitement in her voice.

"Look here, father," she called sharply.

"What's that?" he asked, catching sight of the wad of sheets in her hand.

As he came closer, he could see that the top one was covered with strange characters.

"What on earth. . . ?" he began.

Joan's voice was curt with his stupidity.

"Don't you see?" she cried. "It's written this for us."

The doctor brightened for a moment; then the expression of gloom returned to his face.

"But how can we. . . ?"

"The thing wasn't a fool—it must have learned enough of our language to put a key in somewhere to all this weird stuff, even if it couldn't write the whole thing in English. Look, this might be it; it looks even queerer than the rest."

Several weeks of hard work followed for Joan in her efforts to decipher the curious document, but she held on with painstaking labor until she was able to lay the complete text before her father. That evening he picked up the pile of typed sheets and read steadily, without interrupting, to the end. . . .

ARRIVAL

As we slowed to the end of our journey, Banuff began to show signs of excitement.

"Look," he called to me. "The third planet, at last."

I crossed to stand beside him and together we gazed upon a stranger scene than any other fourth planet eyes have ever seen.

Though we were still high above the surface, there was plenty to cause us astonishment.

In place of our own homely red vegetation, we beheld a brilliant green. The whole land seemed to be covered with it. Anywhere and everywhere it clung and thrived as though it needed no water. On the fourth planet, which the third planet men call Mars, the vegetation grows only in or around the canals, but here we could not even see any canals. The only sign of irrigation was one bright streak of water in the distance, twisting senselessly over the countryside—a symbolic warning of the incredible world we had reached.

Here and there our attention was attracted by outcroppings of various strange rocks amid all this green. Great masses of stone which sent up plumes of black smoke.

"The internal fires must be very near the surface of this world," Banuff said, looking doubtfully at the rising vapors. "See in how many places the smoke breaks out. I should doubt whether it has been possible for animal life to evolve on such a planet. It is possible yet that the ground may be too hot for us—or rather for me."

There was a regret in his tone. The manner in which he voiced the last sentence stirred my sympathy. There are so many disadvantages in human construction which do not occur in us machines, and I knew that he was eager to obtain first hand knowledge of the third planet.

For a long time we gazed in silent speculation at this queer, green world. At last Banuff broke the silence.

"I think we'll risk a landing there, Zat," he said, indicating a smooth, open space.

"You don't think it might be liquid," I suggested, "it looks curiously level."

"No," he replied, "I fancy it's a kind of close vegetation. Anyway, we can risk it."

A touch on the lever sent the machine sinking rapidly towards a green rectangle, so regular as to suggest the work of sentient creatures. On one of its sides lay a large stone outcrop, riddled with holes and smoking from the top like the rest, while on the other three sides, thick vegetation rose high and swayed in the wind.

"An atmosphere which can cause such commotion must be very dense," commented Banuff.

"That rock is peculiarly regular," I said, "and the smoking points are evenly spaced. Do you suppose. . . ?

The slight jar of our landing interrupted me.

"Get ready, Zat," Banuff ordered.

I was ready. I opened the inner door and stepped into the

air-lock. Banuff would have to remain inside until I could find out whether it was possible for him to adjust. Men may have more power of originality than we, and they do possess a greater degree of adaptability than any other form of life, but their limitations are, nevertheless, severe. It might require a deal of ponderous apparatus to enable Banuff to withstand the conditions, but for me, a machine, adaptation was simple.

The density of the atmosphere made no difference save slightly to slow my movements. The temperature, within very wide limits, had no effect upon me.

"The gravity will be stronger," Banuff had warned me; "this is a much larger planet than ours."

It had been easy to prepare for that by the addition of a fourth pair of legs.

Now, as I walked out of the air-lock, I was glad of them; the pull of the planet was immense.

After a moment or so of minor adjustment, I passed around our machine to the window where Banuff stood, and held up the instruments for him to see. As he read the air pressure meter, the gravity indicator and the gas proportion scale, he shook his head. He might slowly adapt himself partway to the conditions, but an immediate venture was out of the question.

It had been agreed between us that in such an event I should perform the exploration and specimen collecting while he examined the neighborhood from the machine.

He waved his arm as a signal and, in response, I set off at a good pace for the surrounding green and brown growths. I looked back as I reached them to see our silvery craft floating slowly up into the air.

A second later, there came a stunning explosion; a wave of sound so strong in this thick atmosphere that it almost shattered my receiving diaphragm.

The cause of the disaster must always remain a mystery: I only know that when I looked up, the vessel was nowhere to be seen—only a rain of metal parts dropping to earth all about me.

Cries of alarm came from the large stone outcrop; and simultaneously human figures appeared at the lowest of its many openings.

They began to run towards the wreck, but my speed was far greater than theirs. They can have made but half the distance while I completed it. As I flashed across, I could see them falter and stop with ludicrous expressions of dismay on their faces.

"Lord, did you see that?" cried one of them.

"What the devil was it?" called another.

"Looked like a coffin on legs," somebody said. "Moving some, too."

FLIGHT

Banuff lay in a ring of scattered débris.

Gently I raised him on my fore-rods. A very little examination showed that it was useless to attempt any assistance: he was too badly broken. He managed to smile faintly at me and then slid into unconsciousness.

I was sorry. Though Banuff was not of my own kind, yet he was of my own world and on the long trip I had grown to know him well. These humans are so fragile. Some little thing here or there breaks—they stop working and then, in a short time, they are decomposing. Had he been a machine, like myself, I could have mended him, replaced the broken parts and made him as good as new, but with these animal structures one is almost helpless.

I became aware, while I gazed at him, that the crowd of men and women had drawn closer, and I began to suffer for the first time from what has been my most severe disability on the third planet—I could not communicate with them.

Their thoughts were understandable, for my sensitive plate was tuned to receive human mental waves, but I could not make myself understood. My language was unintelligible to them, and their minds, either from lack of development or some other cause, were unreceptive of my thought-radiations.

As they approached, huddled into a group, I made an astonishing discovery—they were afraid of me.

Men afraid of a machine.

It was incomprehensible. Why should they be afraid? Surely man and machine are natural complements: they assist one another. For a moment I thought I must have misread their minds—it was possible that thoughts registered differently on this planet, but it was a possibility I soon dismissed.

There were only two reasons for this apprehension. The one, that they had never seen a machine or, the other, that third planet machines had pursued a line of development inimical to them.

I turned to show Banuff lying inert on my fore-rods. Then, slowly, so as not to alarm them, I approached. I laid him down softly on the ground nearby and retired a short distance. Experience has taught me that men like their own broken forms to be dealt with by their own kind. Some stepped forward to examine him, the rest held their ground, their eyes fixed upon me.

Banuff's dark coloring appeared to excite them not a little. Their own skins were pallid from lack of ultra-violet rays in their dense atmosphere.

"Dead?" asked one.

"Quite dead," another one nodded. "Curious looking fellow," he continued. "Can't place him ethnologically at all. Just look at the frontal formation of the skull—very odd. And the size of his ears, too, huge: the whole head is abnormally large."

"Never mind him now," one of the group broke in, "he'll keep. That's the thing that puzzles me," he went on, looking in my direction. "What the devil do you suppose it is?"

They all turned wondering faces towards me. I stood motionless and waited while they summed me up.

"About six feet long," ran the thought of one of them. "Two feet broad and two deep. White metal, might be—(his thought conveyed nothing to me). Four legs to a side, fixed about halfway up—joined rather like a crab's, so are the arm-like things in front: but all metal. Wonder what the array of instruments and lenses on this end are? Anyhow, whatever kind of power it uses, it seems to have run down now. . . ."

Hesitatingly he began to advance.

I tried a word of encouragement.

The whole group froze rigid.

"Did you hear that?" somebody whispered. "It—it spoke."

"Loud speaker," replied the one who had been making an inventory of me. Suddenly his expression brightened.

"I've got it," he cried. "Remote control—a telephony and television machine worked by remote control."

So these people did know something of machinery, after all. He was far wrong in his guess, but in my relief I took a step forward.

An explosion roared: something thudded on my body case and whirred away. I saw that one of the men was pointing a hollow rod at me, and I knew that he was about to make another explosion.

The first had done no injury but another might crack one of my lenses.

I turned and made top speed for the high, green vegetation. Two or three more bursts roared behind, but nothing touched me. The weapon was very primitive and grossly inaccurate.

DISAPPOINTMENT

For a day and a night I continued on among the hard stemmed growths.

For the first time since my making, I was completely out of touch with human control, and my existence seemed meaningless. The humans have a curious force they call ambition. It drives them, and, through them, it drives us. This force which keeps them active, we lack. Perhaps, in time, we machines will acquire it. Something of the kind—self-preservation which is allied to it—must have made me leave the man with the explosive tube and taken me into the strange country. But it was not enough to give me an objective. I seemed to go on because —well, because my machinery was constructed to go on.

On the way I made some odd discoveries.

Every now and then my path would be crossed by a band of hard matter, serving no useful purpose which I could then understand. Once, too, I found two unending rods of iron fixed horizontally to the ground and stretching away into the distance on either side. At first I thought they might be a method of guarding the land beyond, but they presented no obstacle.

Also, I found that the frequent outcroppings of stone were not natural, but laboriously constructed. Obviously this primitive race, with insufficient caves to hold its growing numbers, had been driven to construct artificial caves. The puzzling smoke arose from their method of heating these dwellings with naked fire—so wasteful a system of generating heat that no flame has been seen on the fourth planet, save in an accident, for thousands of years.

It was during the second day that I saw my first machine on this planet.

It stood at the side of one of the hard strips of land which had caused me so much wonder. The glitter of light upon its bright parts caught my lenses as I came through the bushes. My delight knew no bounds—at last I had found a being of my own kind. In my excitement I gave a call to attract its attention.

There was a flurry of movement round the far side and a human figure raised its head to look at me.

I was able to tell that she was a woman despite the strange coverings that the third planet humans put upon themselves. She stared at me, her eyes widening in surprise while I could feel the shock in her mind. A spanner dropped from her hand and then, in a flash, she was into the machine, slamming the door behind her. There came a frantic whirring as she pressed a knob, but it produced no other result.

Slowly I continued to advance and as I came, the agitation in her mind increased. I had no wish to alarm her—it would have been more peaceful had her thought waves ceased to bombard me—but I was determined to know this machine.

As I drew clear of the bushes, I obtained a full view of the thing for the first time and disappointment hit me like a blow. The thing had wheels. Not just necessary parts of its internal arrangements, but wheels actually in contact with the ground. In a flash the explanation of all these hard streaks came to me. Unbelievable though it may seem, this thing could only follow a track specially built for it.

Later I found that this was more or less true of all third planet land machines, but my first discouragement was painful. The primitive barbarity of the thing saddened me more than any discovery yet made.

Forlornly, and with little hope, I spoke to it.

There was no answer.

It stood there dumbly inert upon its foolish wheels as though it were a part of the ground itself.

Walking closer, I began to examine with growing disgust its crude internal arrangements. Incredibly, I found that its only means of propulsion was by a series of jerks from frequent explosions. Moreover, it was so ludicrously unorganized that both driving engine and brakes could be applied at the same time.

Sadly, as I gazed at the ponderous parts within, I began to feel that I was indeed alone. Until this encounter, my hope of discovering an intelligent machine had not really died. But now I knew that such a thing could not exist in the same world with this monster.

One of my fore-rods brushed against a part of it with a rasping sound, and there came a startled cry of alarm from within. I looked up to the glass front where the woman's face peered affrightedly. Her mind was in such a state of confusion that it was difficult to know her wants clearly.

She hoped that I would go away—no, she wished the car would start and carry her away—she wondered whether I were an animal, whether I even really existed. In a jumble of emotions she was afraid and at the same time was angry with herself for being afraid. At last I managed to grasp that the machine was unable to run. I turned to find the trouble.

As I labored with the thing's horrible vitals, it became clear to me why men, such as I had met, showed fear of me. No wonder they feared machines when their own mechanisms were as inefficient and futile as this. What reliance or trust could they place in a machine so erratic—so helpless that it could not even temporarily repair itself? It was not under its own control and only partially under theirs. Third planet men's attitude became understandable—commendable—if all their machines were as uncertain as this.

The alarm in the woman's mind yielded to amazement as she leaned forward and watched me work. She seemed to think me unreal, a kind of hallucination:

"I must be dreaming," she told herself. "It's impossible; some kind of horrid nightmare. . . ."

There came a flash of panic at the thought of madness, but her mind soon rebalanced.

"I just don't understand it," she said firmly and then, as though that settled it, proceeded to wait with a growing calm.

At last I had finished. As I wiped the thing's coarse, but necessary oil from my fore-rods, I signalled her to push again on the black knob. The whirr this time was succeeded by a roar—never would I have believed that a machine could be so inefficient.

Through the pandemonium I received an impression of gratitude on my thought plate. Mingling traces of nervousness remained, but first stood gratitude.

Then she was gone. Down the hard strip I watched the disgusting machine dwindle away to a speck.

Then I turned back to the bushes and went slowly on my way. Sadly I thought of the far away, red fourth planet and knew that my fate was sealed. I could not build a means of return. I was lost—the only one of my kind upon this primitive world.

THE BEASTS

They came upon me as I crossed one of the smooth, green spaces so frequent on this world.

My thought-cells were puzzling over my condition. On the fourth planet I had felt interest or disinterest, inclination or the lack of it, but little more. Now I had discovered reactions in myself which, had they lain in a human being, I should have called emotions. I was, for instance, lonely: I wanted the company of my own kind. Moreover, I had begun to experience excitement or, more particularly, apathy.

An apathetic machine!

I was considering whether this state was a development from the instinct of self-preservation, or whether it might not be due to the action of surrounding matter on my chemical cells, when I heard them coming.

First there was a drumming in my diaphragm, swelling gradually to a thunderous beat which shook the ground. Then I turned to see them charging down upon me.

Enormous beasts, extinct on my planet a million years, covered with hair and bearing spikes on their heads. Four-footed survivals of savagery battering across the land in unreasoning ferocity.

Only one course was possible since my escape was cut off by the windings of one of the imbecile-built canals. I folded my legs beneath me, crossed my fore-rods protectingly over my lenses and diaphragms, and waited.

They slowed as they drew close. Suspiciously they came up to me and snuffled around. One of them gave a rap to my side with his spiked head, another pawed my case with a hoofed foot. I let them continue: they did not seem to offer any immediate danger. Such primitive animals, I thought, would be incapable of sustaining interest and soon move off elsewhere.

But they did not. Snuffling and rooting continued all around me. At last I determined to try an experimental waving of my fore-rods. The result was alarming. They plunged and milled around, made strange bellowing noises and stamped their hooves, but they did not go away. Neither did they attack, though they snorted and pawed the more energetically.

In the distance I heard a man's voice; his thought reached me faintly.

"What the 'ell's worritin' them dam' cattle, Bill?" he called.

"Dunno," came the reply of another. "Let's go an' 'ave a look."

The beasts gave way at the approach of the man and I could hear some of them thudding slowly away, though I did not, as yet, care to risk uncovering my lenses.

The men's voices drew quite near.

"'Strewth," said the first, "'ow did that get 'ere, Bill?"

"Search me," answered the other. "Wasn't 'ere 'arf an hour ago—that I'll swear. What is it, any'ow?"

"'Anged if I know. 'Ere, give us a 'and and we'll turn it over."

At this moment it seemed wise to make a movement; my balancers might be slow in adjusting to an inverted position.

There was a gasp, then:

"Bill," came an agitated whisper, "did you see that rod there at the end? It moved, blessed if it didn't."

"Go on," scoffed the other. "'Ow could a thing like that move? You'll be sayin' next that it. . . ."

I unfolded my legs and turned to face them.

For a moment both stood rooted, horror on their faces; then, with one accord, they turned and fled towards a group of their buildings in the distance. I followed them slowly: it seemed as good a direction as any other.

The buildings, not all of stone, were arranged so as almost to enclose a square. As the men disappeared through an opening in one side, I could hear their voices raised in warning and others demanding the reason for their excitement. I turned the corner in time to face a gaggling group of ten or twelve. Abruptly it broke as they ran to dark openings in search of safety. All, save one.

I halted and looked at this remaining one. He stared back, swaying a little as he stood, his eyes blinking in a vague uncertainty.

"What is it?" he exclaimed at last with a strange explosiveness, but as though talking to himself.

He was a sorely puzzled man. I found his mental processes difficult to follow. They were jumbled and erratic, hopping from this mind picture to that in uncontrolled jerks. But he was unafraid of me and I was glad of it. The first third planet man I had met who was not terror-ridden. Nevertheless, he seemed to doubt my reality.

"You fellowsh shee the shame s'I do?" he called deafeningly. Muffled voices all around assured him that this was so.

"Thash all right, then," he observed with relief, and took a step forward.

I advanced slowly not to alarm him and we met in the middle of the yard. Laying a rough hand on my body case he seemed to steady himself; then he patted me once or twice.

"Goo' ol' dog," he observed seriously. "Goo' ol' feller. Come 'long, then."

Looking over his shoulder to see that I followed and making strange whistling noises the while, he led the way to a building made of the hard, brown vegetable matter. At openings all about us scared faces watched our progress with incredulous amazement.

He opened the door and waved an uncertain hand in the direction of a pile of dried stalks which lay within.

"Goo' ol' dog," he repeated. "Lie down. There'sh a goo' dog."

In spite of the fact that I, a machine, was being mistaken for a primitive animal, I obeyed the suggestion—after all, he, at least, was not afraid.

He had a little difficulty with the door fastening as he went out.

THE CIRCUS

There followed one of those dark periods of quiet. The animal
origin of human beings puts them under the disability of requiring frequent periods of recuperation, and since they cannot
use the infra-red rays for sight, as we do, their rests take place
at times when they are unable to see.

With the return of sunlight came a commotion outside the
door. Expostulations were being levelled at one named Tom—
he who had led me here the previous day.

"You ain't really goin' to let it out?" one voice was asking
nervously.

"'Course I am. Why not?" Tom replied.

"The thing don't look right to me. I wouldn't touch it," said
another.

"Scared, that's what you are," Tom suggested.

"P'raps I am—and p'raps you'd 've been scared last night
if you 'adn't been so far gone."

"Well, it didn't do nothin' to me when I'd had a few,"
argued Tom, "so why should it now?"

His words were confident enough, but I could feel a trepida-
tion in his mind.

"It's your own funeral," said the other. "Don't say afterwards
that I didn't warn you."

I could hear the rest of them retire to what they considered a
safe distance. Tom approached, making a show of courage with
his words.

"Of course I'm goin' to let it out. What's more, I'm takin' it
to a place I know of—it ought to be worth a bit."

"You'll never. . . ."

"Oh, won't I?"

He rattled open the door and addressed me in a fierce voice
which masked a threatening panic.

"Come on," he ordered, "out of it."

He almost turned to run as he saw me rise, but managed to master the impulse with an effort. Outwardly calm, he led the way to one of those machines which use the hard tracks, opened a rear door and pointed inside.

"In you get," he said.

I doubt if ever a man was more relieved and surprised than he, when I did so.

With a grain of triumph he turned around, gave a mocking sweep with his cap to the rest, and climbed into the front seat.

My last sight as we roared away was of a crowd of open-mouthed men.

The sun was high when we reached our destination. The limitations of the machine were such that we had been delayed more than once to replenish fuel and water before we stopped, at last, in front of large gates set in a wooden fence.

Over the top could be seen the upper parts of pieces of white cloth tightly stretched over poles and decorated by further pieces of colored cloth flapping in the wind. I had by this time given up the attempt to guess the purposes of third planet constructions; such incredible things managed to exist on this primitive world that it was simpler to wait and find out.

From behind the fence a rhythmical braying noise persisted; then there came the sound of a man's voice shouting above the din:

"What do you want—main entrance is round the other side."

"Where's the boss?" called Tom. "I got something for him."

The doors opened for us.

"Over there in his office," said the man, jerking a thumb over his shoulder.

As we approached I could see that the third planet mania for wheels had led them even to mount the "office" thus.

Tom entered and reappeared shortly, with another man.

"There it is," he said, pointing to me, "and there ain't another like it nowhere. The only all-metal animal in the world —how'll that look on the posters?"

The other regarded me with no enthusiasm in his eyes and a deal of disbelief in his mind.

"That long box thing?" he inquired.

"Sure, 'that box thing.' Here, you," he added to me, "get out of it."

Both retreated a step as I advanced; the new man looked apprehensively at my fore-rods.

"You're sure it's safe?" he asked nervously.

"Safe?" said Tom. "'Course it's safe."

To prove it he came across and patted my case.

"I'm offering you the biggest noise in the show business. It's worth ten times what I'm asking for it—I tell you, there ain't another one in the world."

"Well, I ain't heard of another," admitted the showman grudgingly. "Where'd you get it?"

"Made it," said Tom blandly. "Spare time."

The man continued to regard me with little enthusiasm.

"Can it do anything?" he asked at last.

"Can it—?" began Tom indignantly. "Here you," he added, "fetch that lump of wood."

When I brought it, the other looked a trifle less doubtful.

"What's inside it?" he demanded.

"Secrets," said Tom shortly.

"Well, it's got to stop bein' a secret before I buy it. What sort of fool do you take me for? Let's have a look at the thing's innards."

"No," said Tom, sending a nervous look sideways at me. "Either you take it or leave it."

"Ho, so that's your little game, is it? I'm to be the sucker who buys the thing and then finds the kid inside, workin' it. It wouldn't surprise me to find that the police'd like to know about this."

"There ain't no kid inside," denied Tom; "it's just—just secret works. That's what it is."

"I'll believe you when I see."

Tom waited a moment before he answered.

"All right," he said desperately, "we'll get the blasted lid off of it. . . . Here, hey, come back you."

The last was a shout to me but I gave it no notice. It was one thing to observe the curious ways of these humans, but it was quite a different matter to let them pry into my machinery. The clumsiness of such as Tom was capable of damaging my arrangements seriously.

"Stop it," bawled Tom, behind me.

A man in my path landed a futile blow on my body case as I swept him aside. Before me was the biggest of all the cloth covered erections.

"Here," I thought, "there will be plenty of room to hide."

I was wrong. Inside, in a circular space, stood a line of four footed animals. They were unlike the others I had met, in that they had no spikes on their heads and were of a much slenderer build, but they were just as primitive. All around, in tier upon tier of rings, sat hundreds of human beings.

Just a glimpse, I had, and then the animals saw me. They bolted in all directions and shouts of terror arose from the crowd.

I don't remember clearly what happened to me, but somewhere and somehow in the confusion which followed I found Tom in the act of starting his car. His first glance at me was one of pure alarm; then he seemed to think better of it.

"Get in," he snapped, "we've got to get clear of this somehow —and quick."

Although I could make far better speed than that preposterous machine, it seemed better to accompany him than to wander aimlessly.

THE CRASH

Sadly, that night I gazed up at the red, fourth planet.

There rolled a world which I could understand, but here, all around me, was chaos, incredible, unreasoning madness.

With me, in the machine, sat three friends of Tom's whom he had picked up at the last town, and Tom himself who was steering the contraption. I shut my plate off from their thoughts and considered the day I had spent.

Once he was assured that we were free from pursuit, Tom had said to himself:

"Well, I guess that deserves a drink."

Then he stopped on a part of the hard strip which was bordered by a row of artificial caves.

Continually, as the day wore on, he led me past gaping crowds into places where every man held a glass of colored liquid. Strange liquids they were, although men do not value water on the third planet. And each time he proudly showed me to his friends in these places, he came to believe more firmly that he had created me.

Towards sunset something seemed to go seriously wrong with his machinery. He leaned heavily upon me for support, and his voice became as uncertain as his thoughts were jumbled.

"Anybody comin' my way?" he had inquired at last, and at that invitation the other three men had joined us.

The machine seemed to have become as queer as the men. In the morning it had held a straight line, but now it swayed from side to side, sometimes as though it would leave the track. Each time it just avoided the edge, all four men would break off their continuous wailing sounds to laugh senselessly and loudly.

It was while I struggled to find some meaning in all this madness that the disaster occurred.

Another machine appeared ahead. Its lights showed its approach and ours must have been as plain. Then an astounding thing happened. Instead of avoiding one another as would two intelligent machines, the two lumbering masses charged blindly together. Truly this was an insane world.

There came a rending smash. Our machine toppled over on its side. The other left the hard strip, struck one of the growths at the side of the road and burst into naked flames.

None of the four men seemed more than a little dazed. As one of them scrambled free, he pointed to the blaze.

"Thash good bonfire," he said. "Jolly good bonfire. Wonder if anybody'sh inshide?"

They all reeled over to examine the wreck while I, forgotten, waited for the next imbecility to occur on this nightmare world.

"It'sh a girl," said Tom's voice.

One of the others nodded solemnly.

"I think you're right," he agreed with difficult dignity.

After an interval, there came the girl's voice:

"But what shall I do? I'm miles from home."

"'S'all righ'," said Tom. "Quite all righ'. You come along with me. Nishe fellow I am."

I could read the intention behind his words—so could the girl.

There was the sound of a scuffle.

"No, you don't, my beauty. No runnin' away. Dangeroush for li'l girlsh—'lone in the dark."

She started to scream, but a hand quickly stifled the sound.

I caught the upsurge of terror in her mind and at that moment I knew her.

The girl whose machine I had mended—who had been grateful.

In a flash I was amongst them. Three of the men started back in alarm, but not Tom. He was contemptuous of me because I had obeyed him. He lifted a heavy boot to send it crashing at my lens. Human movement is slow: before his leg had completed the back swing, I had caught it and whirled him away. The rest started futilely to close in on me.

I picked the girl up in my fore-rods and raced away into the darkness out of their sight.

DISCOURAGEMENT

At first she was bewildered and not a little frightened, though our first meeting must have shown that I intended no harm.

Gently I placed her on top of my case-work and, holding her there with my fore-rods, set off in the direction of her journey. She was hurt, blood was pouring down her right arm.

We made the best speed my eight legs could take us. I was

afraid lest from lack of blood her mind might go blank and fail
to direct me. At length it did. Her mental vibrations had been
growing fainter and fainter until they ceased altogether. But she
had been thinking ahead of us, picturing the way we should go,
and I had read her mind.

At last, confronted by a closed door she had shown me, I
pushed it down and held her out on my fore-rods to her father.

"Joan. . . ?" he said, and for the moment seemed unsur-
prised at me—the only third planet man who ever was. Not until
he had dressed his daughter's wounds and roused her to consciousness did he even look at me again.

There is little more. They have been kind, those two. They
have tried to comprehend, though they cannot. He once removed a piece of my casing—I allowed him to do so, for he
was intelligent—but he did not understand. I could feel him
mentally trying to classify my structure among electrically
operated devices—the highest form of power known to him, but
still too primitive.

This whole world is too primitive. It does not even know the
metal of which I am made. I am a freak . . . a curiosity outside comprehension.

These men long to know how I was built; I can read in their
minds that they want to copy me. There is hope for them: some
day, perhaps, they will have real machines of their own. . . .
But not through my help will they build them, nothing of
me shall go to making them.

. . . I know what it is to be an intelligent machine in a
world of madness. . . .

The doctor looked up as he turned the last page.

"And so," he said, "it dissolved itself with my acids."

He walked slowly over to the window and gazed up to Mars,
swimming serenely among a myriad stars.

"I wonder," he murmured, "I wonder."

He handed the typewritten sheets back to his daughter.

"Joan, my dear, I think it would be wisest to burn them.
We have no desire to be certified."

Joan nodded.

"As you prefer, father," she agreed.

The papers curled, flared and blackened on the coals—but Joan kept a copy.

All the while this anthology was being assembled, we were especially glad about one thing—that still another classic "Kelleryarn" would be getting back into print where it belongs. We also knew that Colonel Keller himself—nearing his eighty-sixth year and no longer actively writing—would probably get a kick out of hanging on into the sixties and appearing with some of the newer science-fiction masters like Frank Herbert and Isaac Asimov. That last possibility, however, was never meant to be, not for David H. Keller at any rate, for on July 13, 1966, the good doctor died of heart failure. So instead of as one more tribute to a giant from the days of Hugo Gernsback, "The Worm"—its terrifying potency undiminished by the passing years—now memorializes a man who wanted to write great literature—and did.

THE WORM

David H. Keller, M.D.

The miller patted his dog on the head, as he whispered: "We are going to stay here. Our folks, your ancestors and mine, have been here for nearly two hundred years, and queer it would be to leave now because of fear."

The gristmill stood, a solid stone structure, in an isolated Vermont valley. Years ago every day had been a busy one for the mill and the miller, but now only the mill wheel was busy. There was no grist for the mill and no one lived in the valley. Blackberries and hazel grew where once the pastures had been green. The hand of time had passed over the farms, and the only folk left were sleeping in the churchyard. A family of squirrels nested in the pulpit, while on the tombstones silent snails left their cryptic messages in silvery streaks. Thompson's Valley was being handed back to nature. Only the old bachelor miller, John Staples, remained. He was too proud and too stubborn to do anything else.

The mill was his home, even as it had served all of his family for a home during the last two hundred years. The first Staples had built it to stay, and it was still as strong as on the day it was finished. There was a basement for the machinery of the mill, the first floor was the place of grinding and storage, and the upper two floors served as the Staples homestead. The building was warm in winter and cool in summer. Times past it had sheltered a dozen Stapleses at a time; now it provided a home for John Staples and his dog.

He lived there with his books and his memories. He had no friends and desired no associates. Once a year he went to the nearest town and bought supplies of all kinds, paying for them in gold. It was supposed that he was wealthy. Rumor credited him with being a miser. He attended to his own business, asked the world to do the same, and on a winter's evening laughed silently over Burton and Rabelais, while his dog chased rabbits in his heated sleep upon the hearth.

The winter of 1935 was beginning to threaten the valley, but with an abundance of food and wood in the mill, the recluse looked forward to a comfortable period of desuetude. No matter how cold the weather, he was warm and contented. With the inherent ability of his family, he had been able to convert the water power into electricity. When the wheel was frozen, he used the electricity stored in his storage batteries. Every day he puttered around among the machinery which it was his pride to keep in perfect order. He assured the dog that if business ever did come to the mill, he would be ready for it.

It was on Christmas Day of that winter that he first heard the noise. Going down to the basement to see that nothing had been injured by the bitter freeze of the night before, his attention was attracted, even while descending the stone steps, by a peculiar grinding noise that seemed to come from out of the ground. His ancestors, building for permanency, had not only put in solid foundations, but had paved the entire basement with slate flagstones three feet wide and as many inches thick. Between these the dust of two centuries had gathered and hardened.

Once his feet were on this pavement, Staples found that he could not only hear the noise, but he could also feel through the flagstones the vibrations which accompanied it. Even through his heavy leather boots he could feel the rhythmic pulsations. Pulling off his mittens, he stooped over and put his finger tips on the stone. To his surprise it was warm in spite of the fact that the temperature had been below zero the night before. The vibration was more distinct to his finger tips than it had been to his feet. Puzzled, he threw himself on the slate stone and put his ear to the warm surface.

The sound he now heard made him think of the grinding of the millstones when he was a boy and the farmers had brought corn to be ground into meal. There had been no corn meal ground in the mill for fifty years, yet here was the sound of stone scraping slowly and regularly on stone. He could not understand it. In fact, it was some time before he tried to explain it. With the habit born of years of solitary thinking, he first collected all the available facts about this noise. He knew that during the long winter evenings he would have time enough to do his thinking.

Going to his sitting room, he secured a walking stick of ash and went back to the cellar. Holding the handle of the cane lightly, he placed the other end on a hundred different spots on the floor, and each time he held it long enough to determine the presence or absence of vibration. To his surprise he found that while it varied in strength, it was present all over the cellar with the exception of the four corners. The maximum intensity was about in the center.

That evening he concentrated on the problem before him. He had been told by his grandfather that the mill was built on solid rock. As a young man he had helped clean out a well near the mill and recalled that, instead of being dug out of gravel or dirt, it had the appearance of being drilled out of solid granite. There was no difficulty in believing that the earth under the mill was also solid rock. There was no reason for thinking otherwise. Evidently some of these strata of stone had become loose and were slipping and twisting under the mill. The simplest explanation was the most reasonable: it was simply a geological phenomenon. The behavior of the dog, however, was not so easily explained. He had refused to go with his master into the cellar, and now, instead of sleeping in comfort before the fire, he was in an attitude of strained expectancy. He did not bark, or even whine, but crept silently to his master's chair, looking at him anxiously.

The next morning the noise was louder. Staples heard it in his bed, and at first he thought that some bold adventurer had come into the forest and was sawing down a tree. That was what it sounded like, only softer and longer in its rhythm. Buzz-zzzz—Buzzzzz-Buzzzzzz. The dog, distinctly unhappy, jumped up on the bed and crawled uneasily so he could nuzzle the man's hand.

Through the four legs of the bed, Staples could feel the same vibration that had come to him through the handle of his cane the day before. That made him think. The vibration was now powerful enough to be appreciated, not through a walking stick, but through the walls of the building. The noise could be heard as well on the third floor as in the cellar.

He tried to fancy what it sounded like—not what it was—but what it was like. The first idea had been that it resembled a saw going through oak; then came the thought of bees swarming, only these were large bees and millions of them; but finally all he could think of was the grinding of stones in a gristmill, the upper stone against the lower; and now the sound was Grrrrrrr—Grrrrrrrr instead of Bzzzzzzzzz or Hummmmmmmm.

That morning he took longer than usual to shave and was more methodical than was his wont in preparing breakfast for himself and the dog. It seemed as though he knew that sometime he would have to go down into the cellar but wanted to postpone it as long as he could. In fact, he finally put on his coat and beaver hat and mittens and walked outdoors before he went to the basement. Followed by the dog, who seemed happy for the first time in hours, he walked out on the frozen ground and made a circle around the building he called his home. Without knowing it, he was trying to get away from the noise, to go somewhere he could walk without feeling that peculiar tingling.

Finally he went into the mill and started down the steps to the cellar. The dog hesitated on the top step, went down two steps and then jumped back to the top step, where he started to whine. Staples went steadily down the steps, but the dog's behavior did not add to his peace of mind. The noise was much louder than it was the day before, and he did not need a cane to detect the vibration—the whole building was shaking. He sat down on the third step from the bottom and thought the problem over before he ventured out on the floor. He was especially interested in an empty barrel which was dancing around the middle of the floor.

The power of the mill wheel was transferred through a simple series of shafts, cogs, and leather belting to the grinding elements on the first floor. All this machinery for transmitting power was in the basement. The actual grinding had been done on the first floor. The weight of all this machinery, as well as of the heavy millstones on the first floor, was carried entirely by the flooring of the basement. The ceiling of the first floor was built on long pine beams which stretched across the entire building and were sunk into the stone walls at either side.

Staples started to walk around on the slate flagstones when he observed something that made him decide to stay on the steps. The floor was beginning to sink in the middle; not much, but enough to cause some of the shafts to separate from the ceiling. The ceiling seemed to sag. He saw that light objects like the empty barrel were congregating at the middle of the cellar. There was not much light but he was easily able to see that the floor was no longer level; that it was becoming saucer-shaped. The grinding noise grew louder. The steps he sat on were of solid masonry, stoutly connected with and a part of the wall. These shared in the general vibration. The whole building began to sing like a 'cello.

One day he had been to the city and heard an orchestra play. He had been interested in the large violins, especially the one that was so large the player had to stay on his feet to play it. The feeling of the stone step under him reminded him of the notes of this violin the few times it had been played by itself. He sat there. Suddenly he started, realizing that in a few more minutes he would be asleep. He was not frightened but in some dim way he knew that he must not go to sleep—not here. Whistling, he ran up the steps to get his electric torch. With that in his hand, he went back to the steps. Aided by the steady light, he saw that several large cracks had appeared in the floor and that some of the stones, broken loose from their fellows, were moving slowly in a drunken, meaningless way. He looked at his watch. It was only a little after nine.

And then the noise stopped.

No more noise! No more vibration! Just a broken floor and every bit of the machinery of the mill disabled and twisted. In the middle of the floor was a hole where one of the pavement stones had dropped through. Staples carefully walked across and threw the light down this hole. Then he lay down and carefully put himself in such a position that he could look down the hole. He began to sweat. There did not seem to be any bottom!

Back on the solid steps he tried to give that hole its proper value. He could not understand it, but he did not need the whining of the dog to tell him what to do. That hole must be closed as soon as possible.

Like a flash the method of doing so came to him. On the floor above he had cement. There were hundreds of grain sacks. Water was plentiful in the millrace. All that day he worked, carefully closing the hole with a great stopper of bags and wire. Then he placed timbers above and finally covered it all with cement, rich cement. Night came and he still worked. Morning came and still he staggered down the steps, each time with a

bag of crushed stone or cement on his shoulder, or with two
buckets of water in his hands. At noon the next day the floor was
no longer concave but convex. On top of the hole were four feet
of timbers, bags and concrete. Then and only then did he go
and make some coffee. He drank it, cup after cup, and slept.

The dog stayed on the bed at his feet.

When the man woke, the sun was streaming in through the
windows. It was a new day. Though the fire had long since died
out, the room was warm. Such days in Vermont were called
weather breeders. Staples listened. There was no sound except
the ticking of his clock. Not realizing what he was doing, he
knelt by the bed, thanked God for His mercies, jumped into
bed again and slept for another twenty-four hours. This time he
awoke and listened. There was no noise. He was sure that by
this time the cement had hardened. This morning he stayed
awake and shared a Gargantuan meal with the dog. Then it
seemed the proper thing to go to the basement. There was no
doubt that the machinery was a wreck but the hole was closed.
Satisfied that the trouble was over, he took his gun and dog
and went hunting.

When he returned, he did not have to enter the mill to know
that the grinding had begun again. Even before he started down
the steps, he recognized too well the vibration and the sound.
This time it was a melody of notes, a harmony of discords, and
he realized that the thing, which before had cut through solid
rock, was now wearing its way through a cement in which were
bags, timbers and pieces of iron. Each of these gave a different
tone. Together they all wailed over their dissolution.

Staples saw, even with first glance, that it would not be long
before his cement "cork" would be destroyed. What was there
to do next? All that day when hunting, his mind had been
dimly working on that problem. Now he had the answer. He
could not cork the hole, so he would fill it with water. The walls
of the mill were solid, but he could blast a hole through them
and turn the millrace into the cellar. The race, fed by the river,
took only a part of what it could take, if its level were rapidly
lowered. Whatever it was that was breaking down the floor of

the mill could be drowned. If it were alive, it could be killed. If it were fire, it could be quenched. There was no use to wait until the hole was again opened. The best plan was to have everything ready. He went back to his kitchen and cooked a meal of ham and eggs. He ate all he could. He boiled a pot of coffee. Then he started to work. The wall reached three feet down below the surface. A charge of powder, heavy enough to break through, would wreck the whole building, so he began to peck at the wall, like a bird pecking at a nut. First a period of drilling and then a little powder and a muffled explosion. A few buckets of loosened rock. Then some more drilling and another explosion. At last he knew that only a few inches of rock lay between the water and the cellar.

All this time there had been a symphony of noises, a disharmony of sounds. The constant grinding came from the floor, interrupted by the sound of sledge or crowbar, dull explosion of powder, and crashing of rock fragments on the floor. Staples worked without stop save to drink coffee. The dog stood on the upper steps.

Then without warning the whole floor caved in. Staples jumped to the steps. These held. On the first day there had been a hole a few feet wide. Now the opening occupied nearly the entire area of the floor. Staples, nauseated, looked down to the bottom. About twenty feet below him, a mass of rocks and timbers churned in a peculiar way, but all gradually disappeared in a second hole, fifteen feet wide. Even as he looked they all disappeared in this median hole.

The opening he had been breaking in the wall was directly across from the steps. There was a charge of powder there but no way of going across to light the fuse. Still there was no time to lose and he had to think fast. Running to the floor above he picked up his rifle and went to the bottom of the steps. He was able to throw the beam from his searchlight directly into the hole in the wall. Then he shot—once—twice, and the third time the explosion told him he had succeeded.

The water started to run into the cellar. Not fast at first but more rapidly as the mud and weeds were cleared out. Finally an eight-inch stream flowed steadily into the bottomless hole. Staples sat on the bottom steps. Soon he had the satisfaction of seeing the water fill the larger hole and then cover the floor, what there was left of it. In another hour he had to leave the lower steps. He went out to the millrace and saw that there was still enough water to fill a hundred such holes. A deep sense of satisfaction filled his weary mind.

And again, after eating, he sought sleep.

When he awoke, he heard the rain angrily tapping at the windows with multi-fingers. The dog was on the woven rug by the side of the bed. He was still restless and seemed pleased to have his master awake. Staples dressed more warmly than usual and spent an extra half hour making pancakes to eat with honey. Sausages and coffee helped assuage his hunger. Then with rubber boots and a heavy raincoat, he went out into the valley. The very first thing that he noticed was the millrace. It was practically empty. The little stream of water at the bottom was pouring into the hole he had blasted into the stone wall hours before. The race had contained eight feet of water. Now barely six inches remained, and the dread came to the man that the hole in the cellar was not only emptying the race but was also draining the little river that for thousands of years had flowed through the valley. It had never gone dry. He hastened over to the dam and his worst fears were realized. Instead of a river, there was simply a streak of mud with cakes of dirty ice, all being washed by the torrent of rain. With relief he thought of this rain. Millions of tons of snow would melt and fill the river. Ultimately the hole would fill and the water would rise again in the millrace. Still he was uneasy. What if the hole had no bottom?

When he looked into the basement he was little reassured. The water was still going down, though slowly. It was rising in the basement, and this meant that it was now running in faster than it was running down.

Leaving his coat and boots on the first floor, he ran up the stone steps to the second floor, built a fire in the living room and started to smoke—and think. The machinery of the mill was in ruins; of course it could be fixed, but as there was no more need of it, the best thing was to leave it alone. He had gold saved by his ancestors. He did not know how much, but he could live on it. Restlessly he reviewed the past week, and, unable to rest, hunted for occupation. The idea of the gold stayed in his mind and the final result was that he again put on his boots and coat and carried the entire treasure to a little dry cave in the woods about a half mile from the mill. Then he came back and started to cook his dinner. He went past the cellar door three times without looking down.

Just as he and the dog had finished eating, he heard a noise. It was a different one this time, more like a saw going through wood, but the rhythm was the same—Hrrrrr—Hrrrrr. He started to go to the cellar but this time he took his rifle, and though the dog followed, he howled dismally with his tail between his legs, shivering.

As soon as Staples reached the first floor, he felt the vibration. Not only could he feel the vibration, he could see it. It seemed that the center of the floor was being pushed up. Flashlight in hand, he opened the cellar door. There was no water there now—in fact there was no cellar left! In front of him was a black wall on which the light played in undulating waves. It was a wall and it was moving. He touched it with the end of his rifle. It was hard and yet there was a give to it. Feeling the rock, he could feel it move. Was it alive? Could there be a living rock? He could not see around it but he felt that the bulk of the Thing filled the entire cellar and was pressing against the ceiling. That was it! The Thing was boring through the first floor. It had destroyed and filled the cellar! It had swallowed the river! Now it was working at the first floor. If this continued, the mill was doomed. Staples knew that it was a Thing alive, and *he had to stop it!*

He was thankful that all of the steps in the mill were of stone, fastened and built into the wall. Even though the floor did fall in, he could still go to the upper rooms. He realized that from now on the fight had to be waged from the top floors. Going up the steps, he saw that a small hole had been cut through the oak flooring. Even as he watched, this grew larger. Trying to remain calm, realizing that only by doing so could he retain his sanity, he sat down in a chair and timed the rate of enlargement. But there was no need of using a watch: the hole grew larger—and larger and larger—and now he began to see the dark hole which had sucked the river dry. Now it was three feet in diameter—now four feet—now six. It was working smoothly now—it was not only grinding—*but it was eating.*

Staples began to laugh. He wanted to see what it would do when the big stone grinders slipped silently down into that maw. That would be a rare sight. All well enough to swallow a few pavement stones, but when it came to a twenty-ton grinder, that would be a different kind of a pill. "I hope you choke!" he cried. "Damn you! whatever you are! I hope you choke!" The walls hurled back the echo of his shouts and frightened him into silence. Then the floor began to tilt and the chairs to slide toward the opening. Staples sprang toward the steps.

"Not yet!" he shrieked. "Not today, Elenora! Some other day, but not today!" And then from the safety of the steps, he witnessed the final destruction of the floor and all in it. The stones slipped down, the partitions, the beams, and then, as though satisfied with the work and the food, the Thing dropped down, down, down and left Staples dizzy on the steps looking into a hole, dark, deep, coldly bottomless surrounded by the walls of the mill, and below them a circular hole cut out of the solid rock. On one side a little stream of water, a tiny waterfall, came through the blasted wall and fell below. Staples could not hear it splash at the bottom.

Nauseated and vomiting, he crept up the steps to the second floor, where the howling dog was waiting for him. On the floor he lay, sweating and shivering in dumb misery. It took hours for him to change from a frightened animal to a cerebrating god, but ultimately he accomplished even this, cooked some more food, warmed himself and slept.

And while he dreamed, the dog kept sleepless watch at his feet. He awoke the next morning. It was still raining, and Staples knew that the snow was melting on the hills and soon would change the little valley river into a torrent. He wondered whether it was all a dream, but one look at the dog showed him the reality of the last week. He went to the second floor again and cooked breakfast. After he had eaten, he slowly went down the steps. That is, he started to go, but halted at the sight of the hole. The steps had held and ended on a wide stone platform. From there another flight of steps went down to what had once been the cellar. Those two flights of steps clinging to the walls had the solid stone mill on one side, but on the inside they faced a chasm, circular in outline and seemingly bottomless; but the man knew there was a bottom and from that pit the Thing had come—and would come again.

That was the horror of it! He was so certain that it would come again. Unless he was able to stop it. How could he? Could he destroy a Thing that was able to bore a thirty-foot hole through solid rock, swallow a river and digest grinding stones like so many pills? One thing he was sure of—he could accomplish nothing without knowing more about it. To know more, he had to watch. He determined to cut a hole through the floor. Then he could see the Thing when it came up. He cursed himself for his confidence, but he was sure it would come.

It did. He was on the floor looking into the hole he had sawed through the plank, and he saw it come: but first he heard it. It was a sound full of slithering slidings, wrathful rasping of rock against rock—but, no! That could not be, for this Thing was alive. Could this be rock and move and grind and eat and drink? Then he saw it come into the cellar and finally to the level of the first floor, and then he saw its head and face.

The face looked at the man, and Staples was glad that the hole in the floor was as small as it was. There was a central mouth filling half the space; fully fifteen feet in diameter was that mouth, and the sides were ashen gray and quivering. There were no teeth.

That increased the horror: a mouth without teeth, without any visible means of mastication, and yet Staples shivered as he thought of what had gone into that mouth, down into that mouth, deep into the recesses of that mouth and disappeared. The circular lip seemed made of scales of steel, and they were washed clean with the water from the race.

On either side of the gigantic mouth was an eye, lidless, browless, pitiless. They were slightly withdrawn into the head so the Thing could bore into rock without injuring them. Staples tried to estimate their size: all he could do was to avoid their baleful gaze. Then even as he watched the mouth closed and the head began a semicircular movement, so many degrees to the right, so many degrees to the left and up—and up—and finally the top touched the bottom of the plank Staples was on and then Hrrrrrr—Hrrrrrrr, and the man knew that it was starting upon the destruction of the second floor. He could not see now as he had been able to see before, but he had an idea that after grinding a while the Thing opened its mouth and swallowed the debris. He looked around the room. Here was where he did his cooking and washing, and here was his winter supply of stove wood. A thought came to him.

Working frantically, he pushed the center burner to the middle of the room right over the hole he had cut in the floor. Then he built a fire in it, starting it with a liberal supply of coal-oil. He soon had the stove red hot. Opening the door he again filled the stove with oak and then ran for the steps. He was just in time. The floor, cut through, disappeared into the Thing's maw and with it the red-hot stove. Staples yelled in his glee, "A hot pill for you this time, a *hot pill!*"

If the pill did anything, it simply increased the desire of the Thing to destroy, for it kept on till it had bored a hole in this floor equal in size to the holes in the floors below it. Staples saw his food, his furniture, the ancestral relics disappear into the same opening that had consumed the machinery and mill supplies.

On the upper floor the dog howled.

The man slowly went up to the top floor, and joined the dog, who had ceased to howl and had begun a low whine. There was a stove on this floor, but there was no food. That did not make any difference to Staples: for some reason he was not hungry any more: it did not seem to make any difference—nothing seemed to matter or make any difference any more. Still he had his gun and over fifty cartridges, and he knew that at the last, even a Thing like that would react to bullets in its eyeballs—he just knew that nothing could withstand that.

He lit the lamp and paced the floor in a cold, careless mood. One thing he had determined. He said it over and over to himself.

"This is my home. It has been the home of my family for two hundred years. No devil or beast or worm can make me leave it."

He said it again and again. He felt that if he said it often enough, he would believe it, and if he could only believe it, he might make the Worm believe it. He knew now that it was a Worm, just like the night crawlers he had used so often for bait, only much larger. Yes, that was it. A Worm like a night crawler, only much larger, in fact, very much larger. That made him laugh—to think how much larger this Worm was than the ones he had used for fishing. All through the night he walked the floor and burned the lamp and said, "This is my home. No Worm can make me leave it!" Several times he went down the steps, just a few of them, and shouted the message into the pit as though he wanted the Worm to hear and understand, "This is my home! *No Worm can make me leave it!*"

Morning came. He mounted the ladder that led to the trap door in the roof and opened it. The rain beat in. Still that might be a place of refuge. Crying, he took his Burton and his Rabelais and wrapped them in his raincoat and put them out on the roof, under a box. He took the small pictures of his father and mother and put them with the books. Then in loving kindness he carried the dog up and wrapped him in a woolen blanket. He sat down and waited, and as he did so he recited poetry—anything that came to him, all mixed up, "Come into the garden where there was a man who was so wondrous wise, he jumped into a bramble bush and you're a better man than I am and no one will work for money and the King of Love my Shepherd is"—and on—and then—

He heard the sliding and the slithering rasping, and he knew that the Worm had come again. He waited till the Hrrrrr—Hrrrrr told that the wooden floor he was on was being attacked, and then he went up the ladder. It was his idea to wait till the Thing had made a large opening, large enough so the eyes could be seen, and then use the fifty bullets—where they would do the most good. So, on the roof, beside the dog, he waited.

He did not have to wait long. First appeared a little hole and then it grew wider and wider till finally the entire floor and the furniture had dropped into the mouth, and the whole opening, thirty feet wide and more than that, was filled with the head, the closed mouth of which came within a few feet of the roof. By the aid of the light from the trap door, Staples could see the eye on the left side. It made a beautiful bull's eye, a magnificent target for his rifle and he was only a few feet away. He could not miss. Determined to make the most of his last chance to drive his enemy away, he decided to drop down on the creature, walk over to the eye and put the end of the rifle against the eye before he fired. If the first shot worked well, he could retire to the roof and use the other cartridges. He knew that there was some danger—but it was his last hope. After all he knew that when it came to brains he was a man, and this Thing was only a Worm. He walked over the head. Surely no sensation could go through such massive scales. He even jumped up and down. Meantime the eye kept looking up at the roof. If it saw the man, it made no signs, gave no evidence. Staples pretended to pull the trigger and then made a running jump for the trap door. It was easy. He did it again, and again. Then he sat on the edge of the door and thought.

He suddenly saw what it all meant. Two hundred years before, his ancestors had started grinding at the mill. For over a hundred and fifty years the mill had been run continuously, often day and night. The vibrations had been transmitted downward through the solid rock. Hundreds of feet below the Worm had heard them and felt them and thought it was another Worm. It had started to bore in the direction of the noise. It had taken two hundred years to do it, but it had finished the task, it had found the place where its mate should be. For two hundred years it had slowly worked its way through the primitive rock. Why should it worry over a mill and the things within it? Staples saw then that the mill had been but a slight incident in its life. It was probable that it had not even known it was there—the water, the gristmill stones, the red-hot stove, had meant nothing—they had been taken as a part of the day's work. There was only one thing that the Worm was really interested in, only one idea that had reached its consciousness and remained there through two centuries, and that was to find its mate. The eye looked upward.

Staples, at the end, lost courage and decided to fire from a sitting position in the trap door. Taking careful aim, he pulled the trigger. Then he looked carefully to see what damage had resulted. There was none. Either the bullet had gone into the eye and the opening had closed or else it had glanced off. He fired again and again.

Then the mouth opened—wide—wider—until there was nothing under Staples save a yawning void of darkness.

The Worm belched a cloud of black, nauseating vapor. The man, enveloped in the cloud, lost consciousness and fell.

The Mouth closed on him.

On the roof the dog howled.

Although some readers may argue that "The Runaway Skyscraper"
doesn't properly belong in a collection called *The Best of Amazing*
—since it originally appeared in *Argosy* at least seven years before
Amazing was born—we're including it anyway as a fine example of
Gernsback's judgment in selecting reprints for the early issues of
a "different" kind of magazine—one that hadn't yet had time to
develop a whole new generation of writers with names like Jack
Williamson, Wallace West, David H. Keller, and E. E. Smith. We
have a much better reason, though—it's still a very fine story, the
first piece of science fiction Leinster ever wrote and one of the
main reasons why today—nearly half a century later—we call him
the Dean of Science Fiction.

THE RUNAWAY SKYSCRAPER

Murray Leinster

The whole thing started when the clock on the Metropolitan
Tower began to run backward. It was not a graceful proceeding.
The hands had been moving onward in their customary deliberate fashion, slowly and thoughtfully, but suddenly the people
in the offices near the clock's face heard an ominous creaking and
groaning. There was a slight, hardly discernible shiver through
the tower, and then something gave with a crash. The big hands
on the clock began to move backward.

Immediately after the crash all the creaking and groaning
ceased, and instead the usual quiet again hung over everything.

One or two of the occupants of the upper offices put their heads
out into the halls, but the elevators were running as usual, the
lights were burning, and all seemed calm and peaceful. The
clerks and stenographers went back to their ledgers and type-
writers, the business callers returned to the discussion of their
errands, and the ordinary course of business was resumed.

Arthur Chamberlain was dictating a letter to Estelle Woodward, his sole stenographer. When the crash came he paused,
listened, and then resumed his task.

It was not a difficult one. Talking to Estelle Woodward was at
no time an onerous duty, but it must be admitted that Arthur
Chamberlain found it difficult to keep his conversation strictly
upon his business.

He was at this time engaged in dictating a letter to his principal creditors, the Gary & Milton Company, explaining that
their demand for the immediate payment of the instalment then
due upon his office furniture was untimely and unjust. A young
and budding engineer in New York never has too much money,
and when he is young as Arthur Chamberlain was, and as fond
of pleasant company, and not too fond of economizing, he is
liable to find all demands for payment untimely and he usually
considers them unjust as well. Arthur finished dictating the
letter and sighed.

"Miss Woodward," he said regretfully, "I am afraid I shall
never make a successful man."

Miss Woodward shook her head vaguely. She did not seem
to take his remark very seriously, but then she had learned never
to take any of his remarks seriously. She had been puzzled at
first by his manner of treating everything with a half-joking
pessimism, but now ignored it.

She was interested in her own problems. She had suddenly decided that she was going to be an old maid, and it bothered her.
She had discovered that she did not like any one well enough
to marry, and she was in her twenty-second year.

She was not a native of New York, and the few young men
she had met there she did not care for. She had regretfully decided she was too finicky, too fastidious, but could not seem

to help herself. She could not understand their absorption in boxing and baseball, and she did not like the way they danced.

She had considered the matter and decided that she would have to reconsider her former opinion of women who did not marry. Heretofore she had thought there must be something the matter with them. Now she believed that she would come to their own estate, and probably for the same reason. She could not fall in love and she wanted to.

She read all the popular novels and thrilled at the love-scenes contained in them, but when any of the young men she knew became in the slightest degree sentimental, she found herself bored, and disgusted with herself for being bored. Still, she could not help it, and was struggling to reconcile herself to a life without romance.

She was far too pretty for that, of course, and Arthur Chamberlain often longed to tell her how pretty she really was, but her abstracted air held him at arm's length.

He lay back at ease in his swivel-chair and considered, looking at her with unfeigned pleasure. She did not notice it, for she was so much absorbed in her own thoughts that she rarely noticed anything he said or did when they were not in the line of her duties.

"Miss Woodward," he repeated, "I said I think I'll never make a successful man. Do you know what that means?"

She looked at him mutely, polite inquiry in her eyes.

"It means," he said gravely, "that I am going broke. Unless something turns up in the next three weeks, or a month at the latest, I'll have to get a job."

"And that means—" she asked.

"All this will go to pot," he explained with a sweeping gesture. "I thought I'd better tell you as much in advance as I could."

"You mean you're going to give up your office—and me?" she asked, a little alarmed.

"Giving up you will be the harder of the two," he said with a smile, "but that's what it means. You'll have no difficulty finding a new place, with three weeks in which to look for one, but I'm sorry."

"I'm sorry, too, Mr. Chamberlain," she said, her brow puckered.

She was not really frightened, because she knew she could get another position, but she became aware of rather more regret than she had expected.

There was silence for a moment.

"Jove!" said Arthur, suddenly. "It's getting dark, isn't it?"

It was. It was growing dark with unusual rapidity. Arthur went to his window and looked out.

"Funny," he remarked in a moment or two. "Things don't look just right, down there, somehow. There are very few people about."

He watched in growing amazement. Lights came on in the streets below, but none of the buildings lighted up. It grew darker and darker.

"It shouldn't be dark at this hour!" Arthur exclaimed.

Estelle went to the window by his side.

"It looks awfully queer," she agreed. "It must be an eclipse or something."

They heard doors open in the hall outside, and Arthur ran out. The halls were beginning to fill with excited people.

"What on earth's the matter?" asked a worried stenographer.

"Probably an eclipse," replied Arthur. "Only it's odd we didn't read about it in the papers."

He glanced along the corridor. No one else seemed better informed than he, and he went back into his office.

Estelle turned from the window as he appeared.

"The streets are deserted," she said in a puzzled tone. "What's the matter? Did you hear?"

Arthur shook his head and reached for the telephone.

"I'll call up and find out," he said confidently. He held the receiver to his ear. "What the—" he exclaimed. "Listen to this!"

A small-sized roar was coming from the receiver. Arthur hung up and turned a blank face upon Estelle.

"Look!" she said suddenly, and pointed out of the window.

All the city was now lighted up, and such of the signs as they could see were brilliantly illumined. They watched in silence. The streets once more seemed filled with vehicles. They darted along, their headlamps lighting up the roadway brilliantly. There was, however, something strange even about their motion. Arthur and Estelle watched in growing amazement and perplexity.

"Are—are you seeing what I am seeing?" asked Estelle breathlessly. "I see them *going backward!*"

Arthur watched and collapsed into a chair.

"For the love of Mike!" he exclaimed softly.

ROTATION OF THE EARTH REVERSED

He was roused by another exclamation from Estelle.

"It's getting light again," she said.

Arthur rose and went eagerly to the window. The darkness was becoming less intense, but in a way Arthur could hardly credit.

Far to the west, over beyond the Jersey hills—easily visible from the height at which Arthur's office was located—a faint light appeared in the sky, grew stronger and then took on a reddish tint. That, in turn, grew deeper, and at last the sun appeared, rising unconcernedly *in the west.*

Arthur gasped. The streets below continued to be thronged with people and motor-cars. The sun was traveling with extraordinary rapidity. It rose overhead, and as if by magic the streets were thronged with people. Every one seemed to be running at top speed. The few teams they saw moved at a breakneck pace —backward! In spite of the suddenly topsy-turvy state of affairs, there seemed to be no accidents.

Arthur put his hand to his head.

"Miss Woodward," he said pathetically. "I'm afraid I've gone crazy. Do you see the same things I do?"

Estelle nodded. Her eyes wide open.

"What *is* the matter?" she asked helplessly.

She turned again to the window. The square was almost empty once more. The motor-cars still traveling about the streets were going so swiftly they were hardly visible. Their speed seemed to increase steadily. Soon it was almost impossible to distinguish them, and only a grayish blur marked their paths along Fifth Avenue and Twenty-third Street.

It grew dusk, and then rapidly dark. As their office was on the western side of the building, they could not see the sun had sunk in the east, but subconsciously they realized that this must be the case.

In silence they watched the panorama grow black except for the street-lamps, remain thus for a time, and then suddenly spring into brilliantly illuminated activity.

Again this lasted for a little while, and the west once more began to glow. The sun rose somewhat more hastily from the Jersey hills and began to soar overhead, but very soon darkness fell again. With hardly an interval the city became illuminated, and the west grew red once more.

"Apparently," said Arthur, steadying his voice with a conscious effort, "there's been a cataclysm somewhere, the direction of the earth's rotation has been reversed, and its speed immensely increased. It seems to take only about five minutes for a rotation now."

As he spoke darkness fell for the third time. Estelle turned from the window with a white face.

"What's going to happen?" she cried.

"I don't know," answered Arthur. "The scientific fellows tell us if the earth were to spin fast enough, the centrifugal force would throw us all off into space. Perhaps that's what's going to happen."

Estelle sank into a chair and stared at him, appalled. There was a sudden explosion behind them. With a start, Estelle jumped to her feet and turned. A little gilt clock over her typewriter-desk lay in fragments. Arthur hastily glanced at his own watch.

"Great bombs and little cannon balls!" he shouted. "Look at this!"

His watch trembled and quivered in his hand. The hands were going around so swiftly it was impossible to watch the minute-hand, and the hour-hand traveled like the wind.

While they looked, it made two complete revolutions. In one of them the glory of daylight had waxed, waned, and vanished. In the other, darkness reigned except for the glow from the electric light overhead.

There was a sudden tension and catch in the watch. Arthur dropped it instantly. It flew to pieces before it reached the floor.

"If you've got a watch," Arthur ordered swiftly, "stop it this instant!"

Estelle fumbled at her wrist. Arthur tore the watch from her hand and threw open the case. The machinery inside was going so swiftly it was hardly visible. Relentlessly, Arthur jabbed a penholder in the works. There was a sharp click, and the watch was still.

Arthur ran to the window. As he reached it, the sun rushed up, day lasted a moment, there was darkness, and then the sun appeared again.

"Miss Woodward!" Arthur ordered suddenly. "Look at the ground!"

Estelle glanced down. The next time the sun flashed into view she gasped.

The ground was white with snow.

"What *has* happened?" she demanded, terrified. "Oh, what *has* happened?"

Arthur fumbled at his chin awkwardly, watching the astonishing panorama outside. There was hardly any distinguishing between the times the sun was up and the times it was below now, as the darkness and light followed each other so swiftly the effect was the same as one of the old flickering motion-pictures.

As Arthur watched, this effect became more pronounced. The tall Fifth Avenue Building across the way began to disintegrate. In a moment, it seemed, there was only a skeleton there. Then that vanished, story by story. A great cavity in the earth appeared, and then another building became visible, a smaller, brown-stone, unimpressive structure.

With bulging eyes Arthur stared across the city. Except for the flickering, he could see almost clearly now.

He no longer saw the sun rise and set. There was merely a streak of unpleasantly brilliant light across the sky. Bit by bit, building by building, the city began to disintegrate and become replaced by smaller, dingier buildings. In a little while those began to disappear and leave gaps where they vanished.

Arthur strained his eyes and looked far downtown. He saw a forest of mast and spars along the waterfront for a moment, and when he turned his eyes again to the scenery near him it was almost barren of houses, and what few showed were mean, small residences, apparently set in the midst of farms and plantations.

Estelle was sobbing.

"Oh, Mr. Chamberlain," she cried. "What is the matter? What has happened?"

Arthur had lost his fear of what their fate would be in his absorbing interest in what he saw. He was staring out of the window, wide-eyed, lost in the sight before him. At Estelle's cry, however, he reluctantly left the window and patted her shoulder awkwardly.

"I don't know how to explain it," he said uncomfortably, "but it's obvious that my first surmise was all wrong. The speed of the earth's rotation can't have been increased, because if it had to the extent we see, we'd have been thrown off into space long ago. But—have you read anything about the Fourth Dimension?"

Estelle shook her head hopelessly.

"Well, then, have you ever read anything by Wells? *The Time Machine*, for instance?"

Again she shook her head.

"I don't know how I'm going to say it so you'll understand, but time is just as much a dimension as length and breadth. From what I can judge, I'd say there has been an earthquake, and the ground has settled a little with our building on it, only instead of settling down toward the center of the earth, or side-wise, it's settled in this fourth dimension."

"But what does that mean?" asked Estelle uncomprehending.

"If the earth had settled down, we'd have been lower. If it had settled to one side we'd have been moved one way or another, but as it's settled back in the Fourth Dimension, we're going back in time."

"Then—"

"We're in a runaway skyscraper, bound for some time back before the discovery of America!"

THE SEASONS ARE REVERSED IN ORDER

It was very still in the office. Except for the flickering outside everything seemed very much as usual. The electric light burned steadily, but Estelle was sobbing with fright, and Arthur was trying vainly to console her.

"Have I gone crazy?" she demanded between her sobs.

"Not unless I've gone mad, too," said Arthur soothingly. The excitement had quite a soothing effect upon him. He had ceased to feel afraid, but was simply waiting to see what had happened. "We're way back before the founding of New York now, and still going strong."

"Are you sure that's what has happened?"

"If you look outside," he suggested, "you'll see the seasons following each other in reverse order. One moment the snow covers all the ground, then you catch a glimpse of autumn foliage, then summer follows, and next spring."

Estelle glanced out of the window and covered her eyes.

"Not a house," she said despairingly. "Not a building. Nothing, nothing, nothing!"

Arthur slipped his arm about her and patted hers comfortingly.

"It's all right," he reassured her. "We'll bring up presently, and there we'll be. There's nothing to be afraid of."

She rested her head on his shoulder and sobbed hopelessly

for a little while longer, but presently quieted. Then, suddenly, realizing that Arthur's arm was about her and that she was crying on his shoulder, she sprang away, blushing crimson.

Arthur walked to the window.

"Look there!" he exclaimed, but it was too late. "I'll swear to it I saw the *Half-Moon*, Hudson's ship," he declared excitedly. "We're way back now, and don't seem to be slackening up, either."

Estelle came to the window by his side. The rapidly changing scene before her made her gasp. It was no longer possible to distinguish night from day.

A wavering streak, moving first to the right and then to the left, showed where the sun flashed across the sky.

"What makes the sun wabble so?" she asked.

"Moving north and south of the equator," Arthur explained casually. "When it's farthest south—to the left—there's always snow on the ground. When it's farthest right it's summer. See how green it is?"

A few moments' observation corroborated his statement.

"I'd say," Arthur remarked reflectively, "that it takes about fifteen seconds for the sun to make the round trip from farthest north to farthest south." He felt his pulse. "Do you know the normal rate of the heart-beat? We can judge time that way. A clock will go all to pieces, of course."

"Why did your watch explode—and the clock?"

"Running forward in time unwinds a clock, doesn't it?" asked Arthur. "It follows, of course, that when you move it backward in time it winds up. When you move it too far back, you wind it so tightly that the spring just breaks to pieces."

He paused a moment, his fingers on his pulse.

"Yes, it takes about fifteen seconds for all the four seasons to pass. That means we're going backward in time about four years a minute. If we go on at this rate in another hour we'll be back in the time of the Northmen, and will be able to tell if they did discover America, after all."

"Funny we don't hear any noises," Estelle observed. She had caught some of Arthur's calmness.

"It passes so quickly that though our ears hear it, we don't separate the sounds. If you'll notice, you do hear a sort of humming. It's very high-pitched, though."

Estelle listened, but could hear nothing.

"No matter," said Arthur. "It's probably a little higher than your ears will catch. Lots of people can't hear a bat squeak."

"I never could," said Estelle. "Out in the country, where I come from, other people could hear them, but I couldn't."

They stood a while in silence, watching.

"When are we going to stop?" asked Estelle uneasily. "It seems as if we're going to keep on indefinitely."

"I guess we'll stop all right," Arthur reassured her. "It's obvious that whatever it was, it only affected our own building, or we'd see some other one with us. It looks like a fault or a flaw in the rock the building rests on. And that can only give so far."

Estelle was silent for a moment.

"Oh, I can't be sane!" she burst out semi-hysterically. "This can't be happening!"

"You aren't crazy," said Arthur sharply. "You're sane as I am. Just something queer is happening. Buck up. Say something sensible, and you'll know you're all right. But don't get frightened now. There'll be plenty to get frightened about later."

The grimness in his tone alarmed Estelle. "What are you afraid of?" she asked quickly.

"Time enough to worry when it happens," Arthur retorted briefly.

"You—you aren't afraid we'll go back before the beginning of the world, are you?" asked Estelle in sudden access of fright.

Arthur shook his head.

"Tell me," said Estelle more quietly, getting a grip on herself. "I won't mind. But please tell me."

Arthur glanced at her. Her face was pale, but there was more resolution in it than he had expected to find.

"I'll tell you, then," he said reluctantly. "We're going back a little faster than we were, and the flaw seems to be a deeper one than I thought. At the roughest kind of an estimate, we're all of a thousand years before the discovery of America now, and I think nearer three or four. And we're gaining speed all the time. So, though I am as sure as I can be of anything that we'll stop this cave-in eventually, I don't know where. It's like a crevasse in the earth opened by an earthquake which may be only a few feet deep, or it may be hundreds of yards, or even a mile or two. We started off smoothly. We're going at a terrific rate. *What will happen when we stop?*"

Estelle caught her breath.

"What?" she asked quietly.

"I don't know," said Arthur in an irritated tone, to cover his apprehension. "How could I know?"

Estelle turned from him to the window again.

"Look!" she said, pointing.

The flickering had begun again. While they stared, hope springing up once more in their hearts; it became more pronounced. Soon they could distinctly see the difference between day and night.

They were slowing up! The white snow on the ground remained there for an appreciable time; autumn lasted quite a while. They could catch the flashes of the sun as it made its revolutions now, instead of its seeming like a ribbon of fire. At last day lasted all of fifteen or twenty minutes.

It grew longer and longer. Then half an hour, then an hour. The sun wavered in midheaven and was still.

Far below them, the watchers in the tower of the skyscraper saw trees swaying and bending in the wind. Though there was not a house or a habitation to be seen and a dense forest covered all of Manhattan Island, such of the world as they could see looked normal. Whatever, or rather in whatever epoch of time they were, they had arrived.

INDIANS OCCUPY MADISON SQUARE

Arthur caught at Estelle's arm and the two made a dash for the elevators. Fortunately one was standing still, the door opened, on their floor. The elevator-boy had deserted his post and was looking with all the rest, at the strange landscape that surrounded them.

No sooner had the pair reached the car, however, than the boy came hurrying along the corridor, three or four other people following him also at a run. Without a word the boy rushed inside, the others crowded after him, and the car shot downward, all of the newcomers panting from their sprint.

Theirs was the first car to reach bottom. They rushed out and to the western door.

Here, where they had been accustomed to see Madison Square spread out before them, a clearing of perhaps half an acre in extent showed itself. Where their eyes instinctively looked for the dark bronze fountain, near which soap-box orators aforetime held sway, they saw a tent, a wigwam of hides and bark gaily painted. And before the wigwam were two or three brown-skinned Indians, utterly petrified with astonishment.

Behind the first wigwam were others, painted like the first with daubs of brightly colored clay. From them, too, Indians issued, and stared in incredulous amazement, their eyes growing wider and wider. When the group of white people confronted the Indians, there was a moment's deathlike silence. Then, with a wild yell, the redskins broke and ran, not stopping to gather together their belongings, nor pausing for even a second glance at the weird strangers who invaded their domain.

Arthur took two or three deep breaths of the fresh air and found himself even then comparing its quality with that of the city. Estelle stared about her with unbelieving eyes. She turned and saw the great bulk of the office building behind her, then faced this small clearing with a virgin forest on its farther side.

She found herself trembling from some undefined cause. Arthur glanced at her. He saw the trembling and knew she would have a fit of nerves in a moment if something did not come up demanding instant attention.

"We'd better take a look at this village," he said in an offhand voice. "We can probably find out how long ago it is from the weapons and so on."

He grasped her arm firmly and led her in the direction of the tents. The other people, left behind, displayed their emotions in different ways. Two or three of them—women—sat frankly down on the steps and indulged in tears of bewilderment, fright and relief in a peculiar combination defying analysis. Two or three of the men swore, in shaken voices.

Meantime, the elevators inside the building were rushing and clanging, and the hall filled with a white-faced mob, desperately anxious to find out what had happened and why. The people poured out of the door and stared about blankly. There was a peculiar expression of doubt on every one of their faces. Each one was asking himself if he were awake, and having proved that by pinches, openly administered, the next query was whether they had gone mad.

Arthur led Estelle cautiously among the tents.

The village contained about a dozen wigwams. Most of them were made of strips of birch-bark, cleverly overlapping each other, the seams cemented with gum. All had hide flaps for doors, and one or two were built almost entirely of hides, sewed together with strips of sinew.

Arthur made only a cursory examination of the village. His principal motive in taking Estelle there was to give her some mental occupation to ward off the reaction from the excitement of the cataclysm.

He looked into one or two of the tents and found merely couches of hides, with minor domestic utensils scattered about. He brought from one tent a bow and quiver of arrows. The workmanship was good, but very evidently the maker had no knowledge of metal tools.

Arthur's acquaintance with archeological subjects was very slight, but he observed that the arrow-heads were chipped, and not rubbed smooth. They were attached to the shafts with strips of gut or tendon.

Arthur was still pursuing his investigation when a sob from Estelle made him look at her.

"Oh, what are we going to do?" she asked tearfully. "What *are* we going to do? What are we?"

"You mean, *when* are we," Arthur corrected with a grim smile. "I don't know. Way back before the discovery of America, though. You can see in everything in the village that there isn't a trace of European civilization. I suspect that we are several thousand years back. I can't tell, of course, but this pottery makes me think so. See this bowl?"

He pointed to a bowl of red clay lying on the ground before one of the wigwams.

"If you'll look, you'll see that it isn't really pottery at all. It's a basket that was woven of reeds and then smeared with clay to make it fire-resisting. The people who made that didn't know about baking clay to make it stay put. When America was discovered nearly all the tribes knew something about pottery."

"But what are we going to do?" Estelle tearfully insisted.

"We're going to muddle along as well as we can," answered Arthur cheerfully, "until we can get back to where we started from. Maybe the people back in the twentieth century can send a relief party after us. When the skyscraper vanished, it must have left a hole of some sort, and it may be possible for them to follow us down."

"If that's so," said Estelle quickly, "why can't we climb up it without waiting for them to come after us?"

Arthur scratched his head. He looked across the clearing at the skyscraper. It seemed to rest very solidly on the ground. He looked up. The sky seemed normal.

"To tell the truth," he admitted, "there doesn't seem to be any hole. I said that more to cheer you up than anything else."

Estelle clenched her hands tightly and took a grip on herself.

"Just tell me the truth," she said quietly. "I was rather foolish, but tell me what you honestly think."

Arthur eyed her keenly.

"In that case," he said reluctantly, "I'll admit we're in a pretty bad fix. I don't know what has happened, how it happened, or anything about it. I'm just going to keep on going until I see a way clear to get out of this mess. There are two thousand of us people, more or less, and among all of us we must be able to find a way out."

Estelle had turned very pale.

"We're in no great danger from Indians," went on Arthur thoughtfully, "or from anything else that I know of—except one thing."

"What is that?" asked Estelle quickly.

Arthur shook his head and led her back toward the skyscraper, which was now thronged with the people from all the floors who had come down to the ground and were standing excitedly about the concourse asking each other what had happened.

Arthur led Estelle to one of the corners.

"Wait for me here," he ordered. "I'm going to talk to this crowd."

He pushed his way through until he could reach the confectionery and newsstand in the main hallway. Here he climbed up on the counter and shouted:

"People, listen to me! I'm going to tell you what's happened!"

In an instant there was dead silence. He found himself the center of a sea of white faces, every one contorted with fear and anxiety.

"To begin with," he said confidently, "there's nothing to be afraid of. We're going to get back to where we started from! I don't know how, yet, but we'll do it. Don't get frightened. Now I'll tell you what's happened."

He rapidly sketched out for them, in words as simple as he could make them, his theory that a flaw in the rock on which the foundations rested had developed and let the skyscraper sink, not downward, but into the Fourth Dimension.

"I'm an engineer," he finished. "What nature can do, we can imitate. Nature let us into this hole. We'll climb out. In the meantime, matters are serious. We needn't be afraid of not getting back. We'll do that. What we've got to fight is—starvation!"

PLANNING FOR THE FOOD-SUPPLY

"We've got to fight starvation, and beat it," Arthur continued doggedly. "I'm telling you this now because I want you to begin right at the beginning and pitch in and help. We have very little food and a lot of us to eat it. First, I want some volunteers to help with rationing. Next, I want every ounce of food in this place put under guard where it can be served to those who need it most. Who will help?"

The swift succession of shocks had paralyzed the faculties of most of the people there, but half a dozen moved forward. Among them was a single gray-haired man with an air of accustomed authority. Arthur recognized him as the president of the bank on the ground floor.

"I don't know who you are or if you're right in saying what has happened," said the gray-haired man. "But I see something's got to be done, and—well, for the time being I'll take your word for what that is. Later on we'll thrash this matter out."

Arthur nodded. He bent over and spoke in a low voice to the gray-haired man, who moved away.

"Grayson, Walters, Terhune, Simpson and Forsythe, come here," the gray-haired man called at the doorway.

A number of men began to press dazedly toward him. Arthur resumed his harangue.

"You people—those of you who aren't too dazed to think—are remembering there's a restaurant in the building and no need to starve. You're wrong. There are nearly two thousand of us here. That means six thousand meals a day. We've got to have nearly ten tons of food a day, and we've got to have it at once."

"Hunt," someone suggested.

"I saw Indians," someone else shouted. "Can we trade with them?"

"We can hunt and we can trade with the Indians," Arthur admitted, "but we need food by the ton—by the ton, people! The Indians don't store up supplies, and, besides, they're much too scattered to have a surplus for us. But we've got to have food. Now, how many of you know anything about hunting, fishing, trapping, or any possible way of getting food?"

There were a few hands raised—pitifully few. Arthur saw Estelle's hand up.

"Very well," he said. "Those of you who raised your hands then, come with me up on the second floor, and we'll talk it over. The rest of you try to conquer your fright, and don't go outside for a while. We've got some things to attend to before it will be quite safe for you to venture out. And keep away from the restaurant. There are armed guards over the food. Before we pass it out indiscriminately, we'll see to it there's more for to-morrow and the next day."

He stepped down from the counter and moved toward the stairway. It was not worthwhile to use the elevator for the ride of only one floor. Estelle managed to join him, and they mounted the steps together.

"Do you think we'll pull through all right?" she asked quietly.

"We've got to!" Arthur told her, setting his chin firmly. "We've simply got to."

The gray-haired president of the bank was waiting for them at the top of the stairs.

"My name is Van Deventer," he said, shaking hands with Arthur, who gave his own name.

"Where shall our emergency council sit?" he asked.

"The bank has a board-room right over the safety vault. I dare say we can accommodate everybody there—everybody in the council, anyway."

Arthur followed into the board-room, and the others trooped in after him.

"I'm just assuming temporary leadership," Arthur explained, "because it's imperative some things be done at once. Later on we can talk about electing officials to direct our activities. Right now we need food. How many of you can shoot?"

About a quarter of the hands were raised. Estelle's was among the number.

"How many are fishermen?"

A few more went up.

"What do the rest of you do?"

There was a chorus of "gardener." "I have a garden in my yard," "I grow peaches in New Jersey," and three men confessed that they raised chickens as a hobby.

"We'll want you gardeners in a little while. Don't go yet.

But the most important are huntsmen and fishermen. Have any of you weapons in your offices?"

A number had revolvers, but only one man had a shotgun and shells.

"I was going on my vacation this afternoon straight from the office," he explained, "and have all my vacation tackle."

"Good man!" Arthur exclaimed. "You'll go after the heavy game."

"With a shotgun?" the sportsman asked, aghast.

"If you get close to them, a shotgun will do as well as anything, and we can't waste a shell on every bird or rabbit. Those shells of yours are precious. You other fellows will have to turn fishermen for a while. Your pistols are no good for hunting."

"The watchmen at the bank have riot guns," said Van Deventer, "and there are one or two repeating rifles there. I don't know about ammunition."

"Good! I don't mean about the ammunition, but about the guns. We'll hope for the ammunition. You fishermen get to work to improvise tackle out of anything you can get hold of. Will you do that?"

A series of nods answered his question.

"Now for the gardeners. You people will have to roam through the woods in company with the hunters and locate anything in the way of edibles that grows. Do all of you know what wild plants look like? I mean wild fruits and vegetables that are good to eat."

A few of them nodded, but the majority looked dubious. The consensus seemed to be that they would try. Arthur seemed a little discouraged.

"I guess you're the man to tell about the restaurant," Van Deventer said quietly. "And as this is the food commission, or something of that sort, everybody here will be better for hearing it. Anyway, everybody will have to know it before night. I took over the restaurant as you suggested, and posted some of the men from the bank that I knew I could trust about the doors. But there was hardly any use in doing it.

"The restaurant stocks up in the afternoon, as most of its

business is in the morning and at noon. It only carries a day's stock of foodstuffs, and the—the cataclysm, or whatever it was, came at three o'clock. There is practically nothing in the place. We couldn't make sandwiches for half the women that are caught with us, let alone the men. Everybody will go hungry tonight. There will be no breakfast tomorrow, nor anything to eat until we either make arrangements with the Indians for some supplies or else get food for ourselves."

Arthur leaned his jaw on his hand and considered. A slow flush crept over his cheek. He was getting his fighting blood up. At school, when he began to flush slowly, his schoolmates had known the symptom and avoided his wrath. Now he was growing angry with mere circumstances, but it would be nonetheless unfortunate for those circumstances.

"Well," he said at last deliberately, "we've got to— What's that?"

There was a great creaking and groaning. Suddenly a sort of vibration was felt under foot. The floor began to take on a slight slant.

"Great Heaven!" someone cried. "The building's turning over and we'll be buried in the ruins!"

The tilt of the floor became more pronounced. An empty chair slid to one end of the room. There was a crash.

ARTHUR AND ESTELLE IN CONFERENCE

Arthur woke to find someone tugging at his shoulders, trying to drag him from beneath the heavy table, which had wedged itself across his feet and pinned him fast, while a flying chair had struck him on the head.

"Oh, come and help," Estelle's voice was calling deliberately. "Somebody come and help! He's caught in here!"

She was sobbing in a combination of panic and some unknown emotion.

"Help me, please!" she gasped; then her voice broke despondently, but she never ceased to tug ineffectually at Chamberlain, trying to drag him out of the mass of wreckage.

Arthur moved a little, dazedly.

"Are you alive?" she called anxiously. "Are you alive? Hurry, oh, hurry and wiggle out. The building's falling to pieces."

"I'm all right," Arthur said weakly. "You get out before it all comes down."

"I won't leave you," she declared. "Where are you caught? Are you badly hurt? Hurry, please hurry!"

Arthur stirred, but could not loosen his feet. He half-rolled over, and the table moved as if it had been precariously balanced, and slid heavily to one side. With Estelle still tugging at him, he managed to get to his feet on the slanting floor and stared about him.

Arthur continued to stare about.

"No danger," he said weakly. "Just the floor of the one room gave way. The aftermath of the rock-flaw."

He made his way across the splintered flooring and piled-up chairs.

"We're on top of the safe-deposit vault," he said. "That's why we didn't fall all the way to the floor below. I wonder how we're going to get down."

Estelle followed him, still frightened for fear of the building falling upon them. Some of the long floor-boards stretched over the edge of the vault and rested on a tall, bronze grating that protected the approach to the massive strong-box. Arthur tested them with his foot.

"They seem to be pretty solid," he said tentatively.

His strength was coming back to him every moment. He had been no more than stunned. He walked out on the planking to the bronze grating and turned.

"If you don't get dizzy, you might come on," he said. "We can swing down the grille here to the floor."

Estelle followed gingerly and in a moment they were safely below. The corridor was quite empty.

"When the crash came," Estelle explained, her voice shaking with the reaction from her fear of a moment ago, "everyone thought the building was coming to pieces, and ran out. I'm afraid they've all run away."

"They'll be back in a little while," Arthur said quietly.

They went along the big marble corridor to the same western door, out of which they had first gone to see the Indian village. As they emerged into the sunlight they met a few of the people who had already recovered from their panic and were returning.

A crowd of respectable size gathered in a few moments, all still pale and shaken, but coming back to the building which was their refuge. Arthur leaned wearily against the cold stone. It seemed to vibrate under his touch. He turned quickly to Estelle.

"Feel this!" he exclaimed.

She did so.

"I've been wondering what that rumble was," she said. "I've been hearing it ever since we landed here, but didn't understand where it came from."

"You hear a rumble?" Arthur asked, puzzled. "I can't hear anything."

"It isn't as loud as it was, but I hear it," Estelle insisted. "It's very deep, like the lowest possible bass note of an organ."

"You couldn't hear the shrill whistle when we were coming here," Arthur exclaimed suddenly, "and you can't hear the squeak of a bat. Of course, your ears are pitched lower than usual, and you can hear sounds that are lower than I can hear. Listen carefully. Does it sound in the least like a liquid rushing through somewhere?"

"Y-yes," said Estelle hesitatingly. "Somehow, I don't quite understand how, it gives me the impression of a tidal flow or something of that sort."

Arthur rushed indoors. When Estelle followed him, she found him excitedly examining the marble floor about the base of the vault.

"It's cracked," he said excitedly. "It's cracked! The vault rose all of an inch!"

Estelle looked and saw the cracks.

"What does that crack in the floor mean?"

"It means we're going to get back where we belong," Arthur cried jubilantly. "It means I'm on the track of the whole trouble. It means everything's going to be all right."

He prowled about the vault exultantly, noting exactly how the cracks in the floor ran and seeing in each a corroboration of his theory.

"I'll have to make some inspections in the cellar," he went on happily, "but I'm nearly sure I'm on the right track and can figure out a corrective."

"How soon can we hope to start back?" asked Estelle eagerly.

Arthur hesitated; then a great deal of the excitement ebbed from his face, leaving it rather worried and stern.

"It may be a month, or two months, or a year," he answered gravely. "I don't know. If the first thing I try will work, it won't be long. If we have to experiment, I daren't guess how long we may be. But"—his chin set firmly—"we're going to get back."

Estelle looked at him speculatively. Her own expression grew a little worried, too.

"But in a month," she said dubiously, "we—there is hardly any hope of our finding food for two thousand people for a month, is there?"

"We've got to," Arthur declared. "We can't hope to get that much food from the Indians. It will be days before they'll dare to come back to their village, if they ever come. It will be weeks before we can hope to have them earnestly at work to feed us, and that's leaving aside the question of how we'll communicate with them, and how we'll manage to trade with them. Frankly, I think everybody is going to have to draw his belt tight before we get through—if we do. Some of us will get along, anyway."

Estelle's eyes opened wide as the meaning of his last sentence penetrated her mind.

"You mean—that all of us won't—"

"I'm going to take care of you," Arthur said gravely, "but there are liable to be lively doings around here when people begin to realize they're really in a tight fix for food. I'm going to get Van Deventer to help me organize a police band to enforce martial law. We mustn't have any disorder, that's certain, and I don't trust a city-bred man in a pinch unless I know him."

He stooped and picked up a revolver from the floor, left there by one of the bank watchmen when he fled, in the belief that the building was falling.

WILD PIGEONS DASH AGAINST THE BUILDING

Arthur stood at the window of his office and stared out toward the west. The sun was setting, but upon what a scene!

Where, from this same window Arthur had seen the sun setting behind the Jersey hills, all edged with the angular roofs of factories, with their chimneys emitting columns of smoke, he now saw the same sun sinking redly behind a mass of luxuriant foliage. And where he was accustomed to look upon the tops of high buildings—each entitled to the name of "skyscraper"— he now saw miles and miles of waving green branches.

The wide Hudson flowed on placidly, all unruffled by the arrival of this strange monument upon its shores—the same Hudson Arthur knew as a busy thoroughfare of puffing steamers and chugging launches. Two or three small streams wandered unconcernedly across the land that Arthur had known as the most closely built-up territory on earth. And far, far below him—Arthur had to lean well out of his window to see it— stood a collection of tiny wigwams. Those small bark structures represented the original metropolis of New York.

His telephone rang. Van Deventer was on the wire. The exchange in the building was still working. Van Deventer wanted Arthur to come down to his private office. There were still a great many things to be settled—the arrangements for commandeering offices for sleeping quarters for the women, and numberless other details. The men who seemed to have best kept their heads were gathering there to settle upon a course of action.

Arthur glanced out of the window again. He saw a curiously compact dark cloud moving swiftly across the sky to the west.

"Miss Woodward," he said sharply. "What is that?"

Estelle came to the window and looked.

"They are birds," she told him. "Birds flying in a group. I've often seen them in the country, though never as many as that."

"How do you catch birds?" Arthur asked her. "I know about shooting them, and so on, but we haven't guns enough to count. Could we catch them in traps, do you think?"

"I wouldn't be surprised," said Estelle thoughtfully. "But it would be hard to catch many."

"Come downstairs," directed Arthur. "You know as much as any of the men here, and more than most, apparently. We're going to make you show us how to catch things."

Estelle smiled, a trifle wanly. Arthur led the way to the elevator. In the car he noticed that she looked distressed.

"What's the matter?" he asked. "You aren't really frightened, are you?"

"No," she answered shakily, "but—I'm rather upset about this thing. It's so—so terrible, somehow, to be back here, thousands of miles, or years, away from all one's friends and everybody."

"Please"—Arthur smiled encouragingly at her—"please count me your friend, won't you?"

She nodded, but blinked back some tears. Arthur would have tried to hearten her further, but the elevator stopped at their floor. They walked into the room where the meeting of cool heads was to take place.

No more than a dozen men were in there talking earnestly but dispiritedly. When Arthur and Estelle entered, Van Deventer came over to greet them.

"We've got to do something," he said in a low voice. "A wave of homesickness has swept over the whole place. Look at those men. Every one is thinking about his family and contrasting his cozy fireside with all that wilderness outside."

"You don't seem to be worried," Arthur observed with a smile.

Van Deventer's eyes twinkled.

"I'm a bachelor," he said cheerfully, "and I live in a hotel. I've been longing for a chance to see some real excitement for thirty years. Business has kept me from it up to now, but I'm enjoying myself hugely."

Estelle looked at the group of dispirited men.

"We'll simply have to do something," she said with a shaky smile. "I feel just as they do. This morning I hated the thought of having to go back to my boarding house tonight, but right now I feel as if the odor of cabbage in the hallway would seem like heaven."

Arthur led the way to the flat-topped desk in the middle of the room.

"Let's settle a few of the more important matters," he said in a businesslike tone. "None of us has any authority to act for the rest of the people in the tower, but so many of us are in a state of blue funk that those who are here must have charge for a while. Anybody have any suggestions?"

"Housing," answered Van Deventer promptly. "I suggest that we draft a gang of men to haul all the upholstered settees and rugs that are to be found to one floor, for the women to sleep on."

"M-m. Yes. That's a good idea. Anybody have a better plan?"

No one spoke. They all still looked much too homesick to take any great interest in anything, but they began to listen more or less halfheartedly.

"I've been thinking about coal," said Arthur. "There's undoubtedly a supply in the basement, but I wonder if it wouldn't be well to cut the lights off most of the floors, only lighting up the ones we're using."

"That might be a good idea later," Estelle said quietly, "but light is cheering, somehow, and everyone feels so blue that I wouldn't do it tonight. Tomorrow they'll begin to get up their resolution again, and you can ask them to do things."

"If we're going to starve to death," one of the other men said gloomily, "we might as well have plenty of light to do it by."

"We aren't going to starve to death," retorted Arthur sharply. "Just before I came down I saw a great cloud of birds, greater than I had ever seen before. When we get at those birds—"

"When," echoed the gloomy one.

"They were pigeons," Estelle explained. "They shouldn't be hard to snare or trap."

"I usually have my dinner before now," the gloomy one protested, "and I'm told I won't get anything tonight."

The other men began to straighten their shoulders. The peevishness of one of their number seemed to bring out their latent courage.

"Well, we've got to stand it for the present," one of them said almost philosophically. "What I'm most anxious about is getting back. Have we any chance?"

Arthur nodded emphatically.

"I think so. I have a sort of idea as to the cause of our sinking into the Fourth Dimension, and when that is verified, a corrective can be looked for and applied."

"How long will that take?"

"Can't say," Arthur replied frankly. "I don't know what tools, what materials, or what workmen we have, and what's rather more to the point, I don't even know what work will have to be done. The pressing problem is food."

"Oh, bother the food," someone protested impatiently. "I don't care about myself. I can go hungry tonight. I want to get back to my family."

"That's all that really matters," a chorus of voices echoed.

"We'd better not bother about anything else unless we find we can't get back. Concentrate on getting back," one man stated more explicitly.

"Look here," said Arthur incisively. "You've a family, and so have a great many of the others in the tower, but your family and everybody else's family has got to wait. As an inside limit, we can hope to begin to work on the problem of getting back when we're sure there's nothing else going to happen. I tell you quite honestly that I think I know what is the direct cause of this catastrophe. And I'll tell you even more honestly that I think I'm the only man among us who can put this tower back where it started from. And I'll tell you most honestly of all that any attempt to meddle at this time with the forces that let us down here will result in a catastrophe considerably greater than the one that happened today."

"Well, if you're sure—" someone began reluctantly.

"I am so sure that I'm going to keep to myself the knowledge of what will start those forces to work again," Arthur said quietly. "I don't want any impatient meddling. If we start them too soon, God only knows what will happen."

ORGANIZING THE FOOD-SUPPLY

Van Deventer was eyeing Arthur Chamberlain keenly.

"It isn't a question of your wanting pay in exchange for your services in putting us back, is it?" he asked coolly.

Arthur turned and faced him. His face began to flush slowly. Van Deventer put up one hand.

"I beg your pardon. I see."

"We aren't settling the things we came here for," Estelle interrupted.

She had noted the threat of friction and had hastened to put in a diversion. Arthur relaxed.

"I think that as a beginning," he suggested, "we'd better get sleeping arrangements completed. We can get everybody together somewhere, I dare say, and then secure volunteers for the work."

"Right." Van Deventer was anxious to make amends for his blunder of a moment before. "Shall I send the bank watchmen to go on each floor in turn and ask everyone to come downstairs?"

"You might start them," Arthur said. "It will take a long time for everyone to assemble."

Van Deventer spoke into the telephone on his desk. In a moment he hung up the receiver.

"They're on their way," he said.

Arthur was frowning to himself and scribbling in a notebook.

"Of course," he announced abstractedly, "the pressing problem is food. We've quite a number of fishermen, and a few hunters. We've got to have a lot of food at once, and everything considered, I think we'd better count on the fishermen. At sunrise we'd better have some people begin to dig bait and wake our anglers. They'd better make their tackle tonight, don't you think?"

There was a general nod.

"We'll announce that, then. The fishermen will go to the river under guard of the men we have who can shoot. I think what Indians there are will be much too frightened to try to ambush any of us, but we'd better be on the safe side. They'll keep together and fish at nearly the same spot, with our hunters patrolling the woods behind them, taking pot shots at game, if they see any. The fishermen should make more or less of a success, I think. The Indians weren't extensive fishers that I ever heard of, and the river ought fairly to swarm with fish."

He closed his notebook.

"How many weapons can we count on altogether?" Arthur asked Van Deventer.

"In the bank, about a dozen riot guns and half a dozen repeating rifles. Elsewhere I don't know. Forty or fifty men said they had revolvers, though."

"We'll give revolvers to the men who go with the fishermen. The Indians haven't heard firearms and will run at the report, even if they dare attack our men."

"We can send out the gun-armed men as hunters," someone suggested, "and send gardeners with them to look for vegetables and such things."

"We'll have to take a sort of census, really," Arthur suggested, "finding what everyone can do and getting him to do it."

"I never planned anything like this before," Van Deventer remarked, "and I never thought I should, but this is much more fun than running a bank."

Arthur smiled.

"Let's go and have our meeting," he said cheerfully.

But the meeting was a gloomy and despairing affair. Nearly everyone had watched the sun set upon the strange, wild landscape. Hardly an individual among the whole two thousand of them had ever been out of sight of a house before in his or her life. To look out at a vast, untouched wilderness where hitherto they had seen the most highly civilized city on the globe would have been startling and depressing enough in itself, but to know that they were alone in a whole continent of savages and that there was not, indeed, in all the world a single community of people they could greet as brothers was terrifying.

Few of them thought so far, but there was actually—if Arthur's estimate of several thousand years' drop back through time was correct—there was actually no other group of English-speaking people in the world. The English language was yet to be invented. Even Rome, the synonym for antiquity of culture, might still be an obscure village inhabited by a band of tatterde-malions under the leadership of an upstart Romulus.

Soft in body as these people were, city-bred and unaccustomed to face other than the most conventionalized emergencies of life, they were terrified. Hardly one of them had even gone without a meal in all his life. To have the prospect of having to earn their food, not by the manipulation of figures in a book, or by expert juggling of profits and prices, but by literal wresting of that food from its source in the earth or stream was a really terrifying thing for them.

In addition, every one of them was bound to the life of modern times by a hundred ties. Many of them had families, a thousand years away. All had interests, engrossing interests, in modern New York.

One young man felt an anxiety that was really ludicrous because he had promised to take his sweetheart to the theater that night, and if he did not come, she would be very angry. Another was to be married in a week. Some of the people were, like Van Deventer and Arthur, so situated they could view the episode as an adventure, or, like Estelle, who had no immediate fear because all her family was provided for without her help and lived far from New York, so they would not learn of the catastrophe for some time. Many, however, felt instant and pressing fear for the families whose expenses ran always so close to their incomes that the disappearance of the breadwinner for a week would mean actual want or debt. There are very many such families in New York.

The people, therefore, that gathered hopelessly at the call of Van Deventer's watchmen were dazed and spiritless. Their excitement after Arthur's first attempt to explain the situation to them had evaporated. They were no longer keyed up to a high pitch by the startling thing that had happened to them.

Nevertheless, although only half comprehending what had actually occurred, they began to realize what that occurrence meant. No matter where they might go over the whole face of the globe, they would always be aliens and strangers. If they had been carried away to some unknown shore, some wilderness far from their own land, they might have thought of building ships to return to their homes. They had seen New York vanish before their eyes, however. They had seen their civilization disappear while they watched.

They were in a barbarous world. There was not, for example, a single safety match on the whole earth except those in the runaway skyscraper.

A FOOD-RIOT IN THE BUILDING

Arthur and Van Deventer, in turn with the others of the cooler heads, thundered at the apathetic people, trying to waken them to the necessity for work. They showered promises of inevitable return to modern times; they pledged their honor to the belief that a way would ultimately be found by which they would all yet find themselves safely back home again.

The people, however, had seen New York disintegrate, and Arthur's explanation sounded like some wild dream of an imaginative novelist. Not one person in all the gathering could actually realize that his home might yet be waiting for him, though at the same time he felt a pathetic anxiety for the welfare of its inmates.

Everyone was in a turmoil of contradictory beliefs. On the

one hand they knew that all of New York could not be actually destroyed and replaced by a splendid forest in the space of a few hours, so the accident or catastrophe must have occurred to those in the tower, and on the other hand, they had seen all of New York vanish by bits and fragments, to be replaced by a smaller and dingier town, had beheld that replaced in turn, and at last had landed in the midst of this forest.

Everyone, too, began to feel an unusual and uncomfortable sensation of hunger. It was a mild discomfort as yet, but few of them had experienced it before without an immediate prospect of assuaging the craving, and the knowledge that there was no food to be had somehow increased the desire for it. They were really in a pitiful state.

Van Deventer spoke encouragingly, and then asked for volunteers for immediate work. There was hardly any response. Everyone seemed sunk in despondency. Arthur then began to talk straight from the shoulder and succeeded in rousing them a little, but everyone was still rather too frightened to realize that work could help at all.

In desperation the dozen or so men who had gathered in Van Deventer's office went about among the gathering and simply selected men at random, ordering them to follow and begin work. This began to awaken the crowd, but they wakened to fear rather than resolution. They were city-bred, and unaccustomed to face the unusual or the alarming.

Arthur noted the new restlessness, but attributed it to growing uneasiness rather than selfish panic. He was rather pleased that they were outgrowing their apathy. When the meeting had come to an end, he felt satisfied that by morning the latent resolution among the people would have crystallized, and they would be ready to work earnestly and intelligently on whatever tasks they were directed to undertake.

He returned to the ground floor of the building feeling much more hopeful than before. Two thousand people all earnestly working for one end are hard to down even when faced with such a task as confronted the inhabitants of the runaway skyscraper.

Even if they were never able to return to modern times, they would still be able to form a community that might do much to hasten the development of civilization in other parts of the world.

His hope received a rude shock when he reached the great hallway on the lower floor. There was a fruit and confectionery stand here, and as Arthur arrived at the spot, he saw a surging mass of men about it. The keeper of the stand looked frightened, but was selling off his stock as fast as he could make change. Arthur forced his way to the counter.

"Here," he said sharply to the keeper of the stand, "stop selling this stuff. It's got to be held until we can dole it out where it's needed."

"I—I can't help myself," the keeper said. "They're takin' it anyway."

"Get back there," Arthur cried to the crowd. "Do you call this decent, trying to get more than your share of this stuff? You'll get your portion tomorrow. It is going to be divided up."

"Go to hell!" someone panted. "You c'n starve if you want to, but I'm goin' to look out f'r myself."

The men were not really starving, but had been put into a panic by the plain speeches of Arthur and his helpers, and were seizing what edibles they could lay hands upon in preparation for the hunger they had been warned to expect.

Arthur pushed against the mob, trying to thrust them away from the counter, but his very effort intensified their panic. There was a quick surge and a crash. The glass front of the showcase broke in.

In a flash of rage Arthur struck out viciously. The crowd paid not the slightest attention to him, however. Every man was too panic-stricken, and too intent on getting some of this food before it was all gone, to bother with him.

Arthur was simply crushed back by the bodies of the forty or fifty men. In a moment he found himself alone amid the wreckage of the stand, with the keeper wringing his hands over the remnants of his goods.

Van Deventer ran down the stairs.

"What's the matter?" he demanded as he saw Arthur nursing a bleeding hand cut on the broken glass of the showcase.

"Bolsheviki!" answered Arthur with a grim smile. "We woke up some of the crowd too successfully. They got panic-stricken and started to buy out this stuff here. I tried to stop them, and you see what happened. We'd better look to the restaurant, though I doubt if they'll try anything just now."

He followed Van Deventer up to the restaurant floor. There were picked men before the door, but just as Arthur and the bank president appeared two or three white-faced men went up to the guards and started low-voiced conversations.

Arthur reached the spot in time to forestall bribery.

Arthur collared one man, Van Deventer another, and in a moment the two were sent reeling down the hallway.

"Some fools have got panic-stricken!" Van Deventer explained to the men before the doors in a casual voice, though he was breathing heavily from the unaccustomed exertion. "They've smashed the fruitstand on the ground floor and stolen the contents. It's nothing but blue funk! Only, if any of them start to gather around here, hit them first and talk it over afterward. You'll do that?"

"We will!" the men said heartily.

"Shall we use our guns?" asked another hopefully.

Van Deventer grinned.

"No," he replied, "we haven't any excuse for that yet. But you might shoot at the ceiling, if they get excited. They're just frightened!"

He took Arthur's arm, and the two walked toward the stairway again.

"Chamberlain," he said happily, quickening his pace, "tell me why I've never had as much fun as this before!"

Arthur smiled a bit wearily.

"I'm glad you're enjoying yourself!" he said. "Because I'm not. I'm going outside and walk around a bit. I want to see if any cracks have appeared in the earth anywhere. It's dark, and

I'll borrow a lantern down in the fire-room, but I want to find out if there are any more developments in the condition of the building."

THEORIZING ON THE STRANGE OCCURRENCE

Despite his preoccupation with his errand, which was to find if there were other signs of the continued activity of the strange forces that had lowered the tower through the Fourth Dimension into the dim and unrecorded years of aboriginal America, Arthur could not escape the fascination of the sight that met his eyes. A bright moon shone overhead and silvered the white sides of the tower, while the brightly-lighted windows of the offices within glittered like jewels set into the shining shaft.

From his position on the ground he looked into the dimness of the forest on all sides. Black obscurity had gathered beneath the dark masses of moonlit foliage. The tiny birch-bark teepees of the now deserted Indian village glowed palely. Above the stars looked calmly down at the accusing finger of the tower pointing upward, as if in reproach at their indifference to the savagery that reigned over the whole earth.

Like a fairy tower of jewels the building rose. Alone among a wilderness of trees and streams it towered in a strange beauty; moonlit to silver, lighted from within to a mass of brilliant gems, it stood serenely still.

Arthur, carrying his futile lantern about its base, felt his own insignificance as never before. He wondered what the Indians must think. He knew there must be hundreds of eyes fixed upon the strange sight—fixed in awestricken terror or superstitious reverence upon this unearthly visitor to their hunting grounds.

A tiny figure, dwarfed by the building whose base he skirted, Arthur moved slowly about the vast pile. The earth seemed not to have been affected by the vast weight of the tower.

Arthur knew, however, that long concrete piles reached far down to bedrock. It was these piles that had sunk into the Fourth Dimension, carrying the building with them.

Arthur had followed the plans with great interest when the Metropolitan was constructed. It was an engineering feat, and in the engineering periodicals, whose study was part of Arthur's business, great space had been given to the building and the methods of its construction.

While examining the earth carefully he went over his theory of the cause for the catastrophe. The whole structure must have sunk at the same time, or it, too, would have disintegrated, as the other buildings had appeared to disintegrate. Mentally, Arthur likened the submergence of the tower in the oceans of time to an elevator sinking past the different floors of an office building. All about the building the other skyscrapers of New York had seemed to vanish. In an elevator, the floors one passes seem to rise up.

Carrying out the analogy to its logical end, Arthur reasoned that the building itself had no more cause to disintegrate, as the buildings it passed seemed to disintegrate, than the elevator in the office building would have cause to rise because its surroundings seemed to rise.

Within the building, he knew, there were strange stirrings of emotions. Queer currents of panic were running about, throwing the people to and fro as leaves are thrown about by a current of wind. Yet, underneath all those undercurrents of fear was a rapidly growing resolution, strengthened by an increasing knowledge of the need to work.

Men were busy even then shifting all possible comfortable furniture to a single story for the women in the building to occupy. The men would sleep on the floor for the present. Beds of boughs could be improvised on the morrow. At sunrise on the following morning many men would go to the streams to fish, guarded by other men. All would be frightened, no doubt, but there would be a grim resolution underneath the fear. Other men would wander about to hunt.

There was little likelihood of Indians approaching for some days, at least, but when they did come Arthur meant to avoid hostilities by all possible means. The Indians would be fearful of their strange visitors, and it should not be difficult to convince them that friendliness was safest, even if they displayed unfriendly desires.

The pressing problem was food. There were two thousand people in the building, soft-bodied and city-bred. They were unaccustomed to hardship, and could not endure what more primitive people would hardly have noticed.

They must be fed, but they must be taught to feed themselves. The fishermen would help, but Arthur could only hope that they would prove equal to the occasion. He did not know what to expect from them. From the hunters he expected but little. The Indians were wary hunters, and game would be shy if not scarce.

The great cloud of birds he had seen at sunset was a hopeful sign. Arthur vaguely remembered stories of great flocks of woodpigeons which had been exterminated, as the buffalo was exterminated. As he considered, the remembrance became more clear.

They had flown in huge flocks which nearly darkened the sky. As late as the forties of the nineteenth century they had been an important article of food, and had glutted the market at certain seasons of the year.

Estelle had said the birds he had seen at sunset were pigeons. Perhaps this was one of the great flocks. If it were really so, the food problem would be much lessened, provided a way could be found to secure them. The ammunition in the tower was very limited, and a shell could not be found for every bird that was needed, nor even for every three or four. Great traps must be devised, or bird-lime might possibly be produced. Arthur made a mental note to ask Estelle is she knew anything of bird-lime.

A vague, humming roar, altering in pitch, came to his ears. He listened for some time before he identified it as the sound of the wind playing upon the irregular surfaces of the tower. In the city the sound was drowned by the multitude of other noises, but here Arthur could hear it plainly.

He listened a moment, and became surprised at the number of night noises he could hear. In New York he had closed his ears to incidental sounds from sheer self-protection. Somewhere he heard the ripple of a little spring. As the idea of a spring came into his mind, he remembered Estelle's description of the deep-toned roar she had heard.

He put his hand on the cold stone of the building. There was still a vibrant quivering of the rock. It was weaker than before, but was still noticeable. He drew back from the rock and looked up into the sky. It seemed to blaze with stars, more stars than Arthur had ever seen in the city, and more than he had dreamed existed.

As he looked, however, a cloud seemed to film a portion of the heavens. The stars still showed through it, but they twinkled in a peculiar fashion that Arthur could not understand.

He watched in growing perplexity. The cloud moved very swiftly. Thin as it seemed to be, it should have been silvery from the moonlight, but the sky was noticeably darker where it moved. It advanced toward the tower and seemed to obscure the upper portion. A confused motion became visible among its parts. Wisps of it whirled away from the brilliantly lighted tower, and then returned swiftly toward it.

Arthur heard a faint tinkle, then a musical scraping, which became louder. A faint scream sounded, then another. The tinkle developed into the sound made by breaking glass, and the scraping sound became that of the broken fragments as they rubbed against the sides of the tower in their fall.

The scream came again. It was the frightened cry of a woman. A soft body struck the earth not ten feet from where Arthur stood, then another, and another.

ARTHUR AND ESTELLE IN CONFERENCE AGAIN

Arthur urged the elevator-boy to greater speed. They were speeding up the shaft as rapidly as possible, but it was not fast enough. When they at last reached the height at which the excitement seemed to be centered, the car stopped with a jerk and Arthur dashed down the hall.

Half a dozen frightened stenographers stood there, huddled together.

"What's the matter?" Arthur demanded. Men were running from the other floors to see what the trouble was.

"The—the windows broke, and—and something flew in at us!" one of them gasped. There was a crash inside the nearest office, and the women screamed again.

Arthur drew a revolver from his pocket and advanced to the door. He quickly threw it open, entered, and closed it behind him. Those left out in the hall waited tensely.

There was no sound. The women began to look even more frightened. The men shuffled their feet uneasily, and looked uncomfortably at one another. Van Deventer appeared on the scene, puffing a little from his haste.

The door opened again and Arthur came out. He was carrying something in his hand. He had put his revolver aside and looked somewhat foolish but very much delighted.

"The food question is settled," he said happily. "Look!"

He held out the object he carried. It was a bird, apparently a pigeon of some sort. It seemed to have been stunned, but as Arthur held it out it stirred, then struggled, and in a moment was flapping wildly in an attempt to escape.

"It's a wood-pigeon," said Arthur. "They must fly after dark sometimes. A big flock of them ran afoul of the tower and were dazed by the lights. They've broken a lot of windows, I dare say, but a great many of them ran into the stonework and were stunned. I was outside the tower, and when I came in, they were dropping to the ground by hundreds. I didn't know what they were then, but if we wait twenty minutes or so I think we can go out and gather up our supper and breakfast and several other meals, all at once."

Estelle had appeared and now reached out her hands for the bird.

"I'll take care of this one," she said. "Wouldn't it be a good idea to see if there aren't some more stunned in the other offices?"

In half an hour the electric stoves of the restaurant were going at their full capacity. Men, cheerfully excited men now, were bringing in pigeons by armfuls, and other men were skinning them. There was no time to pluck them, though a great many of the women were busily engaged in that occupation.

As fast as the birds could be cooked they were served out to the impatient but much cheered castaways, and in a little while nearly every person in the place was walking casually about the halls with a roasted, broiled, or fried pigeon in his hands. The ovens were roasting pigeons, the frying-pans were frying them, and the broilers were loaded down with the small but tender birds.

The unexpected solution of the most pressing question cheered everyone amazingly. Many people were still frightened, but less frightened than before. Worry for their families still oppressed a great many, but the removal of the fear of immediate hunger led them to believe that the other problems before them would be solved, too, and in as satisfactory a manner.

Arthur had returned to his office with four broiled pigeons in a sheet of wrapping-paper. As he somehow expected, Estelle was waiting there.

"Thought I'd bring lunch up," he announced. "Are you hungry?"

"Starving!" Estelle replied, and laughed.

The whole catastrophe began to become an adventure. She bit eagerly into the bird. Arthur began as hungrily on another. For some time neither spoke a word. At last, however, Arthur waved the leg of his second pigeon toward his desk.

"Look what we've got here!" he said.

Estelle nodded. The stunned pigeon Arthur had first picked up was tied by one foot to a paperweight.

"I thought we might keep him for a souvenir," she suggested.

"You seem pretty confident we'll get back, all right," Arthur observed. "It was surely lucky those blessed birds came along. They've heartened up the people wonderfully!"

"Oh, I knew you'd manage somehow!" said Estelle confidently.

"I manage?" Arthur repeated, smiling. "What have I done?"

"Why, you've done everything," affirmed Estelle stoutly. "You've told the people what to do from the very first, and you're going to get us back."

Arthur grinned, then suddenly his face grew a little more serious.

"I wish I were as sure as you are," he said. "I think we'll be all right, though, sooner or later."

"I'm sure of it," Estelle declared with conviction. "Why, you—"

"Why I?" asked Arthur again. He bent forward in his chair and fixed his eyes on Estelle's. She looked up, met his gaze and stammered:

"You—you do things," she finished lamely.

"I'm tempted to do something now," Arthur said. "Look here, Miss Woodward, you've been in my employ for three or four months. In all that time I've never had anything but the most impersonal comments from you. Why the sudden change?"

The twinkle in his eyes robbed his words of any impertinence.

"Why, I really—I really suppose I never noticed you before," said Estelle.

"Please notice me hereafter," said Arthur. "I have been noticing you. I've been doing practically nothing else."

Estelle flushed again. She tried to meet Arthur's eyes and failed. She bit desperately into her pigeon drumstick, trying to think of something to say.

"When we get back," went on Arthur meditatively, "I'll have nothing to do—no work or anything. I'll be broke and out of a job."

Estelle shook her head emphatically. Arthur paid no attention.

"Estelle," he said, smiling, "would you like to be out of a job with me?"

Estelle turned crimson.

"I'm not very successful," Arthur went on soberly. "I'm afraid I wouldn't make a very good husband; I'm rather worthless and lazy!"

"You aren't," broke in Estelle; "you're—you're—"

Arthur reached over and took her by the shoulders.

"What?" he demanded.

She would not look at him, but she did not draw away. He held her from him for a moment.

"What am I?" he demanded again. Somehow he found himself kissing the tips of her ears. Her face was buried against his shoulder.

"What am I?" he repeated sternly.

Her voice was muffled by his coat.

"You're—you're dear!" she said.

There was an interlude of about a minute and a half, then she pushed him away from her.

"Don't!" she said breathlessly. "Please don't!"

"Aren't you going to marry me?" he demanded.

Still crimson, she nodded shyly. He kissed her again.

"Please don't!" she protested.

She fondled the lapels of his coat, quite content to have his arms about her.

"Why mayn't I kiss you if you're going to marry me?" Arthur demanded.

She looked up at him with an air of demure primness.

"You—you've been eating pigeon," she told him in mock gravity, "and—and your mouth is greasy!"

A GEYSER EFFECTS A HAPPY RETURN

It was two weeks later. Estelle looked out over the now familiar wild landscape. It was much the same when she looked far away but nearby there were great changes.

A cleared trail led through the woods to the waterfront, and a raft of logs extended out into the river for hundreds of feet. Both sides of the raft were lined with busy fishermen—men and women, too. A little to the north of the base of the building a huge mound of earth smoked sullenly. The coal in the cellar had given out and charcoal had been found to be the best substitute they could improvise. The mound was where the charcoal was made.

It was heartbreaking work to keep the fires going with charcoal, because it burned so rapidly in the powerful draft of the furnaces, but the original fire-room gang had been recruited to several times its original number from among the towerites, and the work was divided until it did not seem hard.

As Estelle looked down, two tiny figures sauntered across the clearing from the woods with a heavy animal slung between them. One was using a gun as a walking-stick. Estelle saw the flash of the sun on its polished barrel.

There were a number of Indians in the clearing, watching with wide-open eyes the activities of the whites. Dozens of birch-bark canoes dotted the Hudson, each with its load of fishermen, industriously working for the white people. It had been hard to overcome the fear in the Indians, and they still paid superstitious reverence to the whites, but fair dealings, coupled with a constant readiness to defend themselves, had enabled Arthur to institute a system of trading for food that had so far proved satisfactory.

The whites had found spare electric-light bulbs valuable currency in dealing with the redmen. Picture-wire, too, was highly prized. There was not a picture left hanging in any of the offices. Metal paper-knives bought huge quantities of provisions from the eager Indian traders, and the story was current in the tower that Arthur had received eight canoe-loads of corn and vegetables in exchange for a broken-down typewriter. No one could guess what the savages wanted with the typewriter, but they had carted it away triumphantly.

Estelle smiled tenderly to herself as she remembered how Arthur had been the leading spirit in all the numberless enterprises in which the castaways had been forced to engage. He would come to her in a spare ten minutes, and tell her how everything was going. He seemed curiously boylike in those moments.

Sometimes he would come straight from the fire-room—he insisted on taking part in all the more arduous duties—having hastily cleaned himself for her inspection, snatch a hurried kiss and then go off, laughing, to help chop down trees for the long fishing-raft. He had told them how to make charcoal, had taken a leading part in establishing and maintaining friendly relations with the Indians, and was now down in the deepest sub-basement, working with a gang of volunteers to try to put the building back where it belonged.

Estelle had said, after the collapse of the flooring in the board-room, that she heard a sound like the rushing of waters. Arthur, on examining the floor where the safe-deposit vault stood, found it had risen an inch. On these facts he had built up his theory. The building, like all modern skyscrapers, rested on concrete piles extending down to bedrock. In the center of one of those piles there was a hollow tube originally intended to serve as an artesian well. The flow had been insufficient and the well had been stopped up.

Arthur, of course, as an engineer, had studied the construction of the building with great care, and happened to remember that this partly hollow pile was the one nearest the safe-deposit vault. The collapse of the board-room floor had suggested that some change had happened in the building itself, and that was found when he saw that the deposit vault had actually risen an inch.

He at once connected the rise in the flooring above the hollow pile with the pipe in the pile. Estelle had heard liquid sounds. Evidently water had been forced into the hollow artesian pipe under an unthinkable pressure when the catastrophe occurred.

From the rumbling and the suddenness of the whole catastrophe, a volcanic or seismic disturbance was evident. The connection of volcanic or seismic action with a flow of water suggested a geyser or a hot spring of some sort, probably a spring which had broken through its normal confines sometime before, but whose pressure had been sufficient to prevent the accident until the failure of its flow.

When the flow ceased the building sank rapidly. For the fact that this "sinking" was in the fourth direction—the Fourth Dimension—Arthur had no explanation. He simply knew that in some mysterious way an outlet for the pressure had developed in that fashion, and that the tower had followed the spring in its fall through time.

The sole apparent change in the building had occurred above the one hollow concrete pile, which seemed to indicate that if access were to be had to the mysterious, and so far only assumed spring, it must be through that pile. While the vault retained its abnormal elevation, Arthur believed that there was still water at an immense and incalculable pressure in the pipe. He dared not attempt to tap the pipe until the pressure had abated.

At the end of the week he found the vault slowly settling back into place. When its return to normal was complete, he dared begin boring a hole to reach the hollow tube in the concrete pile.

As he suspected, he found water in the pile—water whose sulfurous and mineral nature confirmed his belief that a geyser reaching deep into the bosom of the earth, as well as far back in the realms of time, was at the bottom of the extraordinary jaunt of the tower.

Geysers were still far from satisfactory things to explain. There are many of their vagaries which we cannot understand at all. We do know a few things which affect them, and one thing is that "soaping" them will stimulate their flow in an extraordinary manner.

Arthur proposed to "soap" this mysterious geyser when the renewal of its flow should lift the runaway skyscraper back to the epoch from which the failure of the flow had caused it to fall.

He made his preparations with great care. He confidently expected his plan to work, and to see the skyscraper once more towering over mid-town New York as was its wont, but he did not allow the fishermen and hunters to relax their efforts on that account. They labored as before, while deep down in the sub-basement of the colossal building Arthur and his volunteers toiled mightily.

They had to bore through the concrete pile until they reached the hollow within it. Then, when the evidence gained from the water in the pipe had confirmed his surmises, they had to prepare their "charge" of soapy liquids by which the geyser was to be stirred to renewed activity.

Great quantities of the soap used by the scrub-women in scrubbing down the floors were boiled with water until a sirupy mess was evolved. Means had then to be provided by which this could be quickly introduced into the hollow pile, the hole then closed, and then braced to withstand a pressure unparalleled in hydraulic science. Arthur believed that from the hollow pile the soapy liquid would find its way to the geyser proper, where it would take effect in stimulating the lessened flow to its former proportions. When they took place he believed that the building would return to normal, modern times, as swiftly and as surely as it had left them.

The telephone rang in his office, and Estelle answered it. Arthur was on the wire. A signal was being hung out for all the castaways to return to the building from their several occupations. They were about to soap the geyser.

Did Estelle want to come down and watch? She did! She stood in the main hallway as the excited and hopeful people trooped in. When the last was inside, the doors were firmly closed. The few friendly Indians outside stared perplexedly at the mysterious white strangers. The whites, laughing excitedly, began to wave to the Indians. Their leave-taking was premature.

Estelle took her way down into the cellar. Arthur was awaiting her arrival. Van Deventer stood near, with the grinning, grimy members of Arthur's volunteer work gang. The massive concrete pile stood in the center of the cellar. A big steam-boiler was coupled to a tiny pipe that led into the heart of the mass of concrete. Arthur was going to force the soapy liquid into the hollow pile by steam.

At the signal steam began to hiss in the boiler. Live steam from the fire-room forced the soapy sirup out of the boiler, through the small iron pipe, into the hollow that led to the geyser far underground. Six thousand gallons in all were forced into the opening in a space of three minutes. Arthur's grimy gang began to work with desperate haste. Quickly they withdrew the iron pipe and inserted a long steel plug, painfully beaten from a bar of solid metal. Then, girding the colossal concrete pile, ring after ring of metal was slipped on, to hold the plug in place.

The last of the safeguards was hardly fastened firmly when Estelle listened intently. "I hear a rumbling!" she said quietly.

Arthur reached forward and put his hand on the mass of concrete.

"It is quivering!" he reported as quietly. "I think we'll be on our way in a very little while."

The group broke for the stairs, to watch the panorama as the runaway skyscraper made its way back through the thousands of years to the times that had built it for a monument to modern commerce. Arthur and Estelle went high up in the tower. From the window of Arthur's office they looked eagerly, and felt the slight quiver as the tower got under way. Estelle looked up at the sun, and saw it mend its pace toward the west.

Night fell. The evening sounds became highpitched and shrill, then seemed to cease altogether.

In a very little while there was light again, and the sun was speeding across the sky. It sank hastily, and returned almost immediately, *via* the east. Its pace became a breakneck rush. Down behind the hills and up in the east. Down in the west and up in the east. Down and up— The flickering began. The race back toward modern time had started.

Arthur and Estelle stood at the window and looked out as the sun rushed more and more rapidly across the sky until it became a streak of light, shifting first to the right and then to the left as the seasons passed in their turn.

With Arthur's arms about her shoulders, Estelle stared out across the unbelievable landscape, while the nights and days, the winters and summers, and the storms and calms of a thousand years swept past them into the irrevocable aeons.

Presently Arthur drew her to him and kissed her. While he kissed her, so swiftly did the days and years flee by, three generations were born, grew and begot children, and died again! Estelle, held fast in Arthur's arms, thought nothing of such trivial things. She put her arms about his neck and kissed him, while the years passed them unheeded.

Of course you know that the building landed safely, in the exact hour, minute, and second from which it started, so that when the frightened and excited people poured out of it to stand in Madison Square and feel that the world was once more right side up, their hilarious and incomprehensible conduct made such of the world as was passing by to think a contagious madness had broken out.

Days passed before the story of the two thousand was believed, but at last it was accepted as truth, and eminent scientists studied the matter exhaustively.

There has been one rather queer result of the journey of the runaway skyscraper. A certain Isidore Eckstein, a dealer in jewelry novelties, whose office was in the tower when it disappeared into the past, has entered suit in the courts of the United States against all holders of land on Manhattan Island. It seems that during the two weeks in which the tower rested in the wilderness he traded independently with one of the Indian chiefs, and in exchange for two near-pearly necklaces, sixteen finger-rings, and one dollar in money, received a title-deed to the entire island. He claims that his deed is a conveyance made previous to all other sales whatever.

Strictly speaking, he is undoubtedly right, as his deed was signed before the discovery of America. The courts, however, are deliberating the question with a great deal of perplexity.

Eckstein is quite confident that in the end his claim will be allowed and he will be admitted as the sole owner of real estate on Manhattan Island, with all occupiers of building and territory paying his ground-rent at a rate he will fix himself. In the meantime, though the foundations are being reinforced so the catastrophe cannot occur again, his entire office is packed full of articles suitable for trading with the Indians. If the tower makes another trip back through time, Eckstein hopes to become a landholder of some importance.

No less than eighty-seven books have been written by members of the memorable two thousand in description of their trip to the hinterland of time, but Arthur, who could write more intelligently about the matter than anyone else, is too busy to bother with such things. He has two very important matters to look after. One is, of course, the reinforcement of the foundations of the building so that a repetition of the catastrophe cannot occur, and the other is to convince his wife—who is Estelle, naturally—that she is the most adorable person in the universe. He finds the latter task the more difficult, because she insists that *he* is the most adorable person—

Even in a field as far out as this one, Isaac Asimov must be considered remarkable—on at least three counts. First, he was one of the seminal writers in the Campbell group that helped make science fiction modern in the Golden Forties. Then, for most of the next decade, he produced a cluster of major novels that some of us feel culminated with *Caves of Steel*, which so beautifully fuses science fiction with the detective story. Finally, since then he has just about made a runaway of the popular-science writing field, turning out at an incredible pace at least half a dozen books a year on everything from the human brain to the building blocks of the universe. And as if that weren't enough, he is now writing, among other things, a monumental analysis of the Bible.

But if you're still not convinced, then consider what he has done in the following pair of stories written twenty years apart. Where most writers probably would have left well enough alone, Asimov challenged himself—in 1959—to go back to the premise of his first published story—written in the style of the thirties—and try a sequel. The result? A crisp, "modern" piece that if anything turned out better than the original—even though as a first sale "Marooned off Vesta" was exceptional for a young man still in his teens.

MAROONED OFF VESTA

Isaac Asimov

1. WRECK OF THE SILVER QUEEN

"Will you please stop walking up and down like that," said Warren Moore from the couch; "it won't do any of us any good. Think of our blessings; we're airtight, aren't we?"

Mark Brandon whirled and ground his teeth at him. "I'm glad you feel happy about that," he spat out viciously. "Of course you don't know that our air-supply will last only three days." He resumed his interrupted stride with a defiant air.

Moore yawned and stretched, assumed a more comfortable

position, and replied, "Expending all that energy will only use it up faster. Why don't you take a hint from Mike here. He's taking it easy."

"Mike" was Michael Shea, late a member of the crew of the *Silver Queen*. His short, squat body was resting on the only chair in the room and his feet were on the only table. He looked up as his name was mentioned, his mouth widening in a twisted grin.

"You've got to expect things like this to happen sometimes," he said. "Bucking the asteroids is risky business. We should've taken the hop. It takes longer, but it's the only safe way. But no, the captain wanted to make the schedule; he *would* go through," Mike spat disgustedly, "and here we are."

"What's the 'hop'?" asked Brandon.

"Oh, I take it that friend Mike means that we should have avoided the asteroid belt by plotting a course outside the plane of the ecliptic," answered Moore. "That's it, isn't it, Mike?"

Mike hesitated and then replied cautiously, "Yeah—I guess that's it."

Moore smiled blandly and continued, "Well, I wouldn't blame Captain Crane too much. The repulsion screen must have failed five minutes before that chunk of granite barged into us. That's not his fault, though of course we ought to have steered clear instead of relying on the screen." He shook his head meditatively. "The *Silver Queen* just went to pieces. It's really miraculously lucky that this part of the ship remained intact, and what's more, airtight."

"You've got a funny idea of luck, Warren," said Brandon. "Always have for as long as I've known you. Here we are in a tenth part of a spaceship, comprising only three *whole* rooms, with air for three days, and no prospect of being alive after that. And you have the infernal gall to prate about luck."

"Compared to the others who died instantly when the asteroid struck, yes," was Moore's answer.

"You think so, eh? Well, let me tell you that instant death isn't so bad compared with what we're going to have to go through. Suffocation is a damned unpleasant way of dying."

"We may find a way out," Moore suggested hopefully.

"Why not face facts!" Brandon's face was flushed and his voice trembled. "We're done, I tell you! Through!"

Mike glanced from one to the other doubtfully and then coughed to attract their attention. "Well, gents, seeing that we're all in the same fix, I guess there is no use hogging things." He drew a small bottle out of his pocket that was filled with a greenish liquid. "Grade A *Jabra* this is. I ain't too proud to share and share alike."

Brandon exhibited the first signs of pleasure for over a day. "Martian *Jabra* water. Why didn't you say so before?"

But as he reached for it, a firm hand clamped down upon his wrist. He looked up into the calm blue eyes of Warren Moore.

"Don't be a fool," said Moore, "there isn't enough to keep us drunk for three days. What do you want to do? Go on a tear now and then die cold sober? Let's save this for the last six hours when the air gets stuffy and breathing hurts—then we'll finish the bottle among us and never *know* when the end comes, or *care*."

Brandon's hand fell away reluctantly. "Damn it, Warren, you'd bleed ice if you were cut. How can you think straight at a time like this?" He motioned to Mike and the bottle was once more stowed away. Brandon walked to the porthole and gazed out.

Moore approached and placed a kindly arm over the shoulders of the younger man. "Why take it so hard, man?" he asked. "You can't last at this rate. Inside of twenty-four hours you'll be a madman if you keep this up."

There was no answer. Brandon stared bitterly at the globe that filled almost the entire porthole, so Moore continued, "Watching Vesta won't do you any good, either."

Mike Shea lumbered up to the porthole. "We'd be safe if we were only down there on Vesta. There's people there. How far away are we?"

"Not more than three or four hundred miles judging from its apparent size," answered Moore. "You must remember that it is only two hundred miles in diameter."

"Three hundred miles from salvation," murmured Brandon, "and we might as well be a million. If there were only a way to get ourselves out of the orbit this rotten fragment adopted. You know, manage to give ourselves a push so as to start falling. There'd be no danger of crashing if we did, because that midget hasn't got enough gravity to crush a creampuff."

"It has enough to keep us in the orbit," retorted Moore. "It must have picked us up while we were lying unconscious after the crash. Wish it had come closer; we might have been able to land on it."

"Funny place, Vesta," observed Mike Shea. "I was down there two-three times. What a dump! It's all covered with some stuff like snow; only it ain't snow. I forget what they call it."

"Frozen carbon dioxide?" prompted Moore.

"Yeah, dry ice, that carbon stuff, that's it. They say that's what makes Vesta so shiny."

"Of course! That would give it a high albedo."

Mike cocked a suspicious eye at Moore and decided to let it pass. "It's hard to see anything down there on account of the snow, but if you look close," he pointed, "you can see a sort of gray smudge. I think that's Bennett's dome. That's where they keep the observatory. And there is Calorn's dome up there. That's a fuel station, that is. There's plenty more, too, only I don't see them."

He hesitated and then turned to Moore. "Listen, boss, I've been thinking. Wouldn't they be looking for us as soon as they hear about the crash? And wouldn't we be easy to find from Vesta seeing we're so close?"

Moore shook his head. "No, Mike, they won't be looking for us. No one's going to find out about the crash until the *Silver Queen* fails to turn up on schedule. You see, when the asteroid hit, we didn't have time to send out an SOS." He sighed. "And they won't find us down there at Vesta, either. We're so small that even at our distance they couldn't see us unless they knew what they were looking for, and exactly where to look."

"Hmm," Mike's forehead was corrugated in deep thought, "then we got to get to Vesta before three days are up."

"You've got the gist of the matter, Mike. Now, if we only knew how to go about it, eh?"

Brandon suddenly exploded. "Will you two stop this infernal chitter-chatter and do something? For God's sake, do something."

Moore shrugged his shoulders and without answer, returned to the couch. He lounged at ease, apparently carefree, but there was the tiniest crease between his eyes which bespoke concentration.

There was no doubt about it; they *were* in a bad spot. He reviewed the events of the preceding day for perhaps the twentieth time.

After the asteroid had struck, tearing the ship apart, he'd gone out like a light; for how long he didn't know, his own watch being broken and no other timepiece available. When he came to, he found himself, along with Mark Brandon, who shared his room, and Mike Shea, a member of the crew, sole occupants of all that was left of the *Silver Queen*.

This remnant was now careening in an orbit about Vesta. At present, things were fairly comfortable. There was a food supply that would last a week. Likewise there was a regional gravitator under the room that kept them at normal weight and would continue to do so for an indefinite time, certainly for longer than the air would last. The lighting system was less satisfactory but had held on so far.

There was no doubt, however, where the joker in the pack lay. Three days air! Not that there weren't other disheartening features. There was no heating system (though it would take a long time for the ship to radiate enough heat into the vacuum of space to render them too uncomfortable). Far more important was the fact that their part of the ship had neither a means of communication nor a propulsive mechanism. Moore sighed; one fuel jet in working order would fix everything, for one blast in the right direction would send them safely to Vesta.

The crease between his eyes deepened. What was to be done? They had but one spacesuit among them, one heat-ray, and one detonator. That was the sum total of space appliances after a thorough search of the accessible parts of the ship. A pretty hopeless mess, that.

Moore shrugged his shoulders, rose and drew himself a glass of water. He swallowed it mechanically, still deep in thought, when an idea struck him. He glanced curiously at the empty cup in his hand.

"Say, Mike," he said, "what kind of water supply have we? Funny that I never thought of that before."

Mike's eyes opened to their fullest extent in an expression of ludicrous surprise. "Didn't you know, boss?"

"Know *what?*" asked Moore impatiently.

"We've got all the water there was." He waved his hand in an all-inclusive gesture. He paused, but as Moore's expression showed nothing but total mystification, he elaborated. "Don't you see? We've got the main tank, the place where all the water for the whole ship was stored." He pointed to one of the walls.

"Do you mean to say that there's a tank full of water adjoining us?"

Mike nodded vigorously. "Yep! Cubic vat a hundred feet each way. And she's three-quarters full."

Moore was astonished. "750,000 cubic feet of water." Then suddenly, "Why hasn't it run out through the broken pipes?"

"It only has one main outlet, which runs down the corridor just outside this room. I was fixing that main when the asteroid hit and had to shut it off. After I came to I opened the pipe leading to our faucet, but that's the only outlet open now."

"Oh." Moore had a curious feeling way down deep inside. An idea had half-formed in his brain, but for the life of him he could not drag it into the light of day. He knew only that there was something in what he had just heard that had some important meaning but he just could not place his finger on it.

Brandon, meanwhile, had been listening to Shea in silence, and now he emitted a short, humorless laugh. "Fate seems to be having its fill of fun with us, I see. First, it puts us within arm's reach of a place of safety and then sees to it that we have no way of getting there.

"Then she provides us with a week's food, three days air, and *a year's supply of water*. A year's supply, do you hear me? Enough water to drink and to gargle and to wash and to take baths in and—and to do anything else we want. Water—damn the water!"

"Oh, take a less serious view, Mark," said Moore in an attempt to break the younger man's melancholy. "Pretend we're a satellite of Vesta (which we are). We have our own period of revolution and of rotation. We have an equator and an axis. Our 'north pole' is located somewhere toward the top of the porthole, pointing toward Vesta and our 'south' sticks out away from Vesta through the water tank somewhere. Well, as a satellite, we have an atmosphere, and now, you see, we have a newly discovered ocean.

"And seriously, we're not so badly off. For the three days our atmosphere will last, we can eat double rations and drink ourselves soggy. Hell, we have water enough to throw away—"

The idea which had been half-formed before suddenly sprang to maturity and was nailed. The careless gesture with which he had accompanied the last remark was frozen in midair. His mouth closed with a snap and his head came up with a jerk.

But Brandon, immersed in his own thoughts, noticed nothing of Moore's strange actions. "Why don't you complete the analogy to a satellite," he sneered, "or do you, as a Professional Optimist, ignore any and all disagreeable facts? If *I* were you, I'd continue this way." Here he imitated Moore's voice: "The satellite is at present habitable and inhabited but, due to the approaching depletion of its atmosphere in three days, is expected to become a dead world.

"Well, why don't you answer? Why do you persist in making a joke out of this? Can't you see—*what's the matter?*"

The last was a surprised exclamation and certainly Moore's actions did merit surprise. He had arisen suddenly and after giving himself a smart rap on the forehead, remained stiff and silent, staring into the far distance with gradually narrowing eye-lids. Brandon and Mike Shea watched him in speechless as-tonishment.

Suddenly Moore burst out, "Ha! I've got it. Why didn't I think of it before?" His exclamations degenerated into the un-intelligible.

Mike drew out the *Jabra* bottle with a significant look, but Moore waved it away impatiently. Whereupon Brandon, without any warning, lashed out with his right, catching the surprised Moore flush on the jaw and toppling him.

Moore groaned and rubbed his chin. Somewhat indignant, he asked, "What was the reason for that?"

"Stand up and I'll do it again," shouted Brandon, "I can't stand it any more. I'm sick and tired of being preached at, and having to listen to your Pollyanna talk. *You're* the one that's going daffy."

"Daffy, nothing! Just a little overexcited, that's all. Listen, for God's sake. I think I know a way—"

Brandon glared at him balefully. "Oh, you do, do you? Raise our hopes with some silly scheme and then find it doesn't work. I won't take it, do you hear? I'll find a real use for the water: drown you—and save some of the air besides."

Moore lost his temper. "Listen, Mark, you're out of this; I'm going through alone. I don't need your help and I don't want it. If you're that sure of dying and that afraid, why not have the agony over. We've got one heat-ray and one detonator, both reliable weapons. Take your choice and kill yourself. Shea and I won't interfere." Brandon's lip curled in a last weak gesture of defiance and then suddenly he capitulated, completely and abjectly. "All right, Warren, I'm with you. I—I guess I didn't quite know what I was doing. I don't feel well, Warren. I—I—"

"Aw, that's all right, boy." Moore was genuinely sorry for him. "Take it easy. I know how you feel. It's got me, too. But you mustn't give in to it. Fight it, or you'll go stark, raving mad. Now you just try and get some sleep and leave everything to me. Things will turn out right yet."

Brandon, pressing a hand to an aching forehead, stumbled to the couch and tumbled down. Silent sobs shook his frame while Moore and Shea remained in embarrassed silence nearby.

2. A TOUGH JOB

At last, Moore nudged Mike. "Come on," he whispered; "let's get busy. We're going places. Airlock 5 is at the end of the corridor, isn't it?" Shea nodded and Moore continued, "Is it airtight?"

"Well," said Shea after some thought, "the inner door is, of course, but I don't know anything about the outer one. For all I know it may be a sieve. You see, when I tested the wall for airtightness, I didn't dare open the inner door, because if there was anything wrong with the outer one—blooey!" The accompanying gesture was very expressive.

"Then it's up to us to find out about that outer door right now. I've got to get outside some way and we'll just have to take chances. Where's the spacesuit?"

He grabbed the lone suit from its place in the cupboard, threw it over his shoulder and led the way into the long corridor that ran down the side of the room. He passed closed doors behind whose airtight barriers were what once had been passenger quarters but which were now merely cavities, open to space. At the end of the corridor was the tight-fitting door of Airlock 5.

Moore stopped and surveyed it appraisingly. "Looks all right," he observed, "but of course you can't tell what's outside. God, I hope it'll work." He frowned. "Of course we could use the entire corridor as an airlock, with the door to our room as the inner door and this as the outer door, but that would mean the loss of half our air-supply. We can't afford that—yet."

He turned to Shea. "All right, now. The indicator shows that the lock was last used for entrance, so it should be full of air.

Open the door the tiniest crack, and if there's a hissing noise, shut it quick."

"Here goes." And the lever moved one notch. The mechanism had been severely shaken up during the shock of the crash and its former noiseless workings had given way to a harsh, rasping sound; but it was still in commission. A thin black line appeared on the left hand side of the lock, marking where the door had slid a fraction of an inch on the runners.

There was no hiss! Moore's look of anxiety faded somewhat. He took a small pasteboard from his pocket and held it against the crack. If air were leaking that card should have held there, pushed by the escaping gas. It fell to the floor.

Mike Shea stuck a forefinger in his mouth and then put it against the crack. "Thank the Lord," he breathed, "not the sign of a draft."

"Good, good. Open it wider. Go ahead."

Another notch and the crack opened further. And still no draft. Slowly, ever so slowly, notch by notch, it creaked its way wider and wider. The two men held their breaths, afraid that while not actually punctured, the outer door might have been so weakened as to give way any moment. But it held! Moore was jubilant as he wormed into the spacesuit.

"Things are going fine so far, Mike," he said. "You sit down right here and wait for me. I don't know how long I'll take but I'll be back. Where's the heat-ray? Have you got it?"

Shea held out the ray and asked, "But what are you going to do? I'd sort of like to know."

Moore paused as he was about to buckle on the helmet. "Did you hear me say inside that we had water enough to throw away? Well, I've been thinking it over and that's not such a bad idea. I'm going to throw it away." With no other explanation, he stepped into the lock, leaving behind him a very puzzled Mike Shea.

It was with a pounding heart that Moore waited for the outer door to open. His plan was an extraordinarily simple one—but it might not be easy to carry out.

There was a sound of creaking gears and scraping ratchets. Air sighed away to nothingness. The door before him slid open a few inches and stuck. Moore's heart sank as for a moment he thought it would not open at all, but after a few preliminary jerks and rattles the barrier slid the rest of the way.

He clicked on the magnetic grapple and, very cautiously, put a foot out into space. Clumsily, he groped his way out to the side of the ship. He had never been outside a ship in open space before and a vast dread overtook him as he clung there, fly-like, to his precarious perch. For a moment dizziness overcame him.

He closed his eyes and for five minutes hung there, clutching the smooth sides of what had once been the *Silver Queen*. The magnetic grapple held him firm, and when he opened his eyes once more he found his self-confidence in a measure returned.

He gazed about him. For the first time since the crash he saw the stars, instead of the vision of bloated Vesta which their porthole afforded. Eagerly, he searched the skies for the little green speck that was Earth. It had often amused him that Earth should always be the first object sought for by space-travelers when star-gazing, but the humor of the situation did not strike him now. However, his search was in vain. From where he lay Earth was invisible. It, as well as the Sun, must be hidden behind Vesta.

Still, there was much else that he could not help but note. Jupiter was off to the left, a brilliant globe the size of a small pea to the naked eye. Moore observed two of its attendant satellites. Saturn was visible, too, as a brilliant star of some negative magnitude, rivaling Venus as seen from Earth.

Moore had expected that a goodly number of asteroids would be visible, marooned as they were in the asteroid belt, but space seemed surprisingly empty. Once he thought he could see a hurtling body pass within a few miles but so fast had the impression come and gone that he could not swear that it was not fancy.

And then, of course, there was Vesta. Almost directly below him it loomed like a balloon filling a quarter of the sky. It floated steadily, snowy white, and Moore gazed at it with earnest longing. A good hard kick against the side of the ship, he thought, might start him falling toward Vesta. He *might* land safely and get help for the others. But the chance was too great that he would merely take on a new orbit about Vesta. No, it would have to be better than that.

This reminded him that he had no time to lose. He scanned the side of the ship, looking for the water tank but all he could see was a jungle of jutting walls, jagged, crumbling, and pointed. He hesitated. Evidently, the only thing to do was to make for the lighted porthole to their room and proceed to the tank from there.

Carefully he dragged himself along the wall of the ship. Not five yards from the lock, the smoothness stopped abruptly. There was a yawning cavity which Moore recognized as having once been the room adjoining the corridor at the far end. He shuddered. Suppose he were to come across a bloated dead body in one of those rooms. He had known most of the passengers, many of them personally. But he overcame his squeamishness and forced himself to continue his precarious journey toward its goal.

And here he encountered his first practical difficulty. The room itself was made of nonferrous material in many parts. The magnetic grapple was intended for use only on outer hulls and was useless throughout much of the ship's interior. Moore had forgotten this when suddenly he found himself floating down an incline, his grapple out of use. He gasped and clutched at a nearby projection. Slowly, he pulled himself back to safety.

He lay for a moment, almost breathless. Theoretically, he should be weightless out here in space (Vesta's influence being negligible), but the regional gravitator under his room was working. Without the balance of the other gravitators, it tended to place him under variable and sudden-shifting stresses as he kept changing his position. For his magnetic grapple to let go

suddenly might mean being jerked away from the ship altogether. And then what?

Evidently, this was going to be even more difficult than he
had thought.

After that, he inched forward in a crawl, testing each spot to
see if the grapple would hold. Sometimes he had to make long,
circuitous journeys to gain a few feet's headway and at other
times he was forced to scramble and slip across small patches of
nonferrous material. And always there was that tiring pull of the
gravitator, continually changing directions as he progressed,
setting horizontal floors and vertical walls at queer and almost
haphazard angles.

Carefully, he investigated all objects that he came across.
But it was a barren search. Loose articles, chairs, tables had
been jerked away at the first shock probably and now were
independent bodies of the solar system. He did manage, however, to pick up a small field-glass and fountain pen. These he
placed in his pocket. They were valueless under present conditions, but somehow they seemed to make more real this macabre
trip across the sides of a dead ship.

For fifteen minutes, twenty, half an hour, he labored slowly
toward where he thought the porthole should be. Sweat poured
down into his eyes and rendered his hair a matted mass. His
muscles were beginning to ache under the unaccustomed strain.
His mind, already strained by the ordeal of the previous day,
was beginning to waver, to play him tricks.

The crawl began to seem eternal, something that had always
existed and would exist forever. The object of the journey, that
for which he was striving seemed unimportant; he only knew
that it was necessary to move. The time, one hour back, when he
had been with Brandon and Shea, seemed hazy and lost in the
far past. That more normal time, two days ago, wholly forgotten.

Only the jagged walls before him; only the vital necessity of
getting at some uncertain destination existed in his spinning
brain. Grasping, straining, pulling. Feeling for the iron alloy. Up
and into gaping holes that were rooms and then out again. Feel
and pull—feel and pull. And—a light.

Moore stopped: had he not been glued to the wall he would have fallen. Somehow that light seemed to clear things. It was the porthole; not the many dark, staring ones he had passed, but alive and alight. Behind it was Brandon. A deep breath and he felt better, his mind cleared.

And now his way lay plain before him. Toward that spark of life he crept. Nearer, and nearer, and nearer until he could touch it. He was there!

His eyes drank in the familiar room. God knows that it hadn't any happy associations in his mind, but it was something real, something almost natural. Brandon slept on the couch. His face was worn and lined but a smile passed over it now and then.

Moore raised his fist to knock. He felt the urgent desire to talk with someone, if only by sign language; yet at the last instant, he refrained. Perhaps the kid was dreaming of home. He was young and sensitive and had suffered much. Let him sleep! Time enough to wake him when—and if—his idea had been carried through.

He located the wall within the room behind which lay the water tank and then tried to spot it from the outside. Now it was not difficult; its rear wall stood out prominently. Moore marveled, for it seemed a very miracle that it had escaped puncture. Perhaps the Fates had not been so ironic after all.

Passage to it was easy though it was on the other side of the fragment. What was once a corridor led almost directly to it. Once when the *Silver Queen* had been whole, that corridor had been level and horizontal, but now, under the unbalanced pull of the regional gravitator, it seemed more of a steep incline than anything else. And yet it made the path simple. Of uniform beryl-steel, Moore found no trouble holding on as he wormed up the twenty-odd feet to the water supply.

And now the crisis—the last stage—had been reached. He felt that he ought to rest first but his excitement grew rapidly in intensity; it was either now or bust. He pulled himself out to the bottom-center of the tank. There, resting on the small ledge formed by the floor of the corridor that had once extended on that side of the tank, he began operations.

"It's a pity that the main pipe is pointing in the wrong direction," he muttered. "It would have saved me a lot of trouble had it been right. As it is—" He sighed and bent to his work. The heat-ray was adjusted to maximum concentration and the invisible emanations focused at a spot perhaps a foot above the floor of the tank.

Gradually the effect of the excitatory beam upon the molecules of the wall became noticeable. A spot the size of a dime began shining faintly at the point of focus of the ray-gun. It wavered uncertainly, now dimming, now brightening as Moore strove to steady his tired arm. He propped it on the ledge and achieved better results as the tiny circle of radiation brightened.

Slowly the color ascended the spectrum. The dark, angry red that had first appeared lightened to a cherry color. As the heat continued pouring in, the brightness seemed to ripple out in widening areas, like a target made of successively deepening tints of red. The wall for a distance of some feet from the focal point was becoming uncomfortably hot even though it did not glow, and Moore found it necessary to refrain from touching it with the metal of his suit.

Moore cursed steadily, for the ledge itself was also growing hot. It seemed that only imprecations could soothe him. And as the melting wall began to radiate heat in its own right, the chief object of his maledictions were the spacesuit manufacturers. Why didn't they build a suit that could keep heat *out* as well as keep it *in*?

But what Brandon called Professional Optimism crept up. With the salt tang of perspiration in his mouth, he kept consoling himself. "It could be worse, I suppose. At least, the two inches of wall here don't present too much of a barrier. Suppose the tank had been built flush against the outer hull. Whew! Imagine trying to melt through a foot of this." He gritted his teeth and kept on.

The spot of brightness was now flickering into the orange-yellow, and Moore knew that the melting point of the beryl-steel alloy would soon be reached. He found himself forced to watch the spot only at widely-spaced intervals and then only for fleeting moments.

Evidently it would have to be done quickly, if it were to be done at all. The heat-ray had not been fully loaded in the first place, and, pouring out energy at maximum as it had been doing for almost ten minutes now, must be approaching exhaustion. Yet the wall was just barely passing the plastic stage. In a fever of impatience, Moore jammed the muzzle of the gun directly at the center of the spot, drawing it back speedily.

A deep depression formed in the soft metal, but a puncture had not been formed. However, Moore was satisfied. He was almost there, now. Had there been air between himself and the wall, he would undoubtedly have heard the gurgling and the hissing of the steaming water within. The pressure was building up. How long would the weakened wall endure?

Then, so suddenly that Moore did not realize it for a few moments, he was through. A tiny fissure formed at the bottom of that little pit made by the ray-gun and in less time than it takes to imagine, the churning water within had its way.

The soft, liquid metal at that spot puffed out, sticking out raggedly around a pea-sized hole. And from that hole there came a hissing and a roaring. A cloud of steam emerged and enveloped Moore.

Through the mist he could see the steam condense almost immediately to ice droplets and saw these icy pellets shrink rapidly into nothingness.

For fifteen minutes, he watched the steam shoot out.

Then he became aware of a gentle pressure pushing him away from the ship. A savage joy welled up within him as he realized that this was the effect of acceleration on the ship's part. His own inertia was holding him back.

That meant his work had been finished—and successfully. That stream of water was substituting for the rocket blast.

He started back.

If the horrors and dangers of the journey to the tank had been great, those back were greater. He was infinitely more tired, his aching eyes were all but blind, and added to the crazy pull of the gravitator was the force induced by the varying acceleration of the ship. But whatever his labors to return, they did not bother him. In later time, he never even remembered the heartbreaking trip.

How he managed to negotiate the distance in safety he did not know. Most of the time he was lost in a haze of happiness, scarcely realizing the actualities of the situation. His mind was filled with one thought only—to get back quickly, to tell the happy news of their escape.

Suddenly he found himself before the airlock. He hardly grasped the fact that it *was* the airlock; he almost did not understand why he pressed the signal button. Some instinct told him it was the thing to do.

Mike Shea was waiting. There was a creak and a rumble and the outer door started opening, caught and stopped at the same place as before, but once again it managed to slide the rest of the way. It closed again behind him. Then the inner door opened and Moore stumbled into Shea's arms.

As in a dream he felt himself half pulled, half carried down the corridor to the room. His suit was ripped off and a hot, burning liquid stung his throat. Moore gagged, swallowed and felt better. Shea pocketed the *Jabra* bottle once more.

The blurred, shifting images of Brandon and Shea before him steadied and became solid. Moore wiped the perspiration from his face with a trembling hand and essayed a weak smile.

"Wait," protested Brandon, "don't say anything. You look half dead. Rest, will you!"

But Moore shook his head. In a hoarse, cracked voice he narrated as well as he could the events of the past two hours. The tale was incoherent, scarcely intelligible but marvelously impressive. The two listeners scarcely breathed during the recital.

"You mean," stammered Brandon, "that the water spout is pushing us toward Vesta; like a rocket exhaust."

"Exactly—same thing as—rocket exhaust," panted Moore,

"action and reaction. Is located—on side opposite Vesta—hence pushing us toward Vesta."

Shea was dancing before the porthole. "He's right, Brandon, me boy. You can make out Bennett's dome as clear as day. We are getting there, we're getting there."

"We're approaching in spiral path on account of original orbit." Moore felt himself recovering. "We'll land in five or six hours probably. The water will last for quite a long while and the pressure is still great, since the water issues as steam."

"Steam—at the low temperature of space?" Brandon was surprised.

"Steam—at the low pressure of space!" corrected Moore. "The boiling point of water falls with the pressure. It is very low indeed in a vacuum. Even ice has a vapor pressure sufficient to sublime."

He smiled. "As a matter of fact, it freezes and boils at the same time. I watched it." A short pause, then, "Well, how do you feel now, Brandon? Much better, eh?"

Brandon reddened and his face fell. He groped vainly for words for a few moments. Finally he said in a half-whisper, "You know, I must have acted like a damn fool and a coward at first. I—I guess I don't deserve all this after going to pieces and letting the burden of our escape rest on your shoulders.

"I wish you'd beat me up, or something, for punching you before. It'd make me feel better. I mean it." And he really did seem to mean it.

Moore gave him an affectionate push. "Forget it, you young jackass. You'll never know how near I came to breaking down myself." He raised his voice in order to drown out any further apologies on Brandon's part. "Hey, Mike, stop staring out of that porthole and bring over that *Jabra* bottle."

Mike obeyed with alacrity, bringing with him three shaving mugs to be used as makeshift cups. Moore filled each precisely to the brim. He was going to be drunk with a vengeance.

"Gentlemen," he said solemnly, "a toast." The three raised the mugs in unison. "Gentlemen, I give you the year's supply of good old H_2O *we used to have*."

ANNIVERSARY

Isaac Asimov

The annual ritual was all set. It was the turn of Moore's house this year, of course, and Mrs. Moore and the children had resignedly gone to her mother's for the evening.

Warren Moore surveyed the room with a faint smile. Only Mark Brandon's enthusiasm kept it going at the first, but he himself had come to like this mild remembrance. It came with age, he supposed; twenty additional years of it. He had grown paunchy, thin-haired, soft-jowled, and—worst of all—sentimental.

So all the windows were polarized into complete darkness and the drapes were drawn. Only occasional stipples of wall were illuminated, thus celebrating the poor lighting and the terrible isolation of that day of wreckage long ago.

There were spaceship rations in sticks and tubes on the table and, of course, in the center an unopened bottle of sparkling green *Jabra* water, the potent brew that only the chemical activity of Martian fungi could supply.

Moore looked at his watch. Brandon would be here soon; he was never late for this occasion. The only thing that disturbed him was the memory of Brandon's voice on the tube: "Warren, I have a surprise for you this time. Wait and see. Wait and see."

Brandon, it always seemed to Moore, aged little. The younger man had kept his slimness, and the intensity with which he greeted all in life, to the verge of his fortieth birthday. He retained the ability to be in high excitement over the good and in deep despair over the bad. His hair was going gray, but except for that, when Brandon walked up and down, talking rapidly at the top of his voice about anything at all, Moore didn't even have to close his eyes to see the panicked youngster on the wreck of the *Silver Queen*.

The door-signal sounded and Moore kicked the release without turning round. "Come, Mark."

It was a strange voice that answered, though; softly, tentatively, "Mr. Moore?"

Moore turned quickly. Brandon was there, to be sure, but only in the background, grinning with excitement. Someone else was standing before him; short, squat, quite bald, nut-brown and with the feel of space about him.

Moore said wonderingly, "Mike Shea— *Mike Shea*, by all Space."

They pounded hands together, laughing.

Brandon said, "He got in touch with me through the office. He remembered I was with Atomic Products—"

"It's been *years*," said Moore. "Let's see, you were on Earth twelve years ago—"

"He's never been here on an anniversary," said Brandon. "How about that? He's retiring now. Getting out of space to a place he's buying in Arizona. He came to say, hello, before he left; stopped off at the city just for that, and I was sure he came for the anniversary. 'What anniversary?' says the old jerk."

Shea nodded, grinning. "He said you made a kind of celebration out of it every year."

"You bet," said Brandon, enthusiastically, "and this will be the first one with all three of us here, the first *real* anniversary. It's twenty years, Mike; twenty years since Warren scrambled over what was left of the wreck and brought us down to Vesta."

Shea looked about. "Space-ration, eh? That's old-home-week to me. And *Jabra*. Oh, sure, I remember. . . . Twenty years. I never give it a thought and now, all of a sudden, it's yesterday. Remember when we got back to Earth finally?"

"Do I!" said Brandon. "The parades. The speeches. Warren was the only real hero of the occasion and we kept saying so, and they kept paying no attention. Remember?"

"Oh, well," said Moore. "We were the first three men ever to survive a spaceship crash. We were unusual and anything unusual is worth a celebration. These things are irrational."

"Hey," said Shea, "any of you remember the songs they wrote. That marching one? 'You can sing of routes through Space and the weary maddened pace of the—'"

Brandon joined in with his clear tenor and even Moore added his voice to the chorus so that the last line was loud enough to shake the drapes. "On the *wreck* of the *Silver* Que-e-en," they roared out and ended laughing wildly.

Brandon said, "Let's open the *Jabra* for the first little sip. This one bottle has to last all of us all night."

Moore said, "Mark insists on complete authenticity. I'm surprised he doesn't expect me to climb out the window and human-fly my way around the building."

"Well, now, that's an idea," said Brandon.

"Remember the last toast we made?" Shea held his empty glass before him and intoned, " 'Gentlemen, I give you the year's supply of good old H_2O *we used to have.*' Three drunken bums when we landed. —Well, we were kids. I was thirty and

I thought I was old. And now," his voice was suddenly wistful, "they've retired me."

"Drink!" said Brandon. "Today you're thirty again, and we remember the day on the *Silver Queen* even if no one else does. Dirty, fickle public."

Moore laughed. "What do you expect? A national holiday every year with space-ration and *Jabra* the ritual food and drink?"

"Listen, we're still the only men ever to survive a spaceship crash and now look at us. We're in oblivion."

"It's pretty good oblivion. We had a good time to begin with and the publicity gave us a healthy boost up the ladder. We are doing well, Mark. And so would Mike Shea be if he hadn't wanted to return to space."

Shea grinned and shrugged his shoulder. "That's where I like to be. I'm not sorry, either. What with the insurance compensation I got, I have a nice piece of cash now to retire on."

Brandon said reminiscently, "The wreck set back Trans-space Insurance a real packet. Just the same, there's still something missing. You say 'Silver Queen' to anyone these days, and he can only think of Quentin, if he can think of anyone."

"Who?" said Shea.

"Quentin. Dr. Horace Quentin. He was one of the non-survivors on the ship. You say to anyone, 'What about the three men who survived?' and they'll just stare at you. 'Huh,' they'll say."

Moore said, calmly, "Come, Mark, face it. Dr. Quentin was one of the world's great scientists and we three are just three of the world's nothings."

"We survived. We're still the only men on record to survive."

"So? Look, John Hester was on the ship, and he was an important scientist, too; not in Quentin's league, but important. As a matter of fact, I was next to him at the last dinner before the rock hit us. Well, just because Quentin died in the same wreck, Hester's death was drowned out. No one ever remembers Hester died on the *Silver Queen*. They only remember Quentin. We may be forgotten, too, but at least we're alive."

"I tell you what," said Brandon, after a period of silence during which Moore's rationale had obviously failed to take. "We're marooned again. Twenty years ago today, we were marooned off Vesta. Today, we're marooned in oblivion. Now here are the three of us back together again at last, and what happened before can happen again. Twenty years ago, Warren pulled us down to Vesta. Now let's solve this new problem."

"Wipe out the oblivion, you mean?" said Moore. "Make ourselves famous?"

"Sure. Why not? Do you know of any better way of celebrating a twentieth anniversary?"

"No, but I'd be interested to know where you expect to start. I don't think people remember the *Silver Queen* at all, except for Quentin, so you'll have to think of some way of bringing the wreck back to mind. That's just to begin with."

Shea stirred uneasily and a thoughtful expression crossed his blunt countenance. "Some people remember the *Silver Queen*. The insurance company does, and you know that's a funny thing, now that you bring up the matter. I was on Vesta about ten-eleven years ago, and I asked if the piece of the wreck we brought down was still there and they said sure, who would cart it away? So I thought I'd take a look at it and shot over by reaction motor strapped to my back. With Vestan gravity, you know, a reaction motor is all you need. —Anyway, I didn't get to see it except from a distance. It was circled off by force-field."

Brandon's eyebrows went skyhigh. "Our *Silver Queen?* For what reason?"

"I went back and asked how come they didn't tell me, and they said they didn't know I was going there. They said it belonged to the insurance company."

Moore nodded. "Surely. They took over when they paid off. I signed a release, giving up my salvage rights when I accepted the compensation check. You did too, I'm sure."

Brandon said, "But why the force-field? Why all the privacy?"

"I don't know."

"The wreck isn't worth anything even as scrap metal. It would cost too much to transport it."

Shea said, "That's right. Funny thing, though; they were bringing pieces back from space. There was a pile of it there. I could see it and it looked like just junk, twisted pieces of frame, you know. I asked about it and they said ships were always landing and unloading more scrap, and the insurance company had a standard price for any piece of the *Silver Queen* brought back, so ships in the neighborhood of Vesta were always looking. Then, on my last voyage in, I went to see the *Silver Queen* again and that pile was a lot bigger."

"You mean they're still looking?" Brandon's eyes glittered.

"I don't know. Maybe they've stopped, but the pile was bigger than it was ten-eleven years ago, so they were still looking then."

Brandon leaned back in his chair and crossed his legs. "Well, now, that's very queer. A hard-headed insurance company is spending all kinds of money, sweeping space near Vesta trying to find pieces of a twenty-year-old wreck."

"Maybe they're trying to prove sabotage," said Moore.

"After twenty years? They won't get their money back even if they do. It's a dead issue."

"They may have quit looking years ago."

Brandon stood up with decision. "Let's ask. There's something funny here and I'm just *Jabrified* enough and anniversaried enough to want to find out."

"Sure," said Shea, "but ask who?"

"Ask Multivac," said Brandon.

Shea's eyes opened wide. "Multivac! Say, Mr. Moore, do you have a Multivac outlet here?"

"Yes."

"I've never seen one, and I've always wanted to."

"It's nothing to look at, Mike. It just looks like a typewriter. Don't confuse a Multivac outlet with Multivac itself. I don't know anyone who's seen Multivac."

Moore smiled at the thought. He doubted if ever in his

life he would meet any of the handful of technicians that spent most of their working days in a hidden spot in the bowels of Earth tending a mile-long super-computer that was the repository of all the facts known to man; that guided man's economy; directed his scientific research; helped make his political decisions—and had millions of circuits left over to answer individual questions that did not violate the ethics of privacy.

Brandon said as they moved up the power-ramp to the second floor, "I've been thinking of installing a Multivac, Jr. outlet for the kids. Homework and things, you know. And yet I don't want to make it just a fancy and expensive crutch for them. How do you work it, Warren?"

Moore said, tersely, "They show me the questions first. If I don't pass them, Multivac does not see them."

The Multivac outlet was indeed a simple typewriter arrangement and little more.

Moore set up the co-ordinates that opened his portion of the planet-wide network of circuits and said, "Now listen. For the record, I'm against this and I'm only going along because it's the anniversary and because I'm just jackass enough to be curious. Now how ought I to phrase the question?"

Brandon said, "Just ask: Are pieces of the wreck of the *Silver Queen* still being searched for in the neighborhood of Vesta by Trans-space Insurance? It only requires a simple yes or no."

Moore shrugged and tapped it out, while Shea watched with awe.

The spaceman said, "How does it answer? Does it talk?"

Moore laughed gently. "Oh, no. I don't spend *that* kind of money. This model just prints the answer on a slip of tape that comes out that slot."

A short strip of tape did come out as he spoke. Moore removed it and after a glance, said, "Well, Multivac says yes."

"Hah!" cried Brandon. "Told you. Now ask why?"

"Now that's silly. A question like that would be obviously against privacy. You'll just get a yellow state-your-reason."

"Ask and find out. They have not made the search for the pieces secret. Maybe they're not making the reason secret."

Moore shrugged. He tapped out: Why is Trans-space Insurance conducting its *Silver Queen* search-project to which reference was made in the previous question?

A yellow slip clicked out almost at once: *State Your Reason For Requiring The Information Requested.*

"All right," said Brandon, unabashed. "You tell it we're the three survivors and have a right to know. Go ahead. Tell it."

Moore tapped that out in unemotional phrasing and another yellow slip was pushed out at them: *Your Reason Is Insufficient. No Answer Can Be Given.*

Brandon said, "I don't see they have a right to keep that secret."

"That's up to Multivac," said Moore. "It judges the reasons given it and if it decides the ethics of privacy is against answering, that's it. The government itself couldn't break those ethics without a court order, and the courts don't go against Multivac once in ten years. So what are you going to do?"

Brandon jumped to his feet and began the rapid walk up and down the room that was so characteristic of him. "All right, then let's figure it out for ourselves. It's something important to justify all their trouble. We're agreed they're not trying to find evidence of sabotage, not after twenty years. But Trans-space must be looking for *something;* something so valuable that it's worth looking for all this time. Now what could be that valuable?"

"Mark, you're a dreamer," said Moore.

Brandon obviously didn't hear him. "It can't be jewels or money or securities. There just couldn't be enough to pay them back for what the search has already cost them; not if the *Silver Queen* were pure gold. What would be more valuable?"

"You can't judge value, Mark," said Moore. "A letter might be worth a hundredth of a cent as waste-paper and yet make a difference of a hundred million dollars to a corporation, depending on what's in the letter."

Brandon nodded his head vigorously. "Right. Documents. Valuable papers. Now who would be most likely to have papers worth billions in his possession on that trip?"

"How could anyone possibly say?"

"How about Dr. Horace Quentin? How about that, Warren? He's the one people remember because he was so important. What about the papers he might have had with him; details of a new discovery, maybe. —Damn it, if I had only seen him on that trip. He might have told me something, just in casual conversation, you know. Did *you* ever see him, Warren?"

"Not that I recall. Not to talk to. So casual conversation with me is out, too. Of course, I might have passed him at some time without knowing it."

"No, you wouldn't have," said Shea, suddenly thoughtful. "I think I remember something. There was one passenger who never left his cabin. The steward was talking about it. He wouldn't even come out for meals."

"And that was Quentin?" said Brandon, stopping his pacing and staring at the spaceman eagerly.

"It might have been, Mr. Brandon. It might have been him. I don't know that anyone *said* it was. I don't remember. But it must have been a big shot, because on a spaceship you don't fool around bringing meals to a man's cabin unless he *is* a big shot."

"And Quentin was *the* big shot on the trip," said Brandon, with satisfaction. "So he had something in his cabin. Something very important. Something he was concealing."

"He might just have been space-sick," said Moore, "except that—" He frowned and fell silent.

"Go ahead," said Brandon, urgently. "You remember something, too?"

"Maybe. I told you I was sitting next to Dr. Hester at the last dinner. He was saying something about hoping to meet Dr. Quentin on the trip and not having any luck."

"Sure," cried Brandon, "because Quentin wouldn't come out of his cabin."

"He didn't *say* that. We got to talking about Quentin, though. Now what was it he said?" Moore put his hands to his temples as though trying to squeeze out the memory of twenty years ago by main force. "I can't give you the exact words, of course, but it was something about Quentin being very theatrical or a slave of drama or something like that, and they were heading out to some scientific conference on Ganymede and Quentin wouldn't even announce the title of his paper."

"It all fits." Brandon resumed his rapid pacing. "He had a new, great discovery, which he was keeping absolutely secret, because he was going to spring it on the Ganymede conference and get maximum drama out of it. He wouldn't come out of his cabin because he probably thought Hester would pump him—and Hester would, I'll bet. And then the ship hit the rock and Quentin was killed. Trans-space Insurance investigated, got rumors of this new discovery and figured that if they gained control of it, they could make back their losses and plenty more. So they took ownership of the ship and have been hunting for Quentin's papers among the pieces ever since."

Moore smiled, in absolute affection for the other man. "Mark, that's a beautiful theory. The whole evening is worth it, just watching you make something out of nothing."

"Oh, yeah. Something out of nothing? Let's ask Multivac again. I'll pay the bill for it this month."

"It's all right. Be my guest. If you don't mind, though, I'm going to bring up the bottle of *Jabra*. I want one more little shot to catch up with you."

"Me, too," said Shea.

Brandon took his seat at the typewriter. His fingers trembled with eagerness as he tapped out: What was the nature of Dr. Horace Quentin's final investigations?

Moore had returned with the bottle and glasses, when the answer came back; on white paper this time. The answer was long and the print was fine, consisting for the most part of references to scientific papers in journals twenty years old.

Moore went over it. "I'm no physicist, but it looks to me as though he were interested in optics."

Brandon shook his head impatiently. "But all that is published. We want something he had not published yet."

"We'll never find out anything about that."

"The insurance company did."

"That's just your theory."

Brandon was kneading his chin with an unsteady hand. "Let me ask Multivac one more question."

He sat down again and tapped out: "Give me the name and tube-number of the surviving colleagues of Dr. Horace Quentin from among those associated with him at the university on whose faculty he served."

"How do you know he was on a university faculty?" asked Moore.

"If not, Multivac will tell us."

A slip popped out. It contained only one name.

Moore said, "Are you planning to call the man?"

"I sure am," said Brandon. "—Otis Fitzimmons, with a Detroit tube-number. Warren, may I—"

"Be my guest, Mark. It's still part of the game."

Brandon set up the combination on Moore's tube keyboard. A woman's voice answered. Brandon asked for Dr. Fitzimmons and there was a short wait.

Then a thin voice said, "Hello." It sounded old.

Brandon said, "Dr. Fitzimmons, I'm representing Transspace Insurance in the matter of the late Dr. Horace Quentin—"

("For heaven's sake, Mark," whispered Moore, but Brandon held up a sharply restraining hand.)

There was a pause so long that a tube breakdown began to seem possible and then the old voice said, "After all these years? Again?"

(Brandon snapped his fingers in an irrepressible gesture of triumph.)

But he said smoothly, almost glibly, "We're still trying to find out, doctor, if you have remembered further details about what

Dr. Quentin might have had with him on that last trip that would pertain to his last unpublished discovery."

"Well—" There was an impatient clicking of the tongue. "I've told you, I don't know. I don't want to be bothered with this again. I don't know that there was *anything*. The man hinted, but he was always hinting about some gadget or other."

"What gadget, sir?"

"I tell you I don't know. He used a name once and I told you about that. I don't think it's significant."

"We don't have the name in our records, sir."

"Well, you should have. Uh, what was that name? An optikon, that's it."

"With a *k*?"

"*C* or *k*. I don't know or care. Now, please, I do not wish to be disturbed again about this. Good-bye." He was still mumbling querulously, when the line went dead.

Brandon was pleased.

Moore said, "Mark, that was the stupidest thing you could have done. Claiming a fraudulent identity on the tube is illegal. If he wants to make trouble for you—"

"Why should he? He's forgotten about it already. But don't you see, Warren? Trans-space has been asking him about this. He kept saying he'd explained all this before."

"All right. But you'd assumed that much. What else do you know?"

"We also know," said Brandon, "that Quentin's gadget was called an optikon."

"Fitzimmons didn't sound certain about that. And even so, since we already know he was specializing in optics toward the end, a name like 'optikon' does not push us any further forward."

"And Trans-space Insurance is looking either for the optikon or for papers concerning it. Maybe Quentin kept the details in his hat and just had a model of the instrument. After all, Shea said they were picking up metal objects. Right?"

"There was a bunch of metal junk in the pile," agreed Shea.

"They'd leave that in space if it were papers they were after. So that's what we want, an instrument that might be called an optikon."

"Even if all your theories were correct, Mark, and we're looking for an optikon, the search is absolutely hopeless now," said Moore, flatly. "I doubt that more than ten percent of the debris would remain in orbit about Vesta. Vesta's escape velocity is practically nothing. It was just a lucky thrust in a lucky direction and at a lucky velocity that put our section of the wreck in orbit. The rest is gone, scattered all over the Solar system in any conceivable orbit about the Sun."

"They've been picking up pieces," said Brandon.

"Yes, the ten percent that managed to make a Vestan orbit out of it. That's all."

Brandon wasn't giving up. He said thoughtfully, "Suppose it were there and they hadn't found it. Could someone have beat them to it?"

Mike Shea laughed. "We were right there, but we sure didn't walk off with anything but our skins, and glad to do that much. Who else?"

"That's right," agreed Moore, "and if anyone else picked it up, why are they keeping it a secret?"

"Maybe they don't know what it is."

"Then how do we go about—" Moore broke off and turned to Shea, "What did you say?"

Shea looked blank. "Who me?"

"Just now, about us being there." Moore's eyes narrowed. He shook his head as though to clear it, then whispered, "Great Galaxy!"

"What is it?" asked Brandon, tensely. "What's the matter, Warren?"

"I'm not sure. You're driving me mad with your theories; so mad, I'm beginning to take them seriously, I think. You know, we did take some things out of the wreck with us. I mean besides our clothes and what personal belongings we still had. Or at least I did."

"What?"

"It was when I was making my way across the outside of the wreckage—Space, I seem to be there now, I see it so clearly—I picked up some items and put them in the pocket of my spacesuit. I don't know why; I wasn't myself, really. I did it without thinking. And then, well, I held on to them. Souvenirs, I suppose. I brought them back to Earth."

"Where are they?"

"I don't know. We haven't stayed in one place, you know."

"You didn't throw them out, did you?"

"No, but things do get lost when you move."

"If you didn't throw them out, they must be somewhere in this house."

"If they didn't get lost. I swear I don't recall seeing them in fifteen years."

"What were they?"

Warren Moore said, "One was a fountain pen, as I recall; a real antique, the kind that used an ink-spray cartridge. What gets me, though, is that the other was a small field-glass, not more than about six inches long. You see what I mean? A field-glass?"

"An optikon," shouted Brandon. "Sure!"

"It's just a coincidence," said Moore, trying to remain level-headed. "Just a curious coincidence."

But Brandon wasn't having it. "A coincidence, nuts! Transspace couldn't find the optikon on the wreck and they couldn't find it in space because you had it all along."

"You're crazy."

"Come on, we've got to find the thing now."

Moore blew out his breath. "Well, I'll look, if that's what you want, but I doubt that I'll find it. Okay, let's start with the storage level. That's the logical place."

Shea chuckled. "The logical place is usually the worst place to look." But they all headed for the power-ramp once more and the additional flight upward.

The storage level had a musty, unused odor to it. Moore turned on the precipitron. "I don't think we've precipitated the dust in two years. That shows you how often I'm up here. Now, let's see; if it's anywhere at all, it would be in with the bachelor collection; I mean the junk I've been hanging on to since bachelor days. We can start here."

Moore started leafing through the contents of plastic collapsibles while Brandon kept peering anxiously over his shoulder.

Moore said, "What do you know? My college yearbook. I was a sonist in those days; a real bug on it. In fact, I managed to get a voice recording with the picture of every senior in this book." He tapped its cover fondly. "You could swear there was nothing there but the usual trimensional photos, but each one has an imprisoned—"

He grew aware of Brandon's frown and said, "Okay. I'll keep looking."

He gave up on the collapsibles and opened a trunk of heavy, old-fashioned woodite. He separated the contents of the various compartments.

Brandon said, "Hey, is that it?"

He pointed to a small cylinder that rolled out on the floor with a small clunk.

Moore said, "I don't— Yes! That's the pen. There it is. And here's the field-glass. Neither one works, of course. They're both broken. At least I suppose the pen's broken. Something's loose and rattles in it. Hear? I wouldn't have the slightest idea as to how to fill it so I can check as to whether it really works. They haven't even made ink-spray cartridges in years."

Brandon held it under the light. "It has initials on it."

"Oh? I don't remember noticing any."

"It's pretty worn down. It looks like J.K.Q."

"Q?"

"Right, and that's an unusual letter with which to start a last name. This pen might have belonged to Quentin; an heirloom he kept for luck or sentiment. It might have belonged to a great-grandfather in the days when they used pens like this; a great-grandfather called Jason Knight Quentin or Judah Kent Quentin or something like that. We can check the names of Quentin's ancestors through Multivac."

Moore nodded. "I think maybe we should. See, you've got me as crazy as you are."

"And if this is so, it proves you picked it up in Quentin's room, so you picked up the field-glass there, too."

"Now hold it. I don't remember that I picked them both up in the same place. I don't remember the scrounging over the outside of the wreck that well."

Brandon turned the small field-glass over and over under the light. "No initials here."

"Did you expect any?"

"I don't see anything in fact, except this narrow joining mark here." He ran his thumbnail into the fine groove that circled the glass near its thicker end. He tried to twist it unsuccessfully. "One piece." He put it to his eye. "This thing doesn't work."

"I told you it was broken. No lenses."

Shea broke in. "You've got to expect a little damage when a spaceship hits a good-sized meteor and goes to pieces."

"So even if this were it," said Moore, pessimistic again, "if this were the optikon, it would not do us any good."

He took the field-glass from Brandon and felt along the empty rims. "You can't even tell where the lenses belonged. There's no groove I can feel into which they might have been seated. It's as if there never—*Hey!*" He exploded the syllable violently.

"Hey what?" said Brandon.

"The name! The name of the thing!"

"Optikon, you mean?"

"Optikon, I don't mean! Fitzimmons, on the tube, called it an optikon and we thought he said 'an—optikon.'"

"Well, he did," said Brandon.

"Sure," said Shea. "I heard him."

"You just thought you heard him. He said, 'anoptikon.'— Don't you get it? Not 'an optikon,' two words, 'anoptikon,' one word."

"Oh," said Brandon, blankly. "And what's the difference."

"A hell of a difference. 'An optikon' would mean an instrument with lenses, but 'anoptikon,' one word, has the Greek prefix 'an-' which means 'no.' Words of Greek derivation use it for 'no.' Anarchy means 'no government,' anemia means 'no blood,' anonymous means 'no name' and anoptikon means—"

"No lenses," cried Brandon.

"Right! Quentin must have been working on an optical device without lenses and this may be it and it may not be broken."

Shea said, "But you don't see anything when you look through it."

"It must be set to neutral," said Moore. "There must be some way of adjusting it." Like Brandon, he placed it in both hands and tried to twist it about that circumscribing groove. He placed pressure on it, grunting.

"Don't break it," said Brandon.

"It's giving. Either it's supposed to be stiff or else it's corroded shut." He stopped, looked at the instrument impatiently and put it to his eye again. He whirled, unpolarized a window and looked out at the lights of the city.

"I'll be dumped in Space," he breathed.

Brandon said, "What? What?"

Moore handed the instrument to Brandon wordlessly. Brandon put it to his eyes and cried out sharply, "It's a telescope."

Shea said at once, "Let me see."

They spent nearly an hour with it, converting it into a telescope with turns in one direction, a microscope with turns in the other.

"How does it work?" Brandon kept asking.

"I don't know," Moore kept saying. In the end, he said, "I'm sure it involves concentrated force-fields. We are turning against considerable field resistance. With larger instruments, power-adjustment will be required."

"It's a pretty cute trick," said Shea.

"It's more than that," said Moore. "I'll bet it represents a completely new turn in theoretical physics. It focuses light without lenses, and it can be adjusted to gather light over a wider and wider area without any change in focal length. I'll bet we could duplicate the five-hundred-inch Ceres telescope in one direction and an electron microscope in the other. What's more I don't see any chromatic aberration, so it must bend light of all wave-lengths equally. Maybe it bends radio waves and gamma rays also. Maybe it distorts gravity, if gravity is some kind of radiation. Maybe—"

"Worth money?" asked Shea, breaking in dryly.

"All kinds if someone can figure out how it works."

"Then we don't go to Trans-space Insurance with this. We go to a lawyer first. Did we sign these things away with our salvage rights or didn't we? You had them already in your possession before signing the paper. For that matter, is the paper any good if we didn't know what we were signing away? Maybe it might be considered fraud."

"As a matter of fact," said Moore, "with something like this, I don't know if any private company ought to own it. We ought to check with some Government agency. If there's money in it—"

But Brandon was pounding both fists on his knees. "To *hell* with the money, Warren. I mean I'll take any money that comes my way but that's not the important thing. We're going to be famous, man, famous! Imagine the story. A fabulous treasure lost in space. A giant corporation combing space for twenty years to find it and all the time we, the forgotten ones, have it in our possession. Then, on the twentieth anniversary of the original loss, we find it again. If this thing works; if anoptics becomes a great new scientific technique, they'll *never* forget us."

Moore grinned, then started laughing. "That's right. You did it, Mark. You did just what you set out to do. You've rescued us from being marooned in oblivion."

"We all did it," said Brandon. "Mike Shea started us off with the necessary basic information. I worked out the theory, and you had the instrument."

"Okay. It's late, and the wife will be back soon, so let's get the ball rolling right away. Multivac will tell us which agency would be appropriate and who—"

"No, no," said Brandon. "Ritual first. The closing toast of the anniversary, please, and with the appropriate change. Won't you oblige, Warren?" He passed over the still half-full bottle of *Jabra* water.

Carefully, Moore filled each small glass precisely to the brim. "Gentlemen," he said solemnly, "a toast." The three raised the glasses in unison. "Gentlemen, I give you the *Silver Queen* souvenirs *we used to have.*"

In a special issue that *Fantasy & Science Fiction* recently devoted to him, Isaac Asimov—then a young, still unpublished but avid reader of pulp science fiction in the late '30s—recalled his genuine agony when the latest issue of his favorite magazine failed to appear on the day usually set aside for distribution each month. That was bad enough, naturally—as we all know—but the extra wait was especially intolerable this time because that particular issue was all set for the first part of a new Jack Williamson story—and Asimov knew it! Eventually, of course, Ike got his copy and, we presume —although he really doesn't say—plunged straightway into Williamson's latest, something most of us also do whenever we spot the author's name on the contents page. A very strong habit indeed, one that old-timers will tell you they formed as long ago as 1928, after reading Williamson's first story, "The Metal Man"—which began with the "hero" delivered in a large wooden chest!

THE METAL MAN

Jack Williamson

The Metal Man stands in a dark, dusty corner of the Tyburn College Museum. Just who is responsible for the figure being moved there, or why it was done, I do not know. To the casual eye it looks to be merely an ordinary life-size statue. The visitor who gives it a closer view marvels at the minute perfection of the detail of hair and skin; at the silent tragedy in the set, determined expression and poise; and at the remarkable greenish cast of the metal of which it is composed, but, most of all, at the peculiar mark upon the chest. It is a six-sided blot, of a deep crimson hue, with the surface oddly granular

and strange wavering lines radiating from it—lines of a lighter
shade of red.

Of course it is generally known that the Metal Man was
once Professor Thomas Kelvin of the Geology Department.
There are current many garbled and inaccurate accounts of the
weird disaster that befell him. I believe I am the only one to
whom he entrusted his story. It is to put these fantastic tales
at rest that I have decided to publish the narrative that Kelvin
sent me.

For some years he had been spending his summer vacations
along the Pacific coast of Mexico, prospecting for radium. It
was three months since he had returned from his last expedition. Evidently he had been successful beyond his wildest
dreams. He did not come to Tyburn, but we heard stories of
his selling millions of dollars worth of salts of radium, and
giving as much more to institutions employing radium treat-
ment. And it was said that he was sick of a strange disorder
that defied the world's best specialists, and that he was pouring
out his millions in the establishment of scholarships and en-
dowments as if he expected to die soon.

One cold, stormy day, when the sea was running high on
the unprotected coast which the cottage overlooks, I saw a sail
out to the north. It rapidly drew nearer until I could tell that it
was a small sailing schooner with auxiliary power. She was running with the wind, but a half mile offshore she came up
into it and the sails were lowered. Soon a boat had put off
in the direction of the shore. The sea was not so rough as to
make the landing hazardous, but the proceeding was rather
unusual, and, as I had nothing better to do, I went out in
the yard before my modest house, which stands perhaps two
hundred yards above the beach, in order to have a better view.

When the boat touched, four men sprang out and rushed it
up higher on the sand. As a fifth tall man arose in the stern,
the four picked up a great chest and started up in my direction.
The fifth person followed leisurely. Silently, and without invitation, the men brought the chest up the beach, and into
my yard, and set it down in front of the door.

The fifth man, a hard-faced Yankee skipper, walked up to me and said gruffly, "I am Captain McAndrews."

"I'm glad to meet you, Captain," I said, wondering. "There must be some mistake. I was not expecting—"

"Not at all," he said abruptly. "The man in that chest was transferred to my ship from the liner *Plutonia* three days ago. He has paid me for my services, and I believe his instructions have been carried out. Good day, sir."

He turned on his heel and started away.

"A man in the chest!" I exclaimed.

He walked on unheeding, and the seamen followed. I stood and watched them walk down to the boat and row back to the schooner. I gazed at its sails until they were lost against the dull blue of the clouds. Frankly, I feared to open the chest.

At last I nerved myself to do it. It was unlocked. I threw back the lid. With a shock of uncontrollable horror that left me half sick for hours, I saw in it, stark naked, with the strange crimson mark standing lividly out from the pale green of the breast, the Metal Man, just as you may see him in the Museum.

Of course, I knew at once that it was Kelvin. For a long time I bent, trembling and staring at him. Then I saw an old canteen, purple-stained, lying by the head of the figure, and under it, a sheaf of manuscript. I got the latter out, walked with shaken steps to the easy chair in the house, and read the story that follows:

Dear Russell,

"You are my best—my only—intimate friend. I have arranged to have my body and this story brought to you. I just drank the last of the wonderful purple liquid that has kept me alive since I came back, and I have scant time to finish this necessarily brief account of my adventure. But my affairs are in order and I die in peace. I had myself transferred to the schooner to-day, in order to reach you as soon as could be and to avoid possible complications. I trust Captain McAndrews.

When I left France, I hoped to see you before the end. But Fate ruled othewise.

"You know that the goal of my expedition was the head-waters of El Rio de la Sangre, 'The River of Blood.' It is a small stream whose strangely red waters flow into the Pacific. On my trip last year I had discovered that its waters were powerfully radioactive. Water has the power of absorbing radium emanations and emitting them in turn, and I hoped to find radium-bearing minerals in the bed of the upper river. Twenty-five miles above the mouth the river emerges from the Cordilleras. There are a few miles of rapids and back of them the river plunges down a magnificent waterfall. No exploring party had ever been back of the falls. I had hired an Indian guide and made a muleback journey to their foot. At once I saw the futility of attempting to climb the precipitous escarpment. But the water there was even more powerfully radioactive than at the mouth. There was nothing to do but return.

"This summer I bought a small monoplane. Though it was comparatively slow in speed and able to spend only six hours aloft, its light weight and the small area needed for landing, made it the only machine suitable for use in so rough a country. The steamer left me again on the dock at the little town of Vaca Morena, with my stack of crates and gasoline tins. After a visit to the Alcade I secured the use of an abandoned shed for a hangar. I set about assembling the plane and in a fortnight I had completed the task. It was a beautiful little machine, with a wingspread of only twenty-five feet.

"Then, one morning, I started the engine and made a trial flight. It flew smoothly and in the afternoon I refilled the tanks and set off for the Rio de la Sangre. The stream looked like a red snake crawling out to the sea—there was something serpentine in its aspect. Flying high, I followed it, above the falls and into a region of towering mountain peaks. The river disappeared beneath a mountain. For a moment I thought of landing, and then it occurred to me that it flowed subterraneously for only a few miles, and would reappear farther inland.

"I soared over the cliffs and came over the crater.

"A great pool of green fire it was, fully ten miles across to the black ramparts at the farther side. The surface of the green was so smooth that at first I thought it was a lake, and then I knew that it must be a pool of heavy gas. In the glory of the evening sun the snow-capped summits about were brilliant argent crowns, dyed with crimson, tinged with purple and gold, tinted with strange and incredibly beautiful hues. Amid this wild scenery, nature had placed her greatest treasure. I knew that in the crater I would find the radium I sought.

"I circled about the place, rapt in wonder. As the sun sank lower, a light silver mist gathered on the peaks, half veiling their wonders, and flowed toward the crater. It seemed drawn with a strange attraction. And then the center of the green lake rose in a shining peak. It flowed up into a great hill of emerald fire. Something was rising in the green—carrying it up! Then the vapor flowed back, revealing a strange object, still veiled faintly by the green and silver clouds. It was a gigantic sphere of deep red, marked with four huge oval spots of dull black. Its surface was smooth, metallic, and thickly studded with great spikes that seemed of yellow fire. It was a machine, inconceivably great in size. It spun slowly as it rose, on a vertical axis, moving with a deliberate, purposeful motion.

"It came up to my own level, paused and seemed to spin faster. And the silver mist was drawn to the yellow points, condensing, curdling, until the whole globe was a ball of lambent argent. For a moment it hung, unbelievably glorious in the light of the setting sun, and then it sank—ever faster—until it dropped like a plummet into the sea of green.

"And with its fall a sinister darkness descended upon the desolate wilderness of the peaks, and I was seized by a fear that had been deadened by amazement, and realized that I had scant time to reach Vaca Morena before complete darkness fell. Immediately I put the plane about in the direction of the town. According to my recollections, I had, at the time, no very definite idea of what it was I had seen, or whether the weird exhibition had been caused by human or natural agencies. I

remember thinking that in such enormous quantities as undoubtedly the crater contained it, radium might possess quali-
ties unnoticed in small amounts, or, again, that there might
be present radioactive minerals at present unknown. It occurred
to me also that perhaps some other scientists had already
discovered the deposits and that what I had witnessed had
been the trial of an airship in which radium was utilized as a
propellent. I was considerably shaken, but not much alarmed.
What happened later would have seemed incredible to me then.

"And then I noticed that a pale bluish luminosity was
gathering about the cowl of the cockpit, and in a moment I
saw that the whole machine, and even my own person, was
covered with it. It was somewhat like St. Elmo's Fire, except
that it covered all surfaces indiscriminately, instead of being
restricted to sharp points. All at once I connected the phenomenon with the thing I had seen. I felt no physical discomfort, and the motor continued to run, but as the blue radiance
continued to increase, I observed that my body felt heavier, and
that the machine was being drawn downward! My mind was
flooded with wonder and terror. I fought to retain sufficient
self-possession to fly the ship. My arms were soon so heavy
that I could hold them upon the controls only with difficulty,
and I felt a slight dizziness, due, no doubt, to the blood's being
drawn from my head. When I recovered, I was already almost
upon the green. Somehow, my gravitation had been increased
and I was being drawn into the pit! It was possible to keep
the plane under control only by diving and keeping at a high
speed.

"I plunged into the green pool. The gas was not suffocating,
as I had anticipated. In fact, I noticed no change in the
atmosphere, save that my vision was limited to a few yards
around. The wings of the plane were still distinctly discernible.
Suddenly a smooth, sandy plain was murkily revealed below,
and I was able to level the ship off enough for a safe landing.
As I came to a stop I saw that the sand was slightly luminous,
as the green mist seemed to be, and red. For a time I was

confined to the ship by my own weight, but I noticed that the blue was slowly dissipating, and with it, its effect.

"As soon as I was able, I clambered over the side of the cockpit, carrying my canteen and automatic, which were themselves immensely heavy. I was unable to stand erect, but I crawled off over the coarse, shining red sand, stopping at frequent intervals to lie flat and rest. I was in deathly fear of the force that had brought me down. I was sure it had been directed by intelligence. The floor was so smooth and level that I supposed it to be the bottom of an ancient lake.

"Sometimes I looked fearfully back, and when I was a hundred yards away I saw a score of lights floating through the green toward the airplane. In the luminous murk each bright point was surrounded by a disc of paler blue. I didn't move, but lay and watched them float to the plane and wheel about it with a slow, heavy motion. Closer and lower they came until they reached the ground about it. The mist was so thick as to obscure the details of the scene.

"When I went to resume my flight, I found my excess of gravity almost entirely gone, though I went on hands and knees for another hundred yards to escape possible observation. When I got to my feet, the plane was lost to view. I walked on for perhaps a quarter of a mile and suddenly realized that my sense of direction was altogether gone. I was completely lost in a strange world, inhabited by beings whose nature and disposition I could not even guess! And then I realized that it was the height of folly to walk about when any step might precipitate me into a danger of which I could know nothing. I had a peculiarly unpleasant feeling of helpless fear.

"The luminous red sand and the shining green of the air lay about in all directions, unbroken by a single solid object. There was no life, no sound, no motion. The air hung heavy and stagnant. The flat sand was like the surface of a dead and desolate sea. I felt the panic of utter isolation from humanity. The mist seemed to come closer; the strange evil in it seemed to grow more alert.

"Suddenly a darting light passed meteor-like through the green above and in my alarm I ran a few blundering steps. My foot struck a light object that rang like metal. The sharpness of the concussion filled me with fear, but in an instant the light was gone. I bent down to see what I had kicked.

"It was a metal bird—an eagle formed of metal—with the wings outspread, the talons gripping, the fierce beak set open. The color was white, tinged with green. It weighed no more than the living bird. At first I thought it was a cast model, and then I saw that each feather was complete and flexible. Somehow, a real eagle had been turned to metal! It seemed incredible, yet here was the concrete proof. I wondered if the radium deposits, which I had already used to explain so much, might account for this too. I knew that science held transmutation of elements to be possible—had even accomplished it in a limited way, and that radium itself was the product of the disintegration of ionium, and ionium that of uranium.

"I was struck with fright for my own safety. Might I be changed to metal? I looked to see if there were other metal things about. And I found them in abundance. Half-buried in the glowing sands were metal birds of every kind—birds that had flown over the surrounding cliffs. And, at the climax of my search, I found a pterosant—a flying reptile that had invaded the pit in ages past—changed to ageless metal. Its wingspread was fully fifteen feet—it would be a treasure in any museum.

"I made a fearful examination of myself, and to my unutterable horror, I perceived that the tips of my fingernails, and the fine hairs upon my hands, *were already changed to light green metal!* The shock unnerved me completely. You cannot conceive my horror. I screamed aloud in agony of soul, careless of the terrible foes that the sound might attract. I ran off wildly. I was blind, unreasoning. I felt no fatigue as I ran, only stark terror.

"Bright, swift-moving lights passed above in the green, but I heeded them not. Suddenly I came upon the great sphere that I had seen above. It rested motionless in a cradle of black metal. The yellow fire was gone from the spikes, but the red surface shone with a metallic luster. Lights floated about it.

They made little bright spots in the green, like lanterns swinging in a fog. I turned and ran again, desperately. I took no note of direction, nor of the passage of time.

"Then I came upon a bank of violet vegetation. Waist-deep it was, grass-like, with thick narrow leaves, dotted with clusters of small pink blooms, and little purple berries. And a score of yards beyond I saw a sluggish red stream—El Rio de la Sangre. Here was cover at last. I threw myself down in the violet growth and lay sobbing with fatigue and terror. For a long time I was unable to stir or think. When I looked again at my fingernails, the tips of metal had doubled in width.

"I tried to control my agitation, and to think. Possibly the lights, whatever they were, would sleep by day. If I could find the plane, or scale the walls, I might escape the fearful action of the radioactive minerals before it was too late. I realized that I was hungry. I plucked off a few of the purple berries and tasted them. They had a salty, metallic taste, and I thought they would be valueless for food. But in pulling them I had inadvertently squeezed the juice from one upon my fingers, and when I wiped it off I saw, to my amazement and my inexpressible joy, that the rim of metal was gone from the fingernails it had touched. I had discovered a means of safety! I suppose that the plants were able to exist there only because they had been so developed that they produced compounds counteracting the metal-forming emanations. Probably their evolution began when the action was far weaker than now, and only those able to withstand the more intense radiations had survived. I lost no time in eating a cluster of the berries, and then I poured the water from my canteen and filled it with their juice. I have analyzed the fluid; it corresponds in some ways with the standard formulas for the neutralization of radium burns, and doubtless it saved me from the terrible burns caused by the action of ordinary radium.

"I lay there until dawn, dozing a little at times, only to start into wakefulness without cause. It seemed that some daylight filtered through the green, for at dawn it grew paler, and even the red sand appeared less luminous. After eating a few more of the berries, I ascertained the direction in which the stagnant red water was moving, and set off downstream, toward the west. In order to get an idea of where I was going, I counted my paces. I had walked about two and a half miles, along by the violet plants, when I came to an abrupt cliff. It towered up until it was lost in the green gloom. It seemed to be mostly of black pitchblende. The barrier seemed absolutely unscalable. The red river plunged out of sight by the cliff in a racing whirlpool.

"I walked off north around the rim. I had no very definite plan, except to try to find a way out over the cliffs. If I failed in that, it would be time to hunt the plane. I had a mortal fear of going near it, or of encountering the strange lights I had seen floating about it. As I went I saw none of them. I suppose they slept when it was day.

"I went on until it must have been noon, though my watch had stopped. Occasionally I passed metal trees that had fallen from above, and once, the metallic body of a bear that had slipped off a path above, some time in past ages. And there were metal birds without number. They must have been accumulating through geological ages. All along up to this, the cliff had risen perpendicularly to the limit of my vision, but now I saw a wide ledge, with a sloping wall beyond it, dimly visible above. But the sheer wall rose a full hundred feet to the shelf, and I cursed at my inability to surmount it. For a time I stood there, devising impractical means for climbing it, driven almost to tears by my impotence. I was ravenously hungry, and thirsty as well.

"At last I went on.

"In an hour I came upon it. A slender cylinder of black metal, that towered a hundred feet into the greenish mist, and carried at the top, a great mushroom-shaped orange flame. It was a strange thing. The fire was as big as a balloon, bright and steady. It looked much like a great jet of combustible gas, burning as it streamed from the cylinder. I stood petrified in amazement, wondering vaguely at the what and why of the thing.

"And then I saw more of them back of it, dimly—scores of them—a whole forest of flames.

"I crouched back against the cliff, while I considered. Here I supposed, was the city of the lights. They were sleeping now, but still I had not the courage to enter. According to my calculations I had gone about fifteen miles. Then I must be, I thought, almost diametrically opposite the place where the crimson river flowed under the wall, with half of the rim unexplored. If I wished to continue my journey, I must go around the city, if I may call it that.

"So I left the wall. Soon it was lost to view. I tried to keep in view of the orange flames, but abruptly they were gone in the mist. I walked more to the left, but I came upon nothing but the wastes of red sand, with the green murk above. On and on I wandered. Then the sand and the air grew slowly brighter and I knew that night had fallen. The lights were soon passing to and fro. I had seen lights the night before, but they traveled high and fast. These, on the other hand, sailed low, and I felt that they were searching.

"I knew that they were hunting for me. I lay down in a little hollow in the sand. Vague, mist-veiled points of light came near and passed. And then one stopped directly overhead. It descended and the circle of radiance grew about it. I knew that it was useless to run, and I could not have done so, for my terror. Down and down it came.

"And then I saw its form. The thing was of a glittering, blazing crystal. A great-six-sided, upright prism of red, a dozen feet in length, it was, with a six-pointed structure like a snow-flake about the center, deep blue, with pointed blue flanges running from the points of the star to angles of the prism! Soft scarlet fire flowed from the points. And on each face of the prism, above and below the star, was a purple cone that must have been an eye. Strange pulsating lights flickered in the crystal. It was alive with light.

"It fell straight toward me!

"It was a terribly, utterly alien form of life. It was not human, not animal—not even life as we know it at all. And yet it had intelligence. But it was strange and foreign and devoid of feeling. It is curious to say that even then, as I lay beneath it, the thought came to me, that the thing and its fellows must have crystallized when the waters of the ancient sea dried out of the crater. Crystallizing salts take intricate forms.

"I drew my automatic and fired three times, but the bullets ricocheted harmlessly off the polished facets.

"It dropped until the gleaming lower point of the prism was not a yard above me. Then the scarlet fire reached out caressingly—flowed over my body. My weight grew less. I was lifted, held against the point. You may see its mark upon my chest. The thing floated into the air, carrying me. Soon others were drifting about. I was overcome with nausea. The scene grew black and I knew no more.

"I awoke floating free in a brilliant orange light. I touched no solid object. I writhed, kicked about—at nothingness. I could not move or turn over, because I could get a hold on nothing. My memory of the last two days seemed a nightmare. My clothing was still upon me. My canteen still hung, or rather floated, by my shoulder. And my automatic was in my pocket. I had the sensation that a great space of time had passed. There was a curious stiffness in my side. I examined it and found a red scar. I believe those crystal things had cut into me. And I found, with a horror you cannot understand, the mark upon my chest. Presently it dawned upon me that I was floating, devoid of gravity and free as an object in space, in the orange flame at the top of one of the black cylinders. The crystals knew the secret of gravity. It was vital to them. And peering about, I discerned, with infinite repulsion, a great flashing body, a few yards away. But its inner lights were dead, so I knew that it was day, and that the strange beings were sleeping.

"If I was ever to escape, this was the opportunity. I kicked, clawed desperately at the air, all in vain. I did not move an inch. If they had chained me, I could not have been more secure. I drew my automatic, resolved on a desperate measure.

They would not find me again, alive. And as I had it in my hand, an idea came into my mind. I pointed the gun to the side, and fired six rapid shots. And the recoil of each explosion sent me drifting faster, rocket-wise, toward the edge.

"I shot out into the green. Had my gravity been suddenly restored, I might have been killed by the fall, but I descended slowly, and felt a curious lightness for several minutes. And to my surprise, when I struck the ground, the airplane was right before me! They had drawn it up by the base of the tower. It seemed to be intact. I started the engine with nervous haste, and sprang into the cockpit. As I started, another black tower loomed up abruptly before me, but I veered around it, and took off in safety.

"In a few moments I was above the green. I half expected the gravitational wave to be turned on me again, but higher and higher I rose unhindered until the accursed black walls were about me no longer. The sun blazed high in the heavens. Soon I had landed again at Vaca Morena.

"I had had enough of radium hunting. On the beach, where I landed, I sold the plane to a rancher at his own price, and told him to reserve a place for me on the next steamer, due in three days. Then I went to the town's single inn, ate, and went to bed. At noon the next day, when I got up, I found that my shoes and the pockets of my clothes contained a good bit of the red sand from the crater that had been collected as I crawled about in flight from the crystal lights. I saved some of it for curiosity alone; but when I analyzed it, I found it a radium compound so rich that the little handful was worth millions of dollars.

"But the fortune was of little value, for, despite frequent doses of the fluid from my canteen, and the best medical aid, I have suffered continually, and now that my canteen is empty, I am doomed.

Your friend, Thomas Kelvin"

Thus the manuscript ends. If the reader doubts the truth of the letter, he may see the Metal Man in the Tyburn Museum.

For about a decade—between the late '30s and the late '40s—the Nelson S. Bond name on a science-fiction or fantasy story meant that readers could look for some pretty nimble plotting and a glossy literary style that few of his pulp contemporaries could match no matter how hard they tried. Especially since Bond was turning out —with amazing facility apparently—such memorable tales as "The Fountain" and "Cunning of the Beast"—many of them collected in *Mr. Mergenthwirker's Lobblies* (Coward-McCann, 1946) and *The Thirty-first of February* (Gnome Press, 1949), both alas now out of print but both worth hunting up in the nearest connoisseur's bookshop. Until you find copies, however, here's something—from *31st*—to spur you on. Probably Bond's best story—he thinks so too —under its original title, "The Priestess Who Rebelled," it helped make 1939 a vintage year for *Amazing*.

PILGRIMAGE

Nelson S. Bond

In her twelfth summer the illness came upon Meg and she was afraid. Afraid, yet turbulent with a sense of exaltation unlike anything she had ever before known. She was a woman now. She was become a woman, and she knew suddenly and completely that which was expected of her from this day forth. Knew . . . and dreaded.

She went immediately to the *hoam* of the Mother, for such was the Law. But as she moved down the walk-avenue she stared with eyes newly curious at the Men she passed. At their pale and pitifully hairless bodies. At their soft, futile hands and weak mouths. One lolling on the doorstep of 'Ana's *hoam* returned her gaze brazenly, made a small enticing gesture. Meg shuddered and curled her lips in a refusal-face.

Only yesterday she had been a child. Now suddenly she was a woman. And for the first time Meg saw her people as they really were.

The warriors of the Clan. She looked with distaste upon the tense angularity of their bodies: the corded legs, the tightset jaws, the cold eyes and the brawny arms scarred to the elbow with ill-healed cicatrices. The tiny, thwarted breasts, flat and hard beneath leather harness-plates. Fighters they were, and nothing else.

This was not what she wanted.

She saw, too, the mothers: the full-lipped, flabby-breasted bearers of children; whose skins were soft and white as those of the Men; whose eyes were humid, washed barren of all expression by desires too oft aroused, too often sated. Their bodies bulged at hip and thigh, swayed when they walked like ripe grain billowing in a lush and fertile field. They lived only that the tribe might continue to exist. They reproduced.

This was not what she wanted.

Then there were the workers. Their bodies retained a vestige of womankind's inherent grace and nobility. But if their waists were thin, their hands were blunt-fingered and thick. Their shoulders sagged with the weariness of toil, were coarsened by adze and hod. Their faces grimly mirrored eternal struggle with an unyielding earth. And the earth of which they had made themselves a part had in return made itself a part of them. The workers' hides were browned with soil, their bodies stank of dirt and grime and unwashed perspiration.

This was not what she wanted. No, none of these was what she wanted.

So great was Meg's concentration that she entered into the *hoam* of the Mother without crying out, as was required. Thus it was that she discovered the Mother making great magic to the gods.

In her right hand the Mother held a stick. With it she

scratched upon a smooth, bleached, calf-skin scroll. From time to time she let the stick drink from a pool of midnight cupped in a dish before her. When she moved it again on the hide it left its spoor, a spidery trail of black.

For a long moment Meg stood and watched, wondering. Then dread overcame her; fear-thoughts shook her body. She thought suddenly of the gods. Of austere Jarg, their leader; of lean Ibrim and taciturn Taamuz. Of far-seeing Tedhi, she whose laughter echoes in the roaring summer thunders. What wrath would they visit upon one who had spied into their secrets?

She covered her eyes and dropped to her knees. But there were footsteps before her, and the Mother's hand upon her shoulders. And there was but gentle chiding in the voice of the Mother as she said, "My child, know you not the Law? That all must cry out before entering the Mother's *hoam?*"

Meg's fear-thoughts went away. The Mother was good. It was she who fed and clothed the Clan, warmed them in dark winter and found them meat when meat was scarce. If she who was the gods' spokesman on earth saw no evil in Meg's unintentional prying. . . .

Meg dared look again at the magic stick. There was a question in her eyes. The Mother answered that question. She said:

"It is 'writing,' Meg. Speech without words."

Speech-without-words? Meg crept to the table, bent a curious ear over the spider-marks. But she heard no sound. Then the Mother was beside her again, saying, "No, my child. It does not speak to the ears, but to the eyes. Listen, I will make it speak through my mouth."

She read aloud:

"Report of the month of June, 3478 A.D. There has been no change in the number of the Jinnia Clan. Still we are five score and seven, with chattels of nineteen Men, twelve kine, thirty horses. But there is reason to believe that 'Ana and Sahlee will soon add to our number.

"Last week Darthee, Lina and Alis journeyed into the Clina territory in search of game. They met there several of the Durm Clan and exchanged gifts of salt and bacca. Pledges of friendship were given. On the return trip Darthee was trapped by one of the Wild Ones, but was rescued by her companions before the strain could be crossed. The Wild One was destroyed.

"We have in our village a visitor from the Delwurs of the east, who says that in her territory the Wild Ones have almost disappeared. Illness, she says, has depleted their Men, and she begs that we lend their Clan studs. I have promised her Jak and Ralf, both strong and proven—"

The Mother stopped. "That is as far as I had gone, my child, when you entered."

Meg's eyes were wide with wonder. It was quite true that Darthee, Lina and Alis had recently returned from a trip to Clina. And that there was now a visitor in camp. But how could the speech-without-words know these things, *tell* these things? She said, "But, Mother . . . will not the speech-without-words forget?"

"No, Meg. *We* forget. The books remember always."

"Books, Mother?"

"These are books." The Mother moved to the sleeping part of her *hoam*, selected one of a tumbled pile of calf-skin scrolls. "Here are the records of our Clan from ages past . . . since the time of the Ancient Ones. Not all are here. Some have been lost. Others were ruined by flood or destroyed by fire.

"But it is the Mother's duty to keep these records. That is why the Mother must know the art of making the speech-without-words. It is hard work, my little one. A labor without end."

Meg's eyes were shining. The trouble that had been cold within her before was vanished now. In its place had come a great thought. A thought so great, so daring, that Meg had to open her lips twice before the words came.

"Is it"—she asked breathlessly—"is it very hard to become a Mother?"

The Mother smiled gently. "Very hard, Meg. But you should not think of such things. It is not yet time for you to decide—" She paused, looking at Meg strangely— "Or . . . or is it, my child?"

Meg flushed, and her eyes dropped.

"It is, Mother."

"Then be not afraid, my daughter. You know the Law. At this important hour it is yours to decide what station in life will be yours. What is your wish, Meg? Would you be a warrior, a worker, or a breeding mother?"

Meg looked at the Clan leader boldly.

"I would be," she said, "a Mother!" Then, swiftly, "But not a breeding mother. I mean a *Clan* Mother . . . like you, O Mother!"

The Mother stared. Then the harsh lines melted from her face and she said, thoughtfully, "Thrice before has that request been made of me, Meg. Each time I have refused. It was Beth who asked first, oh, many years ago. She became a warrior, and died gallantly lifting the siege of Loovil. . . .

"Then Haizl. And the last time it was Heln. When I refused, she became the other type of mother.

"But I was younger then. Now I am old. And it is right that there should be someone to take my place when I am gone—"

She stared at the girl intently. "It is not easy, my daughter. There is much work to be done. Labor, not of the body but of the mind. There are great problems to be solved, stern vows to be taken, a hard pilgrimage to be made—"

"All these," swore Meg, "would I gladly do, O Mother! if you will but let me—" Her voice broke suddenly— "I cannot become anything else. I would not be a warrior, harsh and bitter, nor a worker black with dirt. And the breeders. . . . I would sooner mate with a Wild One than with one of the Men. The thought of their soft hands—"

She shuddered. And the Clan Mother nodded, understanding. "Very well, Meg. Tomorrow you will move into this *hoam*. You will live with me and study to become the Jinnia Clan's next Mother. . . ."

So began Meg's training. Nor was the Mother wrong in saying that the task was not an easy one. Many were the times when Meg wept bitterly, striving to learn that which a Mother must know. There was the speech-without-words, which Meg learned to call "writing." It looked like a simple magic when the Mother did it. But that slender stick which moved so fluidly beneath the Mother's aged fingers slipped and skidded and made ugly blotches of midnight on the hide whenever Meg tried to make spider-marks.

Meg learned that these wavering lines were not meaningless. Each line was made of "sentences," each sentence of "words," and each word was composed of "letters." And each letter made a sound, just as each combination of letters made a word-sound.

These were strange and confusing. A single letter out of place could change the whole meaning of a word. Sometimes it altered the meaning of the whole sentence. But Meg's determination was great. There came finally the day when the Mother allowed her to write the monthly report in the Clan history. Meg was thirteen then. But already she was older in wisdom than the others of her Clan.

Then it was that the Mother began to teach her yet another magic. This was the magic of "numbers." Where there had been twenty-six letters, there were only ten numbers. But theirs was a vast and potent magic. Put together they formed other and greater numbers. Yet those same numbers taken from each other formed still a third group. The names of these magics Meg never did quite learn. They were strange-sounding meaningless terms: "multiplication" and "subtraction." But she learned how to do them.

Her task was very hard, for it was about this time that the Evil Ones sent a little pain-imp to torment her. He stole through her ear one night while she was sleeping, and for many months he lurked in her head, above her eyes. Each time she would set herself to study the magic of the numbers he would begin dancing up and down, trying to stop her. But Meg persisted, and finally the pain-imp died or was removed. And Meg knew the numbers. . . .

There were the rites and rituals to be learned. There was the Sacred Song which must be learned by heart. This song had no tune but was accompanied by the beating of the tribal drums. Its words were strange and terrible, echoing the majesty of the gods in its cryptic phrasing.

"Oh, Saken! You see by Tedhi on his early Light—"

This was a great song. A powerful magic. It was the only tribal song Meg learned which dared name one of the gods. And it had to be sung reverently, lest far-seeing Tedhi be displeased and show her monstrous teeth and destroy the invoker with her mirthful thunders.

Meg learned, too, the tribal song of the Jinnia Clan. She had known it from infancy, but its words had been obscure. Now she had learned enough to probe its import. She did not know the meanings of some of the forgotten words, but for the most part it made sense when the tribe gathered on festive nights to sing, *"Caämé back to over Jinnia—"*

And Meg grew in age and stature and wisdom. In her sixteenth summer her legs were long and firm and straight as a warrior's spear. Her body was supple, bronzed by sunlight save where her doeskin breechcloth kept the skin white. Unbound, her hair would have trailed the earth, but she wore it piled upon her head, fastened by a netting woven by the breeding mothers too ancient to bear.

The vanity-god had died long ages since, and Meg had no way of knowing she was beautiful. But sometimes, seeing her reflection in the pool as she bathed, she approved the soft curves of her slim young body, and was more than ever glad and proud that she had become a neophyte to the Mother. She liked her body to be this way. Why, she did not know. But she was glad she had not turned lean and hard, as had those of her age who had become warriors. Or coarse, as had become the workers. Or soft and flabby, as were the breeding mothers. Her skin was clear and clean, brown where the sunlight burnished the fine down on her arms and legs, pure gold in the secret hollow of her high, firm breasts.

And finally there came the day when the Mother let Meg conduct the rites at the Feast of the Blossoms. This was in July, and Meg had then entered upon her seventeenth year. It was a great occasion and a great test. But Meg did not fail. She conducted the elaborate ceremony from beginning to end without a single mistake.

That night in the quiet of their *hoam* the Mother made a final magic. She drew from her collection of aged trophies a curl of parchment. This she blessed. Then she handed it to Meg.

"You are ready now, O my daughter," she said. "In the morning you will leave."

"Leave, Mother?" asked Meg.

"For the final test. This which I give you is a map: a teller-of-places. Here at this joining of mountain and river lies our village in the heart of the Jinnia territory. Far away westward and to the north, as here is shown, is the Place of the Gods. There will all be made clear to you, even that final secret which the Clan must never know."

"I do not understand, Mother."

"You will, my daughter . . . later. And now to sleep. For at dawn tomorrow begins your pilgrimage. . . ."

Off in the hills a wild dog howled his savage tribute to a melancholy moon. His thin song clove the stirring silence of the trees, the incessant movement of the forest. Meg wakened at that cry, wakened and saw that already the red edge of dawn tinged the eastern sky.

She uncurled from the broad tree crotch in which she had spent the night. Her horse was already awake, and with restless movements was nibbling the sparse grass beneath the giant oak. Meg loosed his tether, bathed the sleep-imps from her eyes at a nearby spring, then set about making breakfast. There was not much food in her saddlebags. A side of rabbit carefully saved from last night's dinner. Two biscuits, slightly dry. A precious handful of salt. Meg ate sparingly, resolved to build camp earlier tonight in order to set a few game traps and bake another batch of biscuit.

She cleared a space, scratching a wide circle of earth bare of all leaves and twigs, walking thrice around it widdershins to chase away the fire-demon. Then she scratched the fire-stone against a piece of the black metal from a town of the Ancient Ones—a gift of the Mother—and kindled her little fire.

Two weeks had passed since she had left the Jinnia territory. She had come from the rugged mountainlands of her homeland, through the river valleys of the Hylan Clan. On the flat plains of the Yana section she had made an error. Her map had shown the route clearly, but she had come upon a road built by the Ancient Ones: a road of white *creet*, still in fair repair. And because it was easier to travel on this highway than to thread a way through the jungle, she had let her path drift southward.

It was not until she reached the time-crumbled village of Slooie that friendly Zurries had pointed out her mistake. Then she had turned northward and westward again, going up the Big River to the territory of the Demoys.

Now, her map showed, she was in Braska territory. Two more weeks—perhaps less than that—would bring her to her goal. To the sacred Place of the Gods.

Meg started and roused from her musings as a twig snapped in the forest behind her. In one swift motion she had wheeled, drawn her sword, and was facing the spot from which the sound had come. But the green bushes did not tremble; no further crackling came from the underbrush. Her fears allayed, she turned to the important business of roasting her side of rabbit.

It was always needful to be on the alert. Meg had learned that lesson early, even before her second day's journey had carried her out of Jinnia territory. For as the Mother had warned, there were still many Wild Ones roaming through the land, searching for food, for the precious fire-metal from the ruined villages of the Ancient Ones . . . most of all for mates. The Wild Ones were slowly dying out because there were few females left among them. Most of the Wild Ones were male. But there was little in their shaggy bodies, their thick, brutish faces, their hard, gnarled muscles, to remind one of the Men.

A Wild One had attacked Meg in her second night's camp. Fortunately she had not yet been asleep when he appeared, else her pilgrimage would have ended abruptly. Not that he would have killed her. The Wild Ones did not kill the Women they captured. They took them to their dens. And a priestess could not cross her strain with a Wild One and still become a Mother.

So Meg had fought fiercely, and the Wild One's bones lay deep in the Jinnia hills, picked white by the vultures. But since that escape Meg had slept nightly in trees, her sword clenched in her hand.

The food was cooked now. Meg removed it from the spit, blew upon it, and began to eat. She had many things on her mind. The end of her pilgrimage was nigh. The hour when she would enter into the Place of the Gods, and learn the last and most carefully guarded secret.

That is why her senses failed her. That is why she did not even know the Wild One lurked near until with a roar of throaty satisfaction he had leaped from the shrubbery, seized her, and pinioned her struggling arms to her sides.

It was a silent struggle but a bitter one. For all her slimness, Meg's body was sturdy. She fought pantherlike, using every weapon with which the gods had endowed her: her fists, her legs, her teeth. But the Wild One's strength was as great as his ardor was strong. He crushed Meg to him fiercely; the stink of his sweat burned her nostrils. His arms bruised her breasts, choked the breath from her straining lungs. One furry arm tensed about her throat, cutting off the precious air.

Meg writhed, broke free momentarily, buried her strong teeth in his arm. A howl of hurt and rage broke from the Wild One's lips. Meg tugged at her sword. But again the Wild One threw himself upon her, this time with great fists flailing. Meg saw a hammerlike hand smashing down upon her, felt the shocking concussion of the Wild One's strength. A lightning flashed. The ground leaped up to meet her. Then all was darkness. . . .

She woke, moaning weakly. Her head was splitting and the bones of her body ached. She started to struggle to her feet, had risen halfway before she discovered with a burst of hope that she *could* move! She was not bound. Then the Wild One. . . .

She glanced about her swiftly. She was still lying in the little glade where she had been attacked. The sun's full orb had crept over the horizon, threading a lacework of light through the tiny glen. Her fire smoldering still. And beside it crouched a—a—

Meg could not decide *what* it was. It looked a little like a Man. But that, of course, was impossible. Its body was bronzed by the sun, smooth and almost as hairless as her own. But it was not the weak, soft body of a Man. It was muscular, hard, firm; taller and stronger than that of a warrior.

Flight was Meg's first thought. But her curiosity was even stronger than her fear. This was a mystery. And her sword was beside her. Whoever or whatever this Thing might be it did not seem to wish her harm. She spoke to it.

"Who are you?" asked Meg. "And where is the Wild One?"

The stranger looked up, and a happy-look spread over his even features. He pointed briefly to the shrubbery. Meg's eyes followed the gesture, saw lying there the dead body of the Wild One. Her puzzled gaze returned to the Man-thing.

"You killed him? Then you are not one of the Wild Ones? But I do not understand. You are not a Man."

"You," said the Man-thing in a voice deeper than Meg had ever heard from a human throat, "talk too much. Sit down and eat, Woman."

He tossed Meg a piece of her own rabbit-meat. Half unaware that she did so, Meg took it and began eating. She stared at the stranger as he finished his own repast, wiped his hands on his clout and moved toward her. Meg dropped her half-eaten breakfast, rose hastily and groped for her sword.

"Touch me not, Hairless One!" she cried. "I am a priestess of the Jinnia Clan. It is not for such as you to—"

The stranger brushed by her without even seeming to hear her words. He reached the spot where her horse had been tethered, shook ruefully a section of broken rein.

"You Women!" he snorted. "You do not know how to train a horse. See, he ran away."

Meg thought anger-thoughts. Her face burned with the sun though the sun's rays were dim in the glade. She cried, "Man-thing, know you no better than to talk thus to a Woman and a master? By Jarg, I should have you whipped."

"You talk too much," repeated the Man-thing wearily. Once more he squatted on his hunkers, studied her thoughtfully. "But you interest me. Who are you? What are you doing so far from the Jinnia territory? Where are you going?"

"A priestess," said Meg coldly, "does not answer the questions of a Man-thing."

"I'm not a Man-*thing*," said the stranger pettishly, "I am a Man. A Man of the Kirki tribe which lives many days walking south of here. I am Daiv, known as He-who-would-learn. So tell me, Woman."

His candor confused Meg. Despite herself, she found the words leaving her lips. "I . . . I am Meg. I am making pilgrimage to the Place of the Gods. It is my final task ere I become Mother of my clan."

The Man's eyes appraised her with embarrassing frankness. "So?" he said. "Mother of a Clan? Meg, would you not rather stay with me and mother your own clan?"

Meg gasped. Men were the mates of Women, yes, but never had any Man had the audacity to *suggest* such a thing. Matings were arranged by the Mother with the agreement of the Women. And surely this Man must know that priestesses did not mate.

"Man," she cried, "know you not the Law? I am soon to become a Clan Mother. Guard your words, or the wrath of the Gods—"

The Man, Daiv, made happy-sounds again. "It was I who saved you from the Wild One," he chuckled, "not the Gods. In my land, Golden One, we think it does no harm to ask. But if you are unwilling—" He shrugged— "I will leave you now."

He rose and started to leave. Meg's face reddened. She cried out angrily, "Man!"

He turned. "Yes?"

"I have no horse. How am I to get to the Place of the Gods?"

"Afoot, Golden One. Or are you Women too weak to make such a journey?"

He laughed . . . and was gone.

For a long moment Meg stared after him, watching the green fronds close behind the disappearing form, feeling the stark desolation of utter aloneness close in upon and envelop her. Then she did a thing she herself could not understand. She put down her foot upon the ground, hard, in an angry-movement.

The sun was high and growing warmer. The journey to the Place of the Gods was longer now that she had no mount. But the pilgrimage was a sacred obligation. Meg scraped dirt over the smoldering embers of her fire. She tossed her saddlebags across her shoulder and faced westward. And she pressed on.

The way was long, the day hot and tedious. Before the sun rode overhead, Meg was sticky with sweat and dust. Her feet were sore and her legs ached with the unaccustomed exercise of walking. By afternoon every step was an agony. And while the sun was too strong to be looked at, she found a small spring of fresh water and decided to make camp there for the night.

She set out two snares for small game, took the flour and salt from her saddlebags, and set about making a batch of biscuit. As the rocks heated she went to the stream and put her feet in it, letting the water-god lick the fever from her tender soles.

From where she sat she could not see the fire. She had been there perhaps half an hour when a strange, unfamiliar smell wrinkled her nostrils. It was at once a sweet-and-bitter smell, a pungent odor like strong herbs, but one that set the water to running in her mouth.

She went back to her camp hastily and found there the Man, Daiv, once again crouching over her fireplace. He was watching a pot on the stones. From time to time he stirred the pot with a long stick. Drawing closer, Meg saw a brown water in the pot. It was this which made the aromatic smell. She would have called out to the Man, but he saw her first.

"Hello, Golden One," he said.

Meg said angrily, "What are you doing here?"

The Man shrugged.

"I am Daiv; they call me He-who-would-learn. I got to thinking about this Place of the Gods and decided I, too, would come and see it." He sniffed the brown, bubbling liquid, seemed satisfied. He poured some of it into an earthen bowl and handed it to Meg. "You want some?"

Meg edged toward him cautiously. This might be a ruse of the Man from the Kirki tribe. Perhaps this strange, aromatic liquid was a drug. The Mother of her Clan had the secret of such drinks. There was one which caused the head to pucker, the mouth to dry and the feet to reel.

"What is it?" she demanded suspiciously.

"Cawfi, of course." Daiv looked surprised. "Don't you know? But, no . . . I suppose the bean-tree would not grow in your cold northern climate. It grows near my land. In Sippe and Weezian territories. Drink it."

Meg tasted the stuff. It was like its smell: strong and bitter, but strangely pleasing. Its heat coursed through her, taking the tired-pain from her body as the water of the spring had taken the burn from her feet.

"It is good, Man," she said.

"Daiv," said the Man. "My name is Daiv, Golden One."

"It is not fitting," she said, "that a priestess should call a Man by his name."

Daiv seemed to be given to making happy-sounds. He made one again.

"You have done a lot of things today that are not fitting for a priestess, Golden One. You are not in Jinnia now. Things are different here. And as for me—" He shrugged— "My people do things differently. We come from the Land of the Escape."

"The Escape?" asked Meg.

"Yes." As he talked, Daiv busied himself. He had taken meat from his pouch and was wrapping it now in clay. He tossed the caked lumps into the embers of the crude oven. He also had something Meg had not tasted for many weeks: taters. He took the skins off these, cut them into slices with his hunting-knife, and browned the pieces on the slab of heated rock. "The Escape of the Ancient Ones, you know."

"I don't understand," said Meg.

"Neither do I . . . quite. It happened many years ago. Before my father's father's father's people. There are books in the tribe Master's *hoam* which tell. I have seen some of them.

"Once things were different, you know. In the days of the

Ancient Ones, Men and Women were equal throughout the world. In fact, the Men were usually the Masters. But the Men were war-like and fierce—"

"Like the Wild Ones, you mean?"

"Yes. But they did not fight, like the Wild Ones, with clubs and spears. They made war with great catapults that threw fire and flame and exploding death. With little bows that shot steel arrowheads. With gases that destroy, and waters that burn the skin.

"On earth and sea they made these battles, and even in the air. For in those days the Ancient Ones had wings like birds. They soared high, making great thunders. And when they warred, they dropped huge eggs of fire which killed others."

Meg cried sharply, "Oh—!"

"Don't you believe me?"

"The taters, Daiv. They're burning."

"Oh!" Daiv made a happy-face and carefully turned the scorching tater slices. Then he continued.

"It is written that there came a last and greatest war of all. It was a conflict not only between the Clans but between the forces of the entire earth. For many years this war lasted, but neither side could gain a victory. In those days it was the Men who fought, while the Women remained *hoam* to keep the Men's houses. But the Men died by the thousands. And there came a day when the Women grew tired of the slaughter.

"They banded together, all of them who lived in the civilized places. They decided to rid themselves of the brutal Men. They stopped sending supplies and fire-eggs to the battling Men across the sea. They built walled forts and hid themselves in them.

"The war ended when the Men found they had no more weapons to fight with. They came back to their *hoams*, seeking their Women. But the Women would not receive them. There was bitter warfare once again . . . this time between the sexes. But the Women held their walled cities. And so—"

"Yes?" said Meg.

"The Men," said Daiv somberly, "became the Wild Ones of the forest. Mateless, save for the few Women they could capture.

Their numbers died off. The Clans grew. Only in a few places—
like Kirki, my homeland—did humanity not become a matri-
archy."

He looked at Meg. "You believe?"

Meg shook her head. Suddenly she felt very sorry for this
stranger, Daiv. She knew, now, why he had not harmed her.
Why, when she had been powerless before him, he had not
forced her to mate with him. He was mad. Totally and completely mad. She said, gently, "Shall we eat, Daiv?"

Mad or not, there was great pleasure in having Daiv's company on the long, weary, remaining marches of her pilgrimage.
Thus it was that Meg made no effort to discourage him in his
desire to accompany her. He was harmless, and he was pleasant
company . . . for a Man. And his talk, wild as it was at times,
served to pass wearisome hours.

So the slow days passed, turning into weeks. Not many miles
did they cover in those first few days while Meg's feet were tender and her legs full of jumping little pain-imps. But when hard
walking had destroyed the pain-imps, they traveled faster. And
the time of their journey's ending drew ever nearer. They crossed
the Braska territory and entered at last into the 'Kota country.
Near here at the far western end, near Yomin, was the Place of
the Gods.

"You started, once, to tell about the Escape, Daiv," said Meg
one night, "but you did not finish. What is the legend of the
Escape?"

Daiv sprawled lazily before the fire. His eyes were dreamy.

"It happened in the Zoni territory," he said, "not far from the
land of my own tribe. In those days there was a Man-god named
Renn who foresaw the death of the Ancient Ones. He built a
gigantic sky-bird of metal, and into its bowels climbed two score
Men and Women.

"They flew away, off there"—Daiv pointed to a shining white
dot in the sky above—"to the evening star. But it is said that
one day they will return. That is why our tribe tries to preserve

the customs of the Ancient Ones. Why even misguided tribes like yours preserve the records—"

Meg's face reddened.

"Enough!" she cried. "I have listened to many of your tales without comment, Daiv. But tell me no more such tales as this. This is blasphemy!"

"Blasphemy?"

"It is bad enough that your deranged mind should tell of days when Men ruled. But when you speak of a *Man-god*—"

Daiv looked worried. He said, "But, Golden One, I thought you knew that all the gods were Men."

"Daiv!" Meg swung suddenly to face him, covered his lips with her hands. Her eyes sought the darkness fearfully; she made a swift gesture and a swifter prayer. "Daiv, do not tempt the fury of the Gods! I am a priestess, and I know. All the Gods are —*must be*—Women!"

"But why?"

"Why, because they are," said Meg. "It could not be otherwise. All Women know the gods are great, good and strong. How, then, could they be Men, great Jarg, and mighty Ibrim, strong Taamuz, and the laughing Tedhi—?"

Daiv's eyes narrowed in a wonder-look.

"I do not know those names," he mused. "They are not gods of our tribe. And yet . . . I have heard legends. Ibrim . . . Tedhi. . . ."

There was vast pity and a sorrow in Meg's voice.

"We have been comrades for a long journey, Daiv," she pleaded. "Never before since the world began have a Man and a Woman met as you and I; as friends, almost as equals. Often you have said mad, impossible things. But I have forgiven you because . . . well, because you are, after all, only a Man.

"But tomorrow, or the day after that, we will come to the Place of the Gods. There will my pilgrimage be ended, and I will learn that which is the ultimate secret. Then I shall return to my Clan to become the Mother. So let us not spoil our last hours of comradeship with vain argument."

Daiv sighed.

"The elder ones are gone and their legends tell so little. It may be you are right, Golden One. But I have a feeling that it is *my* tribal lore which does not err. Meg . . . I asked this once before. Now I ask again. Will you give up this quest and mate with me?"

"It is impossible, Daiv. Priestesses and Mothers do not mate. I am a priestess; soon I will be a Mother. But"—Meg's voice was gentle—"I will take you back with me to Jinnia, if you wish. And I will see to it that you are taken care of always, Daiv, as a Man should be taken care of."

Daiv shook his head.

"No, Meg. Our ways are not the same. There is a custom in our tribe . . . a mating custom which you do not know. Let me show you—"

He leaned over swiftly. Meg felt the great, warm strength of his bronzed arms closing about her, drawing her close. Then he was touching his mouth to hers; closely, brutally, frighteningly.

She struggled and tried to cry out, but his lips silenced her. Anger-thoughts swept through her like a flame. But it was not anger, it was something else that gave life to that flame. Suddenly her veins were aflow with liquid fire. Her heart beat upon rising breasts like something captive that would be free. Her fists beat upon his shoulders vainly . . . but there was little strength in her blows.

Then he released her, and Meg fell back exhausted. Her eyes glowed with anger and her voice was husky in her throat. She tried to speak and could not. And in that moment a vast and terrible weakness trembled through Meg. She knew suddenly and helplessly that if Daiv sought now to mate with her not all the wisdom of the priestessdom could save her. There was a body-hunger throbbing within her that hated Daiv's manhood . . . and cried in wanting for it.

But Daiv, too, had stepped back. And his voice was low as he said, "Meg?"

She scrubbed her lips with the back of her hand. Her voice was vibrant, breaking. "What magic is that, Daiv? What custom is that? I hate it. I hate you!"

"It is the touching-of-mouths, Golden One. It is the right of a Man with his Woman. It is my plea that you enter not the Place of the Gods but return with me now to Kirki, there to be my mate."

For a moment indecision swayed Meg. But then, slowly, "No. I must go to the Place of the Gods," she said.

And thus it was. For the next day Meg marked on the teller-of-places the last line that indicated the path of her pilgrimage. And at eventide, when the sun threw long, ruddy rays upon the rounded hills of black, she and Daiv entered into that gateway which she had been told led to the Place of the Gods.

It was here they lingered a moment. There were many words each would have said to the other. But both knew this was the end.

"I know no Law, Daiv," said Meg, "which forbids a Man from entering the Place of the Gods. So you may do so if you wish. But it is not fitting that we should enter together. Therefore I ask you to wait here while I enter alone.

"Here I will learn the secret. And having learned, I will go out by another path and return to Jinnia."

"You will go . . . alone?"

"Yes, Daiv."

Daiv nodded.

"It is yours to decide, Golden One. But . . . should you change your mind—"

"I will not, Daiv."

"But if you should—" he persisted.

"If by some madness I should change my mind," said Meg, "I will return to you here. But it will not happen. Therefore do not wait."

"I will wait, Golden One," said Daiv soberly, "until all hope is dead."

Meg turned away, then hesitated and turned back. A great sorrow was within her. She did not know why. But she knew of one magic that for a little time could heal her heart.

"Daiv—" she whispered.

"Yes, Golden One?"

"No one will ever know. And before I leave you forever . . . could we not once more do the rite of the touching-of-mouths?"

So it was that alone and with the recollection of a moment of stirring glory in her heart, Meg strode proudly at last into the Place of the Gods.

It was a wild and desolate place. Barren hills of sand rose about, and of vegetation there was none save sparse weeds and scrubby stumps that flowered miserly in the bleak, chill air.

The ground was harsh and salt beneath her feet; no insects sang an evensong in that drab wilderness. Afar, a nightjar pierced the sky with its lonely call; the great hills echoed that cry dismally.

Above the other hills towered a greater one. To this, with un-erring footsteps, Meg took her way. She knew not what to expect. It might be that here a band of singing virgins would appear to her, guiding her to a secret altar before which she would kneel and learn the last mystery. Here might she meet those fabled Mothers who rule all the earth. It might be that the Gods themselves reigned here, and that she would fall in awe before the sweeping skirts of austere Jarg, to hear from the Gods' own lips that which she had come so far to learn.

Whatever the secret that would be revealed to her, Meg was ready. Others had gained this place and had survived. She did not fear death. But . . . death-in-life? Coming to the Place of the Gods with a blasphemy in her heart? With the memory of a Man's mouth upon her own?

For a moment, Meg was afraid. She had betrayed her priestess-dom. Her body was inviolate, true . . . but would not the Gods search her soul and know that her heart had forgotten the Law, had mated with a Man?

But if death must be her lot . . . so be it. She pressed on. . . .

So Meg turned down a winding path between two tortuous clefts of rock and came at last unto the Place of the Gods. Nor could she have chosen a better moment for the ultimate reaching of this place. The sun's roundness had now touched the western horizon, bathing the dark valley with an avenue of light. Meg's eyes, wondering, followed that avenue. And then, with awe in her heart, Meg fell to her knees. She had glimpsed that-which-was-not-to-be-seen. The Gods themselves, in omnipotent majesty looking down upon her from the crest of the towering rocks.

For tremulous moments Meg knelt there, whispering the ritual prayers of appeasement. At any moment she expected to hear the voice of Tedhi, thunderous in judgment, or to feel upon her shoulder the weighty hand of Jarg. But there came no sound save the frenzied beating of her own heart, of the wind stirring fretfully through the crevices of the ageless rocks.

And she lifted her head and looked once more. . . .

It was they. A race-recollection deeper and more sure than her own meagre learning told her at once that she had not erred. This was, indeed, the Place of the Gods. And these she faced were indeed the Gods . . . stern, implacable, eternal, carven in timeless stone by hands of the Ancient Ones.

Here they were: the Great Four. Stern Jarg and mighty Taamuz, with ringletted curls framing their stern, judicial faces; sad Ibrim, lean of cheek and hollow of eye; far-seeing Tedhi, whose eyes were concealed behind the giant telescopes; whose lips, even now, were peeled back as though to loose the dreadful laughter.

And the Secret?

Even as the question leaped to her mind it had its answer. Suddenly Meg knew that here was no visitation to be made upon her. Here would appear no circle of singing virgins; here she would have no message from those great stone lips. For the Secret which the Mother had hinted . . . the Secret which the Clanswomen must not know . . . was a truth Daiv had confided to her during the long marches of their pilgrimage.

The Gods . . . Were Men!

Oh, not men like Jak and Ralf, whose pale and furtive bodies were but instruments by which the breeding mothers' bodies were fertilized. Nor male beasts like the Wild Ones. But Men like Daiv . . . lean and hard of jaw, strong of muscle, sturdy of body.

Even the curls could not conceal the strong, clean masculinity of Jarg and Taamuz. Tedhi's lip was covered with Man-hair, clearcut and bristling above his happy-mouth. And Ibrim's cheeks were haired, even as Daiv's before each dawn he made his tribal cut-magic with a keen knife.

The Gods, the rulers, the masters of the Ancient Ones had been Men. It was as Daiv had said: long years ago the Women had rebelled, and now in sterile penance they pursued their cold and loveless courses save where—in a few places like the land of Kirki—the old way still maintained.

It was a great knowledge and a bitter one. Now Meg understood why the Mother's lot was so unhappy. Only the Mother knew how artificial this new life was. How one day the Wild Ones would die out, and the captive Men as well. When that day came there would be no more young. No more Men *or* Women. No more civilization. . . .

The Gods knew this. That is why, here in the gray hills of 'Kota, they stood so sad, forlorn, forgotten, the dying gods of a dying race. The Gods knew that by an ancient folly humankind had doomed itself to slow but certain death. They knew, and grieved because there was no hope. Sharing this secret, Meg must return to her Clan with lips sealed. There, like the Mother before her, she must watch with haunted eyes the slow dwindling of their tiny number . . . see the weak and futile remnants of Man die off. Until, at last. . . .

Then, like the clear, cold vision of the newborn moon, came a burst of hope to Meg.

The Mother had been wrong. For the Mother of *her* pilgrimage had not been so fortunate as had Meg. She had not learned that in the world were still places where Man had preserved himself in the image of the Gods.

But she, Meg, knew! And knowing she was presented with the greatest choice that ever a Woman had been given.

Forward, into the valley, lay the path through which she could return to her Clan. There she would become Mother and would guide and guard her people through a lifetime. She would be all-wise, all-powerful, all-important. But she would be virgin unto death, sterile with the sanctity of tradition.

This she might do. But there was yet another way. And Meg threw her arms high, crying out that the Gods might hear and decide her problem.

The Gods spoke not. Their solemn features, weighted with the sorrows of slow time, moved not nor spoke to her. But as she searched their faces for an answer to her vast despair, there came to Meg a memory. It was a passage from the Prayer of Ibrim. And as her lips framed those remembered words it seemed the slanted rays of the dying sun centered on Ibrim's weary face, and those great, stone eyes were alive for a moment with understanding and approval.

"—shall not perish from the earth, but have everlasting life—"

Then Meg, the priestess, decided. With a cry that broke from her heart she turned and ran. Not toward the sterile valley. But back . . . back to the fecund world on feet that were suddenly stumbling and eager. Back from the shadow of Mount Rushmore to a gateway where waited the Man who had taught her the touching-of-mouths.

Although Edmond Hamilton—author of *The Haunted Stars* (1960) and *The City at World's End* (1951)—hasn't been writing as long as Murray Leinster, the dean of the field, he's a pretty close runner up, having published his first stories in the old *Weird Tales* back in 1926 and "The Comet Doom" (his first sale to *Amazing*) only two years later. But very much like Leinster—perhaps even more so—he has been astonishingly good at keeping up with the various changes in literary style that have come and gone between the editorships of Hugo Gernsback and H. L. Gold. So much so that even recent Hamilton shorts like "Requiem" and "The Stars, My Brothers" have a more modern "ring" than most of what we read elsewhere. And that's especially true of "Sunfire!," in which an Earthman goes a long way to be disinherited—to the sunward side of Mercury!

SUNFIRE!

Edmond Hamilton

Everything in the old house seemed just the same as it had been before he went to space.

It was incredible, thought Hugh Kellard, standing in the front hall and looking around the silent, sunlit rooms, how little it had changed. The life was gone out of it now, all the people and voices and the comings and goings when his grandfather still lived and he had visited here. But that had been long ago, and he was amazed that so much remained still untouched.

Like travelling into the past, thought Kellard, to come back to this part of Earth.

He was tired, in body and mind and nerve, and he stood for a while, just staring. The agent who cared for the old place had let him in and gone away, and there was not a sound in the house. He walked into the living-room where his grandfather's desk still stood beneath a window, and looked out. The window faced northward, along the California coastal cliffs that run north along Morro Bay to Big Sur. The Pacific foamed and surged against the huge broken stones beneath the cliffs, and the hills, somber now with a tinge of autumn, shouldered massively up toward the east from the cliff road. It all looked as lonely as ever, no other houses in sight but this gray, weatherbeaten house that had faced the sea-wind and the sea-fog for over a hundred years.

Kellard walked back along the hall. On its walls still hung the ornately framed family photographs which his grandfather had stubbornly kept in place. His great-grandfather, and his great-aunt something, and all the rest of them, on back into the shadows. They were all there, they had not been touched, nothing in the house had been touched, just as his grandfather's will had enjoined. Keep the old house, he had said. Some of the family will be back some day.

The old man had been right, he thought. One of the family had come back at last, one who had roamed farther than almost anybody on Earth.

"But that's all done with," he told himself. "Here I am, and here I stay. I'm through with space."

He started through the rooms, opening windows, letting in light and air. The furniture was faded and old-fashioned, but the place was not dusty; the agent had seen that it was kept in shape. Kellard picked one of the big upstairs bedrooms for himself, and brought in the blankets and cartons and luggage from the car. He went into the utility room and turned on the power-unit, remembering as he did so how his grandfather had disliked and distrusted the unit, how he had refused to have one until the electric wires were all gone and there was no other way to get power. He checked the stove and freezer, shoved his cartons of food into the latter, and then looked around and wondered what to do next.

Standing in the silent house, he wondered suddenly if he had been foolish to quit everything and come back to Earth and this old place.

No, he thought heavily. Mercury ended it for me. I made my decision and that is that. Forget it.

He strode abruptly out of the house and started walking. And after a little while the dark weight in his mind, the somber knowledge, faded and receded in the new-found, old-remembered interest of the things about him.

His way took him across the road, past the shabby barns and up sloping pastures where once his grandfather had kept the fine horses he bred. Then he was in among the pines, climbing more steeply, with the resinous smell of the trees strong in his nostrils. That smell he had never forgotten, and once he had met a smell vaguely like it, far away from Earth—

Forget all that, Kellard.

The trees took him in and he walked through a dapple of sun and shadows. A deer slipped away through the pines ahead of him, and quail burst up from almost under his feet. He remembered a grove of bigger pines farther up the slope, and an old man and a boy walking up to them. How long ago was that? He had been fifteen—and he was thirty-two now. Seventeen years. Still, he thought he could find the place.

He found it. The big pines were still there, for people did not use wood much any more. The rough dark giants stood at dignified intervals from each other, and he sat down with his back against the massive trunk of the biggest.

Funny, he thought. When I was a boy sitting here dreaming about the future and what I was going to do, I never once imagined that some things would stay much the same. The whole world would somehow be miraculously transformed—but it wasn't. This tree was here when men first reached the Moon, and Mars, and Venus and the rest, but it didn't know about that; it didn't change because of it.

Kellard sat for a long time, still wrapped in a gray weariness, his emotions in a numb trance. He sat listening to the distant, uneasy murmur of the sea, until the sunset light shafting through the trees dazzled his eyes, and then he got up and went back down to the house. He heated food, ate it, and then went out to the porch in front of the house and sat watching the sun sink toward the vast golden sheet of the Pacific. He thought of the little dot close to the sun that he could not see, the little world and the strange, terrible place upon it where Morse and Binetti had died.

The telephone rang.

Kellard did not stir, and it rang and rang again.

Go ahead and ring your head off, he thought. You're not getting me back. I told you. I've had it.

The ringing stopped. The sun sank and darkness came with the hosts of wheeling stars, and there was no sound but the vast voices rolling in from sea, as Kellard sat staring and drinking.

He finally got up, as the fog started coming in. He moved with gravity, feeling much better. He went in and turned on the lights, and then looked at the faces that stared from the long row of framed photographs.

He raised the bottle to them in a gesture of salutation.

"You see, Kellards, that your prodigal son—or great-grandson —has come home again from space."

He gravely drank, and continued to stand looking along the faded faces.

"You were lucky—you know that? Back in your time, there were hopes, and dreams, and man's road would go on forever, from triumph to triumph everlasting. But that road was a blind alley, all the time, even if I'm the only one who knows it."

The faces looked back at him, unchanging, but he read reproach in their steady gaze, their lined features.

"I'm sorry," said Kellard. "You had your own troubles, I know. I apologize, Kellards. I am very tired and a little drunk, and I am going to bed."

The next morning he was making coffee when there came a banging of the old-fashioned knocker on the front door. A certain tightness came into Kellard's face. He had expected them to send someone.

He had not expected the man who stood at the door. He was not in Survey uniform, although he was the highest brass there was. He was a big, slow-moving man with a heavy face and blue eyes that seemed mild if you didn't know him.

"Well," said Kellard. And after a moment, "Come on in."

Halfrich came in. He sat down and looked interestedly around at the old room and furniture.

"Nice," he murmured. Then he looked at Kellard and said, "All right, let's have it. Why did you quit?"

Kellard shrugged. "It was all in my letter of resignation. I'm getting a bit old and tired for Survey, I—"

"Bull," said Halfrich, "It was something about that crack-up on Sunside, wasn't it?"

Kellard said slowly, "Yes. The deaths of Binetti and Morse, and the after-effects of that shock, made me feel I didn't have it any more."

Halfrich looked at him. "You've had crack-ups before. You've seen men die. You've had almost as many years in Survey as I have, and you've taken as many jolts. You're lying, Kellard."

Kellard got up, and walked a few steps and swung around again.

"So I'm lying. I want out, and what difference does it make why?"

"It makes a difference," Halfrich said grimly. "I remember from away back at Academy, even though you were two years after me. You were the space-craziest cadet there was. You spouted the glories of the conquest of space until we were all sick of it. You haven't changed in all the years in Survey—until now. I want to know what can change a man like that."

Kellard said nothing. He went to the window and looked out at the long rollers coming endlessly in and crashing against the rocks.

"What did you see on Sunside, Kellard?"

He turned around sharply at that.

"What do you mean? What would there be to see there, but hot rocks and volcanoes and a cross-section of hell generally? It's all in my report."

Halfrich sat like a judge, and spoke like one pronouncing sentence. "You saw something, you *met* something there. You covered by tearing out the film of the automatic sweep-camera. Whatever it had recorded, you didn't want us to see, did you?"

Kellard came toward him and spoke angrily and rapidly. "Do you realize that we flamed out and crashed there? A crash like that can do damage. It killed Binetti and mortally injured Morse, and smashed the sweep-camera."

Halfrich nodded. "That's what we thought, at first. But the radar-sweep had an automatic recorder too. It was something new. Binetti knew about it, as communications officer, but I guess he hadn't told you, or you'd have smashed it too. Its record shows something."

A cold feeling came over Kellard. He had thought that he had covered everything, but he had calculated from insufficient data.

He kept his nerve. A radar record was not like a photograph, they couldn't prove much from that; they certainly couldn't guess the truth from it. They *must* not guess the truth.

He laughed mirthlessly. "A radar record made on Sunside isn't worth the paper it's on. The storms of radiation there make radar practically unreliable."

Halfrich was watching him keenly. "But not entirely. And over and above the static and the fake bogies, the record shows quite clearly that you went outside the ship after the crash, that you walked about a thousand yards, and that you were approached by some things that register vaguely but unmistakably."

He paused and then he asked, "Who—or what—did you meet there, Kellard?"

Kellard was cold inside, but all the same he made a disgusted sound that he hoped was convincing.

"Who would I meet on Sunside? Beautiful lightly-clad maidens? After all, you know, it's only four hundred degrees Centigrade there, and practically no atmosphere, and nothing much else but solar radiation and hot rock and volcanoes. I tell you, the radar record is worthless."

Halfrich was studying him with that mild estimating look that Kellard knew well, and didn't like at all. It was the look that came into Halfrich's face when friendship didn't matter and the good of the Survey did.

"You're still lying," he said. "You met or saw something there. And it did something to you—something that made you resign. Something that's taken all the life and eagerness out of you."

"Oh, hell, be reasonable!" said Kellard angrily. "You know no kind of life can exist on Sunside. My mission was the second time even Survey has landed there. Pavlik's mission, the first, didn't see anything. Neither did I. Quit dreaming it up. Go back to Mojave and your job, and leave me be."

Halfrich rose. "All right," he said. "I'll go back to the base. And you're going with me."

"Oh, no," said Kellard. "I'm through, quit, resigned."

"Your resignation has not been accepted," Halfrich told him. "You're still liable to Survey discipline. You'll obey orders just as you always did, or you'll go up before a court-martial."

"So that's it," said Kellard.

Halfrich nodded. "That is it. I don't like to do this. You're an old friend. But—"

"But the Survey comes first," Kellard said, between his teeth.

"The Survey," said Halfrich, "comes first. It has to. It's why we've got stations on Venus and Mars and Ganymede, not to say the Moon. It's why we'll someday be able to hit for deep space and the starworlds. And when one of my best officers suddenly goes off the deep end and won't say why, I'll damn well wring it out of him. Whatever you found on Mercury doesn't belong to you, it belongs to us, and we'll have it."

Kellard looked at him and started to say something and didn't, and then turned his back on Halfrich and looked out the window at the sea. In a low voice he said,

"Let it be, John. I'm telling you now, you'll be sorry if you don't."

There was no answer to that at all, and the silence was his answer. He turned back around.

"All right, you have a rope around my neck. I'll go back to base with you. I'll tell you not one thing more than here."

"In which case," Halfrich said, "we'll go on out to Sunside, and you'll go right along with us."

A rage born of desperation came to Kellard. He had tried to spare people this—Halfrich, the Survey, the whole human race. But they would not let it be so. Damn them, he thought; if they must do this, they have it coming to them.

"All right," he said flatly. "I'll get my jacket. I take it that you have a flier waiting."

The fast flier, less than an hour later, whizzed down over the gaunt mountains and across the desert, and the glitter and splendor of Mojave Base sprang up to meet them. The tall ships shone like silver, and something about them, something about the feel of the place, made you think that this bit of desert did not belong to Earth at all but was part of space, a way-station, the first way-station of all, to the stars.

That, thought Kellard, was what he had thought when he had first come here, years ago. And it had not been just a youngster's passing enthusiasm; it had deepened and strengthened through all the years of work and danger—until Sunside. And oh God, he thought, why did I have to go there, at that place, at that moment? I could have lived my whole life and done my work, all of us could have, without ever dreaming the truth.

He knew now that he had no choice. He must go back to Sunside with them. For even if he told them the truth, they would not believe; they would insist on going to see for themselves. He would keep silent, and that was all he could do now.

* * *

Four days later a Y-90 experimental cruiser, outfitted for space research and with full anti-heater equipment, took off from Mojave. Kellard had kept silent. And still silent he sat in his recoil-harness and took the jolts, and heard Halfrich grunting beside him, and viciously hoped that he was not liking it.

Halfrich had brought along a consulting biophysicist, a keen-faced man of middle age named Morgenson, who did not look as though he was enjoying the mission either. But the three-man crew of the little Y-90 were young men in their twenties. They spoke to Halfrich and to Kellard as though they were heroes out of legend, for in the Survey twelve to fifteen years of space-missions was an age.

It was only after they had gone a long way and a long time through the sun-washed spaces that one of the three, Shay, the navigator, ventured to put a question to Kellard.

"You were with the first mission to Ganymede, sir, weren't you?"

Kellard nodded. "Yes, I was."

"Wouldn't that have been something!" said Shay. "I mean, to be the first."

"It was something," said Kellard.

"Maybe someday I——" Shay began, and broke off and then went on, "I mean, if the star-drive is perfected as soon as some people say it will be, I could maybe be one of the first ones out there? Sir?"

"You could be," said Kellard. "Someone's going to be first. The stars are waiting. All we have to do is go out there and keep going, and the stars will be ours, just like the planets here are, all ours, forever and amen."

Shay looked at him puzzledly, and shuffled, and then went away. Halfrich had been listening, and watching. He said, "Did you have to slap the kid's face?"

Kellard shrugged. "What did I say? I was merely repeating what everyone feels, these days. The glory of the conquest of space."

"I'd give a lot," Halfrich said, "to know what's riding you. We'll soon reach Sunside and we'll find out, but I wish you'd tell me now."

"All right," said Kellard. "I'll tell you. I've been disinherited. That's what's wrong with me."

He would say nothing more, nor did Halfrich ask him another question, until the Y-90 was far in past the orbit of Venus and going into its pattern of approach.

"I assume," said Halfrich, "that you bear none of us any personal ill-will. If there is anything dangerous awaiting us, now would be the time to tell us."

Kellard considered. "You're going to land, I suppose, at the same spot where we crashed."

"Of course."

"Then land," said Kellard. "As far as I know, there is not a thing there to harm you."

In the scanner, he watched Mercury swing slowly toward them, a tiny crescent of white that was hard to see against the Sun. For here the Sun was a monster thing, fringed with writhing flames, paling the stars, drenching this whole area with radiation that already would have killed them but for the ship's anti-heaters.

Kellard remembered that when he had come this way before, Binetti had quoted something, a line from William Blake's poems, he had said. *"The desire of the moth for the star."* And that was what we were, he thought. Three little moths, going right into the furnace, and I was the only one to get out of it, but now I'm going back.

The Y-90 went into its landing pattern. It skimmed over the dark side of Mercury, the black cliffs and peaks and chasms that never saw the Sun, and then light seemed to burst ragingly up from all the horizon ahead of them, and they were over Sunside.

In old days this little world had been called "the moon of the Sun," and it looked like it, the same stark, lifeless rock plains and ridges and cracks, the fang-like look of pinnacles in a place where no atmosphere eroded anything. But the Moon was cold and still, whereas Sunside seemed to throb with sullen hidden fires. Volcanoes spewed ash and lava, and the infernal storm of radiation from overhead made everything quiver in a shimmering haze. The indicator board told them that the temperature of the outside hull was climbing to four hundred as the Y-90 went down.

And the wide valley that haunted his dreams opened up ahead.

Across it the squat volcanic cones still dribbled ash and dust,
and it was all just as it had been when he had last looked back
from the relief cruiser that had come from Venus Station to take
him off. And there gleamed bright on its floor the crumpled
wreck in which Binetti and then Morse had died.

Kellard's gaze flew to the place north of the wreck, the
tumbled, odd-shaped rocks. He felt his palms sweating. Maybe
there would be nothing. After all, could it all happen again?

They set down, and after the crashing rocket uproar, the
steady throb of the anti-heaters was an anti-climactic sound.

"You've got the armor ready?" Halfrich asked of Morgenson.

The biophysicist nodded nervously. "Three suits, with their
anti-heater equipment tested on and off all the way out."

"One suit stays here, for emergencies," Halfrich said. "Kellard
and I will go out, when there's something to go out for. First,
we'll make observations."

The recording telescope-cameras and the radar, Halfrich
ordered focused on the place of the odd-shaped rocks. And then,
sitting there on Sunside, they watched. They waited.

Nothing.

Kellard's hopes began to rise. He was right, he told himself;
it couldn't happen again.

"How long," he asked, "are we going to sit waiting for nothing because a radar made a screwy record? If those anti-heaters
quit for five minutes, we're fried."

Halfrich looked at him bleakly. "I'll tell you how long. Till
you tell the truth, and we see the truth for ourselves. That's how
long."

Kellard shrugged. "If that's the way you want it. I would tell
you to go to hell except that we're already there."

They watched and waited some more.

Morgenson said, on a rising note of excitement, "There's
something——"

Halfrich got to the 'scope fast. Kellard, looking through the
scanner, saw the geyser of flame that was beginning to pour up
from the rocks. It grew slowly, but steadily, in height.

"What is it?" Halfrich asked him.

"Can't you see for yourself?" said Kellard. "There's a blowhole out there and it throws off burning gases from the interior. It did it twice while I was waiting in the wreck."

Halfrich said, "It's in the same location where radar recorded you before, with those other blips. There's something about this —We'll go have a look."

"If you must," said Kellard. "You'll find it's just what I've said."

They got into the heat-armor. It was a clumsy outfit, for it had to have room for an efficient anti-heater, and the long tube of the heat-discharge was a nuisance. Kellard had spent days in one of these suits, waiting for the relief ship after the crack-up, and he did not like the feel of it at all.

Halfrich tested the radio and then said, "All right, Shay, lock us out and stand by. Morgenson, you keep watching."

They stepped upon Sunside.

There beat down upon them such a storm of radiation, such cataracts of heat and light, that instinctively they bowed their heads as before a deluge. It took an effort of will to step forward through that tempest, but Halfrich made it. They walked, slowly and heavily, and at first they saw only the blackened rocks beneath their feet, and the little puddles and rivulets of molten lead, and their own massive armored feet plodding.

Then, as they went forward, they straightened against the impact. Through the face-plate of his armor, dimmed by the many-layered filters, Kellard saw the column of flame ahead. It was a hundred feet high now, and growing higher, and though there was no air-borne sound on this almost airless world, the sound of it came through the rocks and the soles of their feet, a throbbing and roaring that quivered through all their bodies.

They reached the tumbled rocks, and stopped. And now the fire-fountain was so lofty that they had to lean back their heads to look at its topmost crest. Some unthinkable diastole and systole of the fiery planet was at work, and this periodic geyser of flame was its result. The rocks shook and roared, and the fires raged higher, and Kellard thought again, what devil is in the blood of our race that drives us to places like this where we should not be?

"I told you," he said to Halfrich. "Just a blowhole, that's all."

"The blips on the record moved," said Halfrich. "There was more than this."

"Look around you!" cried Kellard desperately. "Do you see anything moving, anything that *could* move? You were wrong, Halfrich. Do you have to keep us here until we all die, because you can't admit you're wrong?"

Halfrich hesitated. "I wasn't wrong. You're still lying. But we'll go back to the ship and wait."

They turned their backs on the fire-fountain, and Kellard felt the sweat pouring on his forehead. It hadn't happened this time, and they couldn't wait forever; they would have to go away and—

Morgenson's voice chattered in their ears. "Blips showing, coming—" And then he suddenly yelled, "I see them! They—"

Halfrich swung around with ponderous swiftness. There was nothing between them and the fire-fountain, nothing around the spouting flames.

"Above you, coming down!" shouted Morgenson. "My God, what—?"

Kellard slowly raised his head. Because he knew what to look for, he saw them while Halfrich was still gazing around searching.

They came flashing down out of the sky. There were four of them this time—no, five. They were like five individual swirls of shining light, so bright that the sun-bleached heavens seemed to darken around them.

Halfrich said bewilderedly, "I don't see—"

Kellard pointed upward. "There."

"Those flakes of flame?"

"Not flakes of flame," said Kellard. "They are the children of the stars."

Halfrich went rigid, staring upward. And now Kellard knew that there was no more hope. No hope at all.

The five bright things had flashed down toward the great fire-fountain. They plunged into it, out of it, climbed swift as the eye could follow, racing up its mighty geyser, frolicking in it joyously. The fountain raved higher and the five sped up and whirled and danced upon its rising plume, and Kellard thought that they were laughing.

In and out of the leaping fires they plunged, and then one of them veered down toward the place where Halfrich and Kellard stood. There was something so humanly purposeful in its sudden movement that Halfrich stepped back.

"Stand still," said Kellard.

"But—" Halfrich protested.

"They won't hurt us," said Kellard, his voice flat and dull. "They're friendly, playful, curious. Stand still."

And now all five of the flashing flames were around them, darting, recoiling, then gliding forward again to touch their heat-armor with questing tendrils of living force, living light.

Halfrich spoke, trying to keep his voice steady but forming the words in a choked fashion.

"Something—in my mind—"

"They're telepathic, in a way you can't even imagine," said Kellard. "And they're curious. They're curious about us, what we are, how we think. They can merge minds with us, somehow." And he added, with a last cruel impulse of dying anger, "You wanted to know. Now know."

He had time to say nothing more before the impact hit him, just as it had that other time, the full stunning shock of unearthly minds interlocking with his own, searching out his thoughts and memories.

Curious, yes. Like children who have found strange, ungainly creatures and wish to know how they live. And as they entered his mind, Kellard's mind entered theirs, fused with them, and there was again the dizzying whirl of memories and feelings that were not his own, that his different, more brutishly physical nature could never apprehend more than dimly.

But that half-apprehension was staggering. He was no longer

Hugh Kellard, a man with flesh and bones who had been born on an air-drowned heavy planet named Earth.

He was one of the children of the stars.

His memory stretched far back, for his life was almost unlimited in time. For long and long beyond human comprehension he had lived with his companions the strange and beautiful life of their kind.

Born of the stars, of the unimaginable forces, pressures, temperatures, atomic conditions within the mighty suns. Born, as the end product of an evolutionary chain almost as old as the universe itself, a grouping of photons that grew toward consciousness, toward individuality and volition. Their bodies were force, rather than matter, their senses had nothing to do with sight or hearing, their movement was an effortless flash and glide as fast as the photons of light itself.

With the other kind of life in the universe, the heavy slow-moving things of matter that grew upon the comparatively cold, dark planets, they had had nothing to do at all. They were of the suns, not the planets, and those chill worlds of fixed, solid matter so repelled them that they would not even approach most of them.

Star-child, star-child, at home in the bursting splendors of the stellar fires, and able to move like light from star to star. And again Kellard felt the agony of that ecstasy that was his in this shared memory.

"We things of matter, we men, who thought that space and the stars would be ours—"

But how could the wide universe belong to solid, heavy, physical creatures who must painfully move in bubbles of air, who crawled between the petty planets encased in metal tombs, who could not even approach the glories of the great suns?

No, the ecstasy was one that men would never know except at secondhand through this brief contact! The glorious rush together of the star-children through the vast abysses, drinking up the energy of the radiation about them. The audacious and dangerous coasting along the shores of dark nebulae, racing the lumbering comets and leaving them behind, on until you felt through all your photons the beckoning warmth of the star you approached. Ignore the cinders called planets that creep around it, speed faster, faster, brothers, the way has been long but we are almost there! And now the radiation that was so weak in the outer darks is strong and lusty-roaring, and the great prominences reach out like arms to gather us in. The shock, the joy, of the first plunge once more into the star. Dive deep, brothers, deep through the outer fires into the throbbing solar furnaces where the atoms are hammered as in forges, changing, shifting their shapes, exploding into force.

Spin in the vortices of the great stellar tornadoes, fling off and fall headlong and then dive laughing in again. Search for the others of your kind; if there are none here there will be at the next star. Up again, out of the boiling fires, and then drift quiet, dreaming, in the pearly glow of the corona, endless afternoon of warmth and light and peace.

But on the sunward side of the tiny planet nearby, a plaything beckons. Fire and light fountain up from the solid rock. There at least we can go, for that place is washed by tides of solar life, not chilled and dead. Speed down toward it, as the fire, the life it spouts higher out of the repellently fixed and solid matter. Frolic in the fountain, through and around it as it rises higher. And what are the things that move on the rock near it, the things that look grotesquely as though matter had been endowed with life? Reach out with your thought-senses and try to apprehend them. Mind, life—in matter! Try to understand how matter thinks, how matter feels, plumb the grotesque memories of them, the vistas of crawling things at the bottom of whelming air-oceans, things of clay too frail to endure, yet things that in their brief living have come here. But the mind recoils from such memories, such a life.

Brothers, we go! First to refresh ourselves in the deepest streams of the star, and then away across the abysses to another star we know. There is nothing to hold us here—

And the oneness was gone from Kellard's mind, and he was

no child of light and stars; he was a man of clay, standing stupid and sick and shaking by the falling fires of the fountain.

He looked at Halfrich. But Halfrich stood, with his head bowed, and Kellard felt only pity.

He touched his arm. "We'll go back to the ship."

For a long moment, Halfrich did not respond. Then he turned and walked, plodding with head down, not looking up once at the flaring sky.

* * *

In the little ship, he sat later with Kellard. He had not spoken yet, and Morgenson and the others, bewildered and awed, had still not dared ask questions. Finally Halfrich looked at Kellard, pain still in his eyes.

"I was thinking," he said. "I was remembering my little boy, years ago. He had just learned to walk, and he started out the door, eager to explore the whole town. He stubbed his toe, and he sat down and cried.

"You tried to spare me this," said Halfrich after a little while. "Thanks for that, Kellard. It didn't work, but thanks anyway."

Kellard said, "Look, no one else knows. No one else is ever likely to know. The only place where the men of matter and the children of stars could meet is a place like Sunside, and how many such meetings would ever by chance happen? We don't have to tell everyone, to take the heart and eagerness out of them by letting them know they'll always be second-best in space."

Halfrich thought about that. And then he shook his head. "No. We've stubbed our toe. We've learned we're not and never will be the sole inheritors of the universe. All right, we'll accept the fact and go on. The planets will be ours, just the same. And someday—" He paused, then said, "—someday, maybe, the sons of the planets and the children of stars will take hands, know each other. No, Kellard. We'll tell them."

Now that *Dune* (Chilton, 1965) has won two awards for best novel of the year—a Nebula and a Hugo, the latter in a tie with Roger Zelazny's "And Call Me Conrad"—we can expect '67, at the least, to be a Frank Herbert year with enterprising publishers making sure that most of his early work reappears both in book form and paperback. But while such exploitation often tends to damage a writer's new-won prestige, in Herbert's case the effect should be just the opposite because his first stories—starting with "Operation Syndrome" (1954) and *The Dragon in the Sea* (Doubleday, 1956) —were remarkably good for a new writer breaking into a tough field. And so is "Try to Remember"—written a few years later—one of the few science-fiction stories to do something like justice to the theme of semantics, and the only one, as far as we know, which begins with a starship that looks like a giant paramecium!

TRY TO REMEMBER

Frank Herbert

Every mind on earth capable of understanding the problem was focused on the spaceship and the ultimatum delivered by its occupants. *Talk or Die!* blared the newspaper headlines.

The suicide rate was up and still climbing. Religious cults were having a field day. A book by a science-fiction author: "What the Deadly Inter-Galactic Spaceship Means to You!" had smashed all previous best-seller records. And this had been going on for a frantic seven months.

The ship had *flapped* out of a gun-metal sky over Oregon, its shape that of a hideously magnified paramecium with edges that rippled like a mythological flying carpet. Its five green-skinned, froglike occupants had delivered the ultimatum, one copy printed on velvety paper to each major government, each copy couched faultlessly in the appropriate native tongue:

"*You are requested to assemble your most gifted experts in human communication. We are about to submit a problem. We will open five identical rooms of our vessel to you. One of us will be available in each room.*

"*Your problem: To communicate with us.*

"*If you succeed, your rewards will be great.*

"*If you fail, that will result in destruction for all sentient life on your planet.*

"*We announce this threat with the deepest regret. You are urged to examine Eniwetok atoll for a small display of our power. Your artificial satellites have been removed from the skies.*

"*You must break away from this limited communication!*"

Eniwetok had been cleared off flat as a table at one thousand feet depth . . . with no trace of explosion! All Russian and United States artificial satellites had been combed from the skies.

All day long a damp wind poured up the Columbia Gorge from the ocean. It swept across the Eastern Oregon alkali flats with a false prediction of rain. Spiny desert scrub bent before the gusts, sheltering blur-footed coveys of quail and flop-eared jackrabbits. Heaps of tumbleweed tangled in the fence lines, and the air was filled with dry particles of grit that crept under everything and into everything and onto everything with the omnipresence of filterable virus.

On the flats south of the Hermiston Ordnance Depot the weird bulk of the spaceship caught pockets and eddies of sand. The thing looked like a monstrous oval of dun canvas draped across upright sticks. A cluster of quonsets and the Army's new desert prefabs dotted a rough half-circle around the north rim. They looked like dwarfed outbuildings for the most gigantic circus tent Earth had ever seen. Army Engineers said the ship was six thousand two hundred and eighteen feet long, one thousand and fifty-four feet wide.

Some five miles east of the site the dust storm hazed across the monotonous structures of the cantonment that housed some thirty thousand people from every major nation: Linguists, anthropologists, psychologists, doctors of every shape and description, watchers and watchers for the watchers, spies, espionage and counter-espionage agents.

For seven months the threat of Eniwetok, the threat of the unknown as well, had held them in check.

Toward evening of this day the wind slackened. The drifted sand began sifting off the ship and back into new shapes, trickling down for all the world like the figurative "sands of time" that here were most certainly running out.

Mrs. Francine Millar, clinical psychologist with the Indo-European Germanic-Root team, hurried across the bare patch of trampled sand outside the spaceship's entrance. She bent her head against what was left of the windstorm. Under her left arm she carried her briefcase tucked up like a football. Her other hand carried a rolled-up copy of that afternoon's *Oregon Journal*. The lead story said that Air Force jets had shot down a small private plane trying to sneak into the restricted area. Three unidentified men killed. The plane had been stolen.

Thoughts of a plane crash made her too aware of the circumstances in her own recent widowhood. Dr. Robert Millar had died in the crash of a trans-Atlantic passenger plane ten days before the arrival of the spaceship. She let the newspaper fall out of her hands. It fluttered away on the wind.

Francine turned her head away from a sudden biting of the sandblast wind. She was a wiry slim figure of about five feet six inches, still trim and athletic at forty-one. Her auburn hair, mussed by the wind, still carried the look of youth. Heavy lids shielded her blue eyes. The lids drooped slightly, giving her a perpetual sleepy look even when she was wide awake and alert—a circumstance she found helpful in her profession.

She came into the lee of the conference quonset, and straightened. A layer of sand covered the doorstep. She opened the door, stepped across the sand only to find more of it on the floor inside, grinding underfoot. It was on tables, on chairs, mounded in corners—on every surface.

Hikonojo Ohashi, Francine's opposite number with the Japanese-Korean and Sino-Tibetan team, already sat at his place on the other side of the table. The Japanese psychologist was grasping, pen fashion, a thin pointed brush, making notes in ideographic shorthand.

Francine closed the door.

Ohashi spoke without looking up: "We're early."

He was a trim, neat little man: flat features, smooth cheeks, an even curve of chin, remote dark eyes behind the inevitable thick lenses of the Oriental scholar.

Francine tossed her briefcase onto the table, and pulled out a chair opposite Ohashi. She wiped away the grit with a handkerchief before sitting down. The ever present dirt, the monotonous landscape, her own frustration—all combined to hold her on the edge of anger. She recognized the feeling and its source, stifled a wry smile.

"No, Hiko," she said. "I think we're late. It's later than we think."

"Much later when you put it that way," said Ohashi. His Princeton accent came out low, modulated like a musical instrument under the control of a master.

"Now we're going to be banal," she said. Immediately, she regretted the sharpness of her tone, forced a smile to her lips.

"They gave us no deadline," said Ohashi. "That is one thing anyway." He twirled his brush across an inkstone.

"Something's in the air," she said. "I can feel it."

"Very much sand in the air," he said.

"You know what I mean," she said.

"The wind has us all on edge," he said. "It feels like rain. A change in the weather." He made another note, put down the brush, and began setting out papers for the conference. All at once, his head came up. He smiled at Francine. The smile made him look immature, and she suddenly saw back through the years to a serious little boy named Hiko Ohashi.

"It's been seven months," she said. "It stands to reason that they're not going to wait forever."

"The usual gestation period is two months longer," he said.

She frowned, ignoring the quip. "But we're no closer today than we were at the beginning!"

Ohashi leaned forward. His eyes appeared to swell behind the thick lenses. "Do you often wonder at their insistence that *we* communicate with *them?* I mean, rather than the other way around?"

"Of course I do. So does everybody else."

He sat back. "What do you think of the Islamic team's approach?"

"You know what I think, Hiko. It's a waste of time to compare all the Galactics' speech sounds to passages from the Koran." She shrugged. "But for all we know actually they could be closer to a solution than anyone else in. . . ."

The door behind her banged open. Immediately, the room rumbled with the great basso voice of Theodore Zakheim, psychologist with the Ural-Altaic team.

"Hah-haaaaaaa!" he roared. "We're all here now!"

Light footsteps behind Zakheim told Francine that he was accompanied by Emile Goré of the Indo-European Latin-Root team.

Zakheim flopped onto a chair beside Francine. It creaked dangerously to his bulk.

Like a great uncouth bear! she thought.

"Do you always have to be so noisy?" she asked.

Goré slammed the door behind them.

"Naturally!" boomed Zakheim. "I am noisy! It's my nature, my little puchkin!"

Goré moved behind Francine, passing to the head of the table, but she kept her attention on Zakheim. He was a thick-bodied man, thick without fat, like the heaviness of a wrestler. His wide face and slanting pale blue eyes carried hints of Mongol ancestry. Rusty hair formed an uncombed brush atop his head.

Zakheim brought up his briefcase, flopped it onto the table, rested his hands on the dark leather. They were flat slab hands with thick fingers, pale wisps of hair growing down almost to the nails.

She tore her attention away from Zakheim's hands, looked down the table to where Goré sat. The Frenchman was a tall, gawk-necked man, entirely bald. Jet eyes behind steel-rimmed bifocals gave him a look of down-nose asperity like a comic bird. He wore one of his usual funereal black suits, every button secured. Knob wrists protruded from the sleeves. His long-fingered hands with their thick joints moved in constant restlessness.

"If I may differ with you, Zak," said Goré, "we are *not* all here. This is our same old group, and we were going to try to interest others in what we do here."

Ohashi spoke to Francine: "Have you had any luck inviting others to our conferences?"

"You can see that I'm alone," she said. "I chalked up five flat refusals today."

"Who?" asked Zakheim.

"The American Indian-Eskimo, the Hyperboreans, the Dravidians, the Malayo-Polynesians and the Caucasians."

"Hagglers!" barked Zakheim. "I, of course, can cover us with the Hamito-Semitic tongues, but. . . ." He shook his head.

Goré turned to Ohashi. "The others?"

Ohashi said: "I must report the polite indifference of the Munda and Mon-Kmer, the Sudanese-Guinean and the Bantu."

"Those are big holes in our information exchange," said Goré. "What are they discovering?"

"No more than we are!" snapped Zakheim. "Depend on it!"

"What of the languages not even represented among the teams here on the international site?" asked Francine. "I mean the Hottentot-Bushmen, the Ainu, the Basque and the Australian-Papuan?"

Zakheim covered her left hand with his right hand. "You always have me, my little dove."

"We're building another Tower of Babel!" she snapped. She jerked her hand away.

"Spurned again," mourned Zakheim.

Ohashi said: *"Go to, let us go down, and there confound their language, that they may not understand one another's speech."* He smiled. "Genesis eleven-seven."

Francine scowled. "And we're missing about twenty percent of Earth's twenty-eight hundred languages!"

"We have all the significant ones," said Zakheim.

"How do *you* know what's significant?" she demanded.

"Please!" Goré raised a hand. "We're here to exchange information, not to squabble!"

"I'm sorry," said Francine. "It's just that I feel so hopeless today."

"Well, what have we learned today?" asked Goré.

"Nothing new with us," said Zakheim.

Goré cleared his throat. "That goes double for me." He looked at Ohashi.

The Japanese shrugged. "We achieved no reaction from the Galactic, Kobai."

"Anthropomorphic nonsense," muttered Zakheim.

"You mean naming him Kobai?" asked Ohashi. "Not at all, Zak. That's the most frequent sound he makes, and the name helps with identification. We don't have to keep referring to him as 'The Galactic' or 'that creature in the spaceship.'"

Goré turned to Francine. "It was like talking to a green statue," she said.

"What of the lecture period?" asked Goré.

"Who knows?" she asked. "It stands there like a bowlegged professor in that black leotard. Those sounds spew out of it as though they'd never stop. It wriggles at us. It waves. It sways. Its face contorts, if you can call it a face. We recorded and filmed it all, naturally, but it sounded like the usual mish-mash!"

"There's something in the gestures," said Ohashi. "If we only had more competent pasimolgists."

"How many times have you seen the same total gesture repeated with the same sound?" demanded Zakheim.

"You've carefully studied our films," said Ohashi. "Not enough times to give us a solid base for comparison. But I do not despair—"

"It was a rhetorical question," said Zakheim.

"We really need more multilinguists," said Goré. "Now is when we most miss the loss of such great linguists as Mrs. Millar's husband."

Francine closed her eyes, took a short, painful breath. "Bob. . . ." She shook her head. *No. That's the past. He's gone. The tears are ended.*

"I had the pleasure of meeting him in Paris shortly before the . . . end," continued Goré. "He was lecturing on the development of the similar sound schemes in Italian and Japanese."

Francine nodded. She felt suddenly empty.

Ohashi leaned forward. "I imagine this is . . . rather painful for Dr. Millar," he said.

"I am *very* sorry," said Goré. "Forgive me."

"Someone was going to check and see if there are any electronic listening devices in this room," said Ohashi.

"My nephew is with our recording section," said Goré. "He assures me there are no hidden microphones here."

Zakheim's brows drew down into a heavy frown. He fumbled with the clasp of his briefcase. "This is very dangerous," he grunted.

"Oh, Zak, you always say that!" said Francine. "Let's quit playing footsy!"

"I do not enjoy the thought of treason charges," muttered Zakheim.

"We all know our bosses are looking for an advantage," she said. "I'm tired of these sparring matches where we each try to get something from the others without giving anything away!"

"If your Dr. Langsmith or General Speidel found out what

you were doing here, it would go hard for you, too," said Zakheim.

"I propose we take it from the beginning and re-examine everything," said Francine. "Openly this time."

"Why?" demanded Zakheim.

"Because I'm satisfied that the answer's right in front of us somewhere," she said.

"In the ultimatum, no doubt," said Goré. "What do you suppose is the *real* meaning of their statement that human languages are *'limited'* communication? Perhaps they are telepathic?"

"I don't think so," said Ohashi.

"That's pretty well ruled out," said Francine. "Our Rhine people say no ESP. No. I'm banking on something else: By the very fact that they posed this question, they have indicated that we *can* answer it with our present faculties."

"*If* they are being honest," said Zakheim.

"I have no recourse but to assume that they're honest," she said. "They're turning us into linguistic detectives for a good reason."

"A good reason for *them*," said Goré.

"Note the phraseology of their ultimatum," said Ohashi. "They *submit* a problem. They *open* their rooms to us. They are *available* to us. They *regret* their threat. Even their display of power—admittedly awe-inspiring—has the significant characteristic of non-violence. No explosion. They offer rewards for success, and this. . . ."

"Rewards!" snorted Zakheim. "We lead the hog to its slaughter with a promise of food!"

"I suggest that they give evidence of being non-violent," said Ohashi. "Either that, or they have cleverly arranged themselves to present the *face* of non-violence."

Francine turned, and looked out the hut's end window at the bulk of the spaceship. The low sun cast elongated shadows of the ship across the sand.

Zakheim, too, looked out the window. "Why did they choose

this place? If it had to be a desert, why not the Gobi? This is not even a good desert! This is a miserable desert!"

"Probably the easiest landing curve to a site near a large city," said Goré. "It is possible they chose a desert to avoid destroying arable land."

"Frogs!" snapped Zakheim. "I do not trust these frogs with their problem of communication!"

Francine turned back to the table, and took a pencil and scratch-pad from her briefcase. Briefly she sketched a rough outline of a Galactic, and wrote "frog?" beside it.

Ohashi said: "Are you drawing a picture of your Galactic?"

"We call it 'Uru' for the same reason you call yours 'Kobai,'" she said. "It makes the sound 'Uru' ad nauseum."

She stared at her own sketch thoughtfully, calling up the memory imagine of the Galactic as she did so. Squat, about five feet ten inches in height, with the short bowed legs of a swimmer. Rippling muscles sent corded lines under the black leotards. The arms were articulated like a human's, but they were more graceful in movement. The skin was pale green, the neck thick and short. The wide mouth was almost lipless, the nose a mere blunt horn. The eyes were large and spaced wide with nictating lids. No hair, but a high crowned ridge from the center of the forehead swept back across the head.

"I knew a Hawaiian distance swimmer once who looked much like these Galactics," said Ohashi. He wet his lips with his tongue. "You know, today we had a Buddhist monk from Java at our meeting with Kobai."

"I fail to see the association between a distance swimmer and a monk," said Goré.

"You told us you drew a blank today," said Zakheim.

"The monk tried no conversing," said Ohashi. "He refused because that would be a form of Earthly striving unthinkable for a Buddhist. He merely came and observed."

Francine leaned forward. "Yes?" She found an odd excitement in the way Ohashi was forcing himself to casualness.

"The monk's reaction was curious," said Ohashi. "He refused

to speak for several hours afterward. Then he said that these Galactics must be very holy people."

"Holy!" Zakheim's voice was edged with bitter irony.

"We are approaching this the wrong way," said Francine. She felt let down, spoke with a conscious effort. "Our access to these Galactics is limited by the space they've opened to us within their vessel."

"What is in the rest of the ship?" asked Zakheim.

"Rewards, perhaps," said Goré.

"Or weapons to demolish us!" snapped Zakheim.

"The pattern of the sessions is wrong, too," said Francine.

Ohashi nodded. "Twelve hours a day is not enough," he said. "We should have them under constant observation."

"I didn't mean that," said Francine. "They probably need rest just as we do. No. I meant the absolute control our team leaders—unimaginative men like Langsmith—have over the way we use our time in those rooms. For instance, what would happen if we tried to break down the force wall or whatever it is that keeps us from actually touching these creatures? What would happen if we brought in dogs to check how *animals* would react to them?" She reached in her briefcase, brought out a small flat recorder, and adjusted it for playback. "Listen to this."

There was a fluid burst of sound: "Pau'timónsh'uego' iklo-prépre 'sauta' urusa'a'a . . ." and a long pause followed by: "tu'kimóomo 'urulig 'lurulil 'oog 'shuquetoé . . ." pause "sum 'a 'suma 'a 'uru 't 'shóap!"

Francine stopped the playback.

"Did you record that today?" asked Ohashi.

"Yes. It was using that odd illustration board with the moving pictures—weird flowers and weirder animals."

"We've seen them," muttered Zakheim.

"And those chopping movements of its hands," said Francine. "The swaying body, the undulations, the facial contortions." She shook her head. "It's almost like a bizarre dance."

"What are you driving at?" asked Ohashi.

"I've been wondering what would happen if we had a leading choreographer compose a dance to those sounds, and if we put it on for. . . ."

"Faaa!" snorted Zakheim.

"All right," said Francine. "But we should be using some kind of random stimulation pattern on these Galactics. Why don't we bring in a nightclub singer? Or a circus barker? Or a magician? Or. . . ."

"We tried a full-blown schizoid," said Goré.

Zakheim grunted. "And you got exactly what such tactics deserve: your schizoid sat there and played with his fingers for an hour!"

"The idea of using artists from the entertainment world intrigues me," said Ohashi. "Some *No* dancers, perhaps." He nodded. "I'd never thought about it. But art is, after all, a form of communication."

"So is the croaking of a frog in a swamp," said Zakheim.

"Did you ever hear about the Paradox Frog?" asked Francine.

"Is this one of your strange jokes?" asked Zakheim.

"Of course not. The Paradox Frog is a very real creature. It lives on the island of Trinidad. It's a very small frog, but it has the opposable thumb on a five-fingered hand, and it. . . ."

"Just like our visitors," said Zakheim.

"Yes. And it uses its hand just like we do—to grasp things, to pick up food, to stuff its mouth, to. . . ."

"To make bombs?" asked Zakheim.

Francine shrugged, turned away. She felt hurt.

"My people believe these Galactics are putting on an elaborate sham," said Zakheim. "We think they are stalling while they secretly study us in preparation for invasion!"

Goré said: "So?" His narrow shoulders came up in a Gallic shrug that said as plainly as words: *Even if this is true, what is there for us to do?*

Francine turned to Ohashi. "What's the favorite theory current with your team?" Her voice sounded bitter, but she was unable to soften the tone.

"We are working on the assumption that this is a language of one-syllable root, as in Chinese," said Ohashi.

"But what of the vowel harmony?" protested Goré. "Surely that must mean the harmonious vowels are all in the same words."

Ohashi adjusted the set of his glasses. "Who knows?" he asked. "Certainly, the back vowels and front vowels come together many times, but. . . ." He shrugged, shook his head.

"What's happening with the group that's working on the historical analogy?" asked Goré. "You were going to find out, Ohashi."

"They are working on the assumption that all primitive sounds are consonants with non-fixed vowels . . . foot-stampers for dancing, you know. Their current guess is that the Galactics are missionaries, their language a religious language."

"What results?" asked Zakheim.

"None."

Zakheim nodded. "To be expected." He glanced at Francine. "I beg the forgiveness of the Mrs. Doctor Millar?"

She looked up, startled from a daydreaming speculation about the Galactic language and dancing. "Me? Good heavens, why?"

"I have been short-tempered today," said Zakheim. He glanced at his wristwatch. "I'm very sorry. I've been worried about another appointment."

He heaved his bulk out of the chair, took up his briefcase. "And it is time for me to be leaving. You forgive me?"

"Of course, Zak."

His wide face split into a grin. "Good!"

Goré got to his feet. "I will walk a little way with you, Zak."

Francine and Ohashi sat on for a moment after the others had gone.

"What good are we doing with these meetings?" she asked.

"Who knows how the important pieces of this puzzle will be fitted together?" asked Ohashi. "The point is: we are doing something different."

She sighed. "I guess so."

Ohashi took off his glasses, and it made him appear suddenly defenseless. "Did you know that Zak was recording our meeting?" he asked. He replaced the glasses.

Francine stared at him. "How do you know?"

Ohashi tapped his briefcase. "I have a device in here that reveals such things."

She swallowed a brief surge of anger. "Well, is it really important, Hiko?"

"Perhaps not." Ohashi took a deep, evenly controlled breath. "I did not tell you one other thing about the Buddhist monk."

"Oh, what did you omit?"

"He predicts that we will fail—that the human race will be destroyed. He is very old and very cynical for a monk. He thinks it is a good thing that all human striving must eventually come to an end."

Anger and a sudden resolve flamed in her. "I don't care! I don't care what anyone else thinks! I know that. . . ." She allowed her voice to trail off, put her hands to her eyes.

"You have been very distracted today," said Ohashi. "Did the talk about your late husband disturb you?"

"I know. I'm. . . ." She swallowed, whispered: "I had a dream about Bob last night. We were dancing, and he was trying to tell me something about this problem, only I couldn't hear him. Each time he started to speak the music got louder and drowned him out."

Silence fell over the room.

Presently, Ohashi said: "The unconscious mind takes strange ways sometimes to tell us the right answers. Perhaps we should investigate this idea of dancing."

"Oh, Hiko! Would you help me?"

"I should consider it an honor to help you," he said.

It was quiet in the semi-darkness of the projection room. Francine leaned her head against the back rest of her chair, looked across at the stand light where Ohashi had been working. He had gone for the films on Oriental ritual dances that had just arrived from Los Angeles by plane. His coat was still draped across the back of his chair, his pipe still smouldered in the ashtray on the worktable. All around their two chairs were stacked the residue of four days' almost continuous research: notebooks, film cans, boxes of photographs, reference books.

She thought about Hiko Ohashi: a strange man. He was fifty and didn't look a day over thirty. He had grown children. His wife had died of cholera eight years ago. Francine wondered what it would be like married to an Oriental, and she found herself thinking that he wasn't really Oriental with his Princeton education and Occidental ways. Then she realized that this attitude was a kind of white snobbery.

The door in the corner of the room opened softly. Ohashi came in, closed the door. "You awake?" he whispered.

She turned her head without lifting it from the chairback. "Yes."

"I'd hoped you might fall asleep for a bit," he said. "You looked so tired when I left."

Francine glanced at her wristwatch. "It's only three-thirty. What's the day like?"

"Hot and windy."

Ohashi busied himself inserting film into the projector at the rear of the room. Presently, he went to his chair, trailing the remote control cable for the projector.

"Ready?" he asked.

Francine reached for the low editing light beside her chair, and turned it on, focusing the narrow beam on a notebook in her lap. "Yes. Go ahead."

"I feel that we're making real progress," said Ohashi. "It's not clear yet, but the points of identity. . . ."

"They're exciting," she said. "Let's see what this one has to offer."

Ohashi punched the button on the cable. A heavily robed Arab girl appeared on the screen, slapping a tambourine. Her hair looked stiff, black and oily. A sooty line of kohl shaded each eye. Her brown dress swayed slightly as she tinkled the tambourine, then slapped it.

The cultured voice of the commentator came through the speaker beside the screen: "This is a young girl of Jebel Tobeyk. She is going to dance some very ancient steps that tell a story of battle. The camera is hidden in a truck, and she is unaware that this dance is being photographed."

A reed flute joined the tambourine, and a twanging stringed instrument came in behind it. The girl turned slowly on one foot, the other raised with knee bent.

Francine watched in rapt silence. The dancing girl made short staccato hops, the tambourine jerking in front of her.

"It is reminiscent of some of the material on the Norse sagas," said Ohashi. "Battle with swords. Note the thrust and parry."

She nodded. "Yes." The dance stamped onward, then: "Wait! Re-run that last section."

Ohashi obeyed.

It started with a symbolic trek on camel-back: swaying, undulating. The dancing girl expressed longing for her warrior. *How suggestive the motions of her hands along her hips,* thought Francine. With a feeling of abrupt shock, she recalled seeing almost the exact gesture from one of the films of the Galactics. "There's one!" she cried.

"The hands on the hips," said Ohashi. "I was just about to stop the reel." He shut off the film, searched through the notebooks around him until he found the correct reference.

"I think it was one of Zak's films," said Francine.

"Yes. Here it is." Ohashi brought up a reel, looked at the scene identifications. He placed the film can on a large stack behind him, re-started the film of Oriental dances.

Three hours and ten minutes later they put the film back in its can.

"How many new comparisons do you make it?" asked Ohashi.

"Five," she said. "That makes one hundred and six in all!" Francine leafed through her notes. "There was the motion of the hands on the hips. I call that one sensual pleasure."

Ohashi lighted a pipe, spoke through a cloud of smoke. "The others: How have you labeled them?"

"Well, I've just put a note on the motions of one of the Galactics and then the commentator's remarks from this dance film. Chopping motion of the hand ties to the end of Sobaya's first dream: 'Now, I *awaken!*' Undulation of the body ties in with swaying of date palms in the desert wind. Stamping of the foot goes with Torak dismounting from his steed. Lifting hands, palms up—that goes with Ali offering his soul to God in prayer before battle."

"Do you want to see this latest film from the ship?" asked Ohashi. He glanced at his wristwatch. "Or shall we get a bite to eat first?"

She waved a hand distractedly. "The film. I'm not hungry. The film." She looked up. "I keep feeling that there's something I should remember . . . something. . . ." She shook her head.

"Think about it a few minutes," said Ohashi. "I'm going to send out these other films to be cut and edited according to our selections. And I'll have some sandwiches sent in while I'm at it."

Francine rubbed at her forehead. "All right."

Ohashi gathered up a stack of film cans, left the room. He knocked out his pipe on a "No Smoking" sign beside the door as he left.

"Consonants," whispered Francine. "The ancient alphabets were almost exclusively made up of consonants. Vowels came later. They were the softeners, the swayers." She chewed at her lower lip. "Language constricts the *ways* you can think." She rubbed at her forehead. "Oh, if I only had Bob's ability with languages!"

She tapped her fingers on the chair arm. "It has something to do with our emphasis on *things* rather than on people and the things people do. Every Indo-European language is the same on that score. If only. . . ."

"Talking to yourself?" It was a masculine voice, startling her because she had not heard the door open.

Francine jerked upright, turned toward the door. Dr. Irving

Langsmith, chief of the American Division of the Germanic-Root team stood just inside, closing the door.

"Haven't seen you for a couple of days," he said. "We got your note that you were indisposed." He looked around the room, then at the clutter on the floor beside the chairs.

Francine blushed.

Dr. Langsmith crossed to the chair Ohashi had occupied, sat down. He was a grey-haired runt of a man with a heavily seamed face, small features—a gnome figure with hard eyes. He had the reputation of an organizer and politician with more drive than genius. He pulled a stubby pipe from his pocket, lighted it.

"I probably should have cleared this through channels," she said. "But I had visions of it getting bogged down in red tape, especially with Hiko . . . I mean with another team represented in this project."

"Quite all right," said Langsmith. "We knew what you were up to within a couple of hours. Now, we want to know what you've discovered. Dr. Ohashi looked pretty excited when he left here a bit ago."

Her eyes brightened. "I think we're onto something," she said. "We've compared the Galactics' movements to known symbolism from primitive dances."

Dr. Langsmith chuckled. "That's very interesting, my dear, but surely you. . . ."

"No, really!" she said. "We've found one hundred and six points of comparison, almost exact duplication of movements!"

"Dances? Are you trying to tell me that. . . ."

"I know it sounds strange," she said, "but we. . . ."

"Even if you *have* found exact points of comparison, that means nothing," said Langsmith. "These are *aliens* . . . from another world. You've no right to assume that their language development would follow the same pattern as ours has."

"But they're humanoid!" she said. "Don't you believe that language started as the unconscious shaping of the *speech* organs to imitate *bodily* gestures?"

"It's highly likely," said Langsmith.

"We can make quite a few pretty safe assumptions about them," she said. "For one thing, they apparently have a rather high standard of civilization to be able to construct—"

"Let's not labor the obvious," interrupted Langsmith, a little impatiently.

Francine studied the team chief a moment, said: "Did you ever hear how Marshal Foch planned his military campaigns?"

Langsmith puffed on his pipe, took it out of his mouth. "Uh . . . are you suggesting that a military. . . ."

"He wrote out the elements of his problem on a sheet of paper," said Francine. "At the top of the paper went the lowest common denominator. There, he wrote: 'Problem—To beat the Germans.' Quite simple. Quite obvious. But oddly enough *beating the enemy* has frequently been overlooked by commanders who got too involved in complicated maneuvers."

"Are you suggesting that the Galactics are enemies?"

She shook her head indignantly. "I am *not!* I'm suggesting that language is primarily an instinctive social reflex. The least common denominator of a social problem is a human being. One single human being. And here we are all involved with getting this thing into mathematical equations and neat word frequency primarily oral!"

"But you've been researching a visual. . . ."

"Yes! But only as it modifies the sounds." She leaned toward Langsmith. "Dr. Langsmith, I believe that this language is a *flexional* language with the flexional endings and root changes contained entirely in the bodily movements!"

"Hmmmmmmmm." Langsmith studied the smoke spiraling ceilingward from his pipe. "Fascinating idea!"

"We can assume that this is a highly standardized language," said Francine. "Basing the assumption on their high standard of civilization. The two usually go hand in hand."

Langsmith nodded.

"Then the gestures, the sounds would tend to be ritual," she said.

"Mmmmm-hmmmm."

"Then . . . may we have the help to go into this idea the way it deserves?" she asked.

"I'll take it up at the next top staff meeting," said Langsmith. He got to his feet. "Don't get your hopes up. This'll have to be submitted to the electronic computers. It probably has been cross-checked and rejected in some other problem."

She looked up at him, dismayed. "But . . . Dr. Langsmith . . . a computer's no better than what's put into it. I'm certain that we're stepping out into a region here where we'll have to build up a whole new approach to language."

"Now, don't you worry," said Langsmith. He frowned. "No . . . don't worry about *this*."

"Shall we go ahead with what we're doing then?" she asked. "I mean—do we have permission to?"

"Yes, yes . . . of course." Langsmith wiped his mouth with the back of his hand. "General Speidel has called a special meeting tomorrow morning. I'd like to have you attend. I'll send somebody to pick you up." He waved a hand at the litter around Francine. "Carry on, now." There was a pathetic emptiness to the way he put his pipe in his mouth and left the room. Francine stared at the closed door.

She felt herself trembling, and recognized that she was deathly afraid. *Why?* she asked herself. *What have I sensed to make me afraid?*

Presently, Ohashi came in carrying a paper bag.

"Saw Langsmith going out," he said. "What did he want?"

"He wanted to know what we're doing."

Ohashi paused beside his chair. "Did you tell him?"

"Yes. I asked for help." She shook her head. "He wouldn't commit himself."

"I brought ham sandwiches," said Ohashi.

Francine's chin lifted abruptly. "Defeated!" she said. "That's it! He acted completely defeated!"

"What?"

"I've been trying to puzzle through the strange way Langsmith was acting. He just radiated defeat."

Ohashi handed her a sandwich. "Better brace yourself for a shock," he said. "I ran into Tsu Ong, liaison officer for our delegation . . . in the cafeteria." The Japanese raised the sandwich sack over his chair, dropped it into the seat with a curious air of preciseness. "The Russians are pressing for a combined attack on the Galactic ship to wrest their secret from them by force."

Francine buried her face in her hands. "The fools!" she whispered. "Oh, the fools!" Abruptly, sobs shook her. She found herself crying with the same uncontrollable wracking that had possessed her when she'd learned of her husband's death.

Ohashi waited silently.

The tears subsided. Control returned. She swallowed, said: "I'm sorry."

"Do not be sorry." He put a hand on her shoulder. "Shall we knock off for the night?"

She put her hand over his, shook her head. "No. Let's look at the latest films from the ship."

"As you wish." Ohashi pulled away, threaded a new film into the projector.

Presently, the screen came alive to a blue-grey alcove filled with pale light: one of the "class" rooms in the spaceship. A squat, green-skinned figure stood in the center of the room. Beside the Galactic was the pedestal-footed projection board that all five used to illustrate their "lectures." The board displayed a scene of a wide blue lake, reeds along the shore stirring to a breeze.

The Galactic swayed. His face moved like a ripple of water. He said: "Ahon'atu'uklah'shoginai' eástruru." The green arms moved up and down, undulating. The webbed hands came out, palms facing and almost touching, began chopping from the wrists: up, down, up, down, up, down. . . .

On the projection board the scene switched to an under-water view: myriad swimming shapes coming closer, closer—large-eyed fish creatures with long ridged tails.

"Five will get you ten," said Ohashi. "Those are the young of this Galactic race. Notice the ridge."

"Tadpoles," said Francine.

The swimming shapes darted through orange shadows and into a space of cold green—then up to splash on the surface, and again down into the cool green. It was a choreographic swinging, lifting, dipping, swaying—lovely in its synchronized symmetry.

"Chiruru'uklia'a'agudav'iaá," said the Galactic. His body undulated like the movements of the swimming creatures. The green hands touched his thighs, slipped upward until elbows were level with shoulders.

"The maiden in the Oriental dance," said Francine.

Now, the hands came out, palms up, in a gesture curiously suggestive of giving. The Galactic said: "Pluainumiuri!" in a single burst of sound that fell on their ears like an explosion.

"It's like a distorted version of the ritual dances we've been watching," said Ohashi.

"I've a hunch," said Francine. "Feminine intuition. The repeated vowels: they could be an adverbial emphasis, like our word *very*. Where it says '*a-a-a*' note the more intense gestures."

She followed another passage, nodding her head to the gestures. "Hiko, could this be a constructed language? Artificial?"

"The thought has occurred to me," said Ohashi.

Abruptly, the projector light dimmed, the action slowed. All lights went out. They heard a dull, booming roar in the distance, a staccato rattling of shots. Feet pounded along the corridor outside the room.

Francine sat in stunned silence.

Ohashi said: "Stay here, please. I will have a look around to see what. . . ."

The door banged open and a flashlight beam stabbed into the room, momentarily blinding them.

"Everything all right in here?" boomed a masculine voice.

They made out a white MP helmet visible behind the light.

"Yes," said Ohashi. "What is happening?"

"Somebody blew up a tower to the main transmission line

from McNary Dam. Then there was an attempt to breach our security blockade on the south. Everything will be back to normal shortly." The light turned away.

"Who?" asked Francine.

"Some crazy civilians," said the MP. "We'll have the emergency power on in a minute. Just stay in this room until we give the all clear." He left, closing the door.

They heard a rattle of machine gun fire. Another explosion shook the building. Voices shouted.

"We are witnessing the end of a world," said Ohashi.

"Our world ended when that spaceship set down here," she said.

Abruptly, the lights came on: glowing dimly, then brighter. The projector resumed its whirring. Ohashi turned it off.

Somebody walked down the corridor outside, rapped on the door, said: "All clear." The footsteps receded down the hall, and they heard another rapping, a fainter "All clear."

"Civilians," she said. "What do you suppose they wanted so desperately to do a thing like that?"

"They are a symptom of the general sickness," said Ohashi. "One way to remove a threat is to destroy it—even if you destroy yourself in the process. These civilians are only a minor symptom."

"The Russians are the big symptom then," she said.

"Every major government is a *big* symptom right now," he said.

"I . . . I think I'll get back to my room," she said. "Let's take up again tomorrow morning. Eight o'clock all right?"

"Quite agreeable," said Ohashi. "If there is a tomorrow."

"Don't *you* get that way, too," she said, and she took a quavering breath. "I refuse to give up."

Ohashi bowed. He was suddenly very Oriental. "There is a primitive saying of the Ainu," he said: *"The world ends every night . . . and begins anew every morning."*

It was a room dug far underground beneath the Ordnance Depot, originally for storage of atomics. The walls were lead.

It was an oblong space: about thirty by fifteen feet, with a very low ceiling. Two trestle tables had been butted end-to-end in the center of the room to form a single long surface. A series of green-shaded lights suspended above this table gave the scene an odd resemblance to a gambling room. The effect was heightened by the set look to the shoulders of the men sitting in spring bottom chairs around the table. There were a scattering of uniforms: Air Force, Army, Marines; plus hard-faced civilians in expensive suits.

Dr. Langsmith occupied a space at the middle of one of the table's sides and directly across from the room's only door. His gnome features were locked in a frown of concentration. He puffed rhythmically at the stubby pipe like a witchman creating an oracle smoke.

A civilian across the table from Langsmith addressed a two-star general seated beside the team chief: "General Speidel, I still think this is too delicate a spot to risk a woman."

Speidel grunted. He was a thin man with a high, narrow face: an aristocratic face that radiated granite convictions and stubborn pride. There was an air about him of spring steel under tension and vibrating to a chord that dominated the room.

"Our choice is limited," said Langsmith. "Very few of our personnel have consistently taken wheeled carts into the ship *and* consistently taken a position close to that force barrier or whatever it is."

Speidel glanced at his wristwatch. "What's keeping them?"

"She may already have gone to breakfast," said Langsmith.

"Be better if we got her in here hungry and jumpy," said the civilian.

"Are you sure you can handle her, Smitty?" asked Speidel.

Langsmith took his pipe from his mouth, peered into the stem as though the answer were to be found there. "We've got her pretty well analyzed," he said. "She's a recent widow, you know. Bound to still have a rather active death-wish structure."

There was a buzzing of whispered conversation from a group of officers at one end of the table. Speidel tapped his fingers on the arm of his chair.

Presently, the door opened. Francine entered. A hand reached in from outside, closed the door behind her.

"Ah, there you are, Dr. Millar," said Langsmith. He got to his feet. There was a scuffling sound around the table as the others arose. Langsmith pointed to an empty chair diagonally across from him. "Sit down, please."

Francine advanced into the light. She felt intimidated, knew she showed it, and the realization filled her with a feeling of bitterness tinged with angry resentment. The ride down the elevator from the surface had been an experience she never wanted to repeat. It had seemed many times longer than it actually was—like a descent into Dante's Inferno.

She nodded to Langsmith, glanced covertly at the others, took the indicated chair. It was a relief to get the weight off her trembling knees, and she momentarily relaxed, only to tense up again as the others resumed their seats. She put her hands on the table, immediately withdrew them to hold them clasped tightly in her lap.

"Why was I brought here like a prisoner?" she demanded.

Langsmith appeared honestly startled. "But I told you last night that I'd send somebody for you."

Speidel chuckled easily. "Some of our Security boys are a little grim-faced," he said. "I hope they didn't frighten you."

She took a deep breath, began to relax. "Is this about the request I made last night?" she asked. "I mean for help in this new line of research?"

"In a way," said Langsmith. "But first I'd like to have you answer a question for me." He pursed his lips. "Uh . . . I've never asked one of my people for just a wild guess before, but I'm going to break that rule with you. What's your guess as to why these Galactics are here?"

"Guess?"

"Logical assumption, then," he said.

She looked down at her hands. "We've all speculated, of course. They might be scientists investigating us for reasons of their own."

"Damnation!" barked the civilian beside her. Then: "Sorry, ma'm. But that's the pap we keep using to pacify the public."

"And we aren't keeping them very well pacified," said Langsmith. "That group that stormed us last night called themselves the *Sons of Truth!* They had thermite bombs, and were going to attack the spaceship."

"How foolish," she whispered. "How pitiful."

"Go on with your guessing, Dr. Millar," said Speidel.

She glanced at the general, again looked at her hands. "There's the military's idea—that they want Earth for a strategic base in some kind of space war."

"It could be," said Speidel.

"They could be looking for more living space for their own kind," she said.

"In which case, what happens to the native population?" asked Langsmith.

"They would either be exterminated or enslaved, I'm afraid. But the Galactics could be commercial traders of some sort, interested in our art forms, our animals for their zoos, our archeology, our spices, our. . . ." She broke off, shrugged. "How do we know what they may be doing on the side . . . secretly?"

"Exactly!" said Speidel. He glanced sidelong at Langsmith. "She talks pretty level-headed, Smitty."

"But I don't believe any of these things," she said.

"What is it you believe?" asked Speidel.

"I believe they're just what they represent themselves to be—representatives of a powerful Galactic culture that is immeasurably superior to our own."

"Powerful, all right!" It was a Marine officer at the far end of the table. "The way they cleaned off Eniwetok and swept our satellites out of the skies!"

"Do you think there's a possibility they could be concealing their true motives?" asked Langsmith.

"A possibility, certainly."

"Have you ever watched a confidence man in action?" asked Langsmith.

"I don't believe so. But you're not seriously suggesting that these. . . ." She shook her head. "Impossible."

"The *mark* seldom gets wise until it's too late," said Langsmith.

She looked puzzled. "Mark?"

"The fellow the confidence men choose for a victim." Langsmith re-lighted his pipe, extinguished the match by shaking it. "Dr. Millar, we have a very painful disclosure to make to you."

She straightened, feeling a sudden icy chill in her veins at the stillness in the room.

"Your husband's death was not an accident," said Langsmith.

She gasped, and turned deathly pale.

"In the six months before this spaceship landed, there were some twenty-eight mysterious deaths," said Langsmith. "More than that, really, because innocent bystanders died, too. These accidents had a curious similarity: In each instance there was a fatality of a foremost expert in the field of language, cryptoanalysis, semantics. . . ."

"The people who might have solved this problem died before the problem was even presented," said Speidel. "Don't you think that's a curious coincidence?"

She was unable to speak.

"In one instance there was a survivor," said Langsmith. "A British jet transport crashed off Ceylon, killing Dr. Ramphit U. The lone survivor, the co-pilot, said a brilliant beam of light came from the sky overhead and sliced off the port wing. Then it cut the cabin in half!"

Francine put a hand to her throat. Langsmith's cautious hand movements suddenly fascinated her.

"Twenty-eight air crashes?" she whispered.

"No. Two were auto crashes." Langsmith puffed a cloud of smoke before his face.

Her throat felt sore. She swallowed, said: "But how can you be sure of that?"

"It's circumstantial evidence, yes," said Speidel. He spoke with thin-lipped precision. "But there's more. For the past four

months all astronomical activity of our nation has been focused
on the near heavens, including the moon. Our attention was
drawn to evidence of activity near the moon crater Theophilus.
We have been able to make out the landing rockets of more
than five hundred space craft!"

"What do you think of that?" asked Langsmith. He nodded
behind his smoke screen.

She could only stare at him; her lips ashen.

"These *frogs* have massed an invasion fleet on the moon!"
snapped Speidel. "It's obvious!"

They're lying to me! she thought. *Why this elaborate pre-
tense?* She shook her head, and something her husband had
once said leapt unbidden into her mind: "*Language clutches at
us with unseen fingers. It conditions us to the way others are
thinking. Through language, we impose upon each other our
ways of looking at things.*"

Speidel leaned forward. "We have more than a hundred
atomic warheads aimed at that moon-base! One of those warheads will do the job if it gets through!" He hammered a fist on
the table. "But first we have to capture this ship here!"

Why are they telling me all this? she asked herself. She drew
in a ragged breath, said: "Are you sure you're right?"

"Of course we're sure!" Speidel leaned back, lowered his
voice. "Why else would they insist we learn their language? The
first thing a conqueror does is impose his language on his new
slaves!"

"No . . . no, wait," she said. "That only applies to recent history. You're getting language mixed up with patriotism because of our own imperial history. Bob always said that such
misconceptions are a serious hindrance to sound historical schol-
arship."

"We know what we're talking about, Dr. Millar," said Speidel.

"You're suspicious of language because our imperialism went
hand in hand with our language," she said.

Speidel looked at Langsmith. "You talk to her."

"If there actually were communication in the sounds these

Galactics make, you know we'd have found it by now," said Langsmith. "You know it!"

She spoke in sudden anger: "I don't know it! In fact, I feel that we're on the verge of solving their language with this new approach we've been working on."

"Oh, come now!" said Speidel. "Do you mean that after our finest cryptographers have worked over this thing for seven months, you disagree with them entirely?"

"No, no, let her say her piece," said Langsmith.

"We've tapped a new source of information in attacking this problem," she said. "Primitive dances."

"Dances?" Speidel looked shocked.

"Yes. I think the Galactics' gestures may be their adjectives and adverbs—the full emotional content of their language."

"Emotion!" snapped Speidel. "Emotion isn't language!"

She repressed a surge of anger, said: "We're dealing with something completely outside our previous experience. We have to discard old ideas. We know that the habits of a native tongue set up a person's speaking responses. In fact, you can define language as the system of habits you reveal when you speak."

Speidel tapped his fingers on the table, stared at the door behind Francine.

She ignored his nervous distraction, said: "The Galactics use almost the full range of implosive and glottal stops with a wide selection of vowel sounds: fricatives, plosives, voiced and unvoiced. And we note an apparent lack of the usual interfering habits you find in normal speech."

"This isn't normal speech!" blurted Speidel. "Those are nonsense sounds!" He shook his head. "Emotions!"

"All right," she said. "Emotions! We're pretty certain that language begins with emotions—pure emotional actions. The baby pushes away the plate of unwanted food."

"You're wasting our time!" barked Speidel.

"I didn't ask to come down here," she said.

"Please." Langsmith put a hand on Speidel's arm. "Let Dr. Millar have her say."

"Emotion," muttered Speidel.

"Every spoken language of Earth has migrated away from emotion," said Francine.

"Can you write an emotion on paper?" demanded Speidel.

"That does it," she said. "That really tears it! You're blind! You say language has to be written down. That's part of the magic! Your mind is tied in little knots by academic tradition! Language, General, is primarily oral! People like you, though, want to make it into ritual noise!"

"I didn't come down here for an egg-head argument!" snapped Speidel.

"Let me handle this, please," said Langsmith. He made a mollifying gesture toward Francine. "Please continue."

She took a deep breath. "I'm sorry I snapped," she said. She smiled. "I think we let emotion get the best of us."

Speidel frowned.

"I was talking about language moving away from emotion," she said. "Take Japanese, for example. Instead of saying, 'Thank you' they say, 'Katajikenai'—'I am insulted.' Or they say, 'Kino doku' which means 'This poisonous feeling!'" She held up her hands. "This is ritual exclusion of showing emotion. Our Indo-European languages—especially Anglo-Saxon tongues—are moving the same way. We seem to think that emotion isn't quite nice, that. . . ."

"It tells you nothing!" barked Speidel.

She forced down the anger that threatened to overwhelm her. "If you can read the emotional signs," she said, "they reveal if a speaker is telling the truth. That's all, General. They just tell you if you're getting at the truth. Any good psychologist knows this, General. Freud said it: 'If you try to conceal your feelings, every pore oozes betrayal.' You seem to think that the opposite is true."

"Emotions! Dancing!" Speidel pushed his chair back. "Smitty, I've had as much of this as I can take."

"Just a minute," said Langsmith. "Now, Dr. Millar, I wanted you to have your say because we've already considered these points. Long ago. You're interested in the gestures. You say this is a dance of emotions. Other experts say with equal emphasis that these gestures are ritual combat! Freud, indeed! They ooze betrayal. This chopping gesture they make with the right hand"—he chopped the air in illustration—"is identical to the karate or judo chop for breaking the human neck!"

Francine shook her head, put a hand to her throat. She was momentarily overcome by a feeling of uncertainty.

Langsmith said: "That outward thrust they make with one hand: that's the motion of a sword being shoved into an opponent! They ooze betrayal all right!"

She looked from Langsmith to Speidel, back to Langsmith. A man to her right cleared his throat.

Langsmith said: "I've just given you two examples. We have hundreds more. Every analysis we've made has come up with the same answer: treachery! The pattern's as old as time: offer a reward; pretend friendship; get the innocent lamb's attention on your empty hand while you poise the ax in your other hand!"

Could I be wrong? she wondered. *Have we been duped by these Galactics?* Her lips trembled. She fought to control them, whispered: "Why are you telling me these things?"

"Aren't you at all interested in revenge against the creatures who murdered your husband?" asked Speidel.

"I don't know that they murdered him!" She blinked back tears. "You're trying to confuse me!" And a favorite saying of her husband's came into her mind: *"A conference is a group of people making a difficult job out of what one person could do easily."* The room suddenly seemed too close and oppressive.

"Why have I been dragged into this conference?" she demanded. "Why?"

"We were hoping you'd assist us in capturing that spaceship," said Langsmith.

"Me? Assist you in. . . ."

"Someone has to get a bomb past the force screens at the door —the ones that keep sand and dirt out of the ship. We've got to have a bomb inside."

"But why me?"

"They're used to seeing you wheel in the master recorder on that cart," said Langsmith. "We thought of putting a bomb in. . . ."

"No!"

"This has gone far enough," said Speidel. He took a deep breath, started to rise.

"Wait," said Langsmith.

"She obviously has no feelings of patriotic responsibility," said Speidel. "We're wasting our time."

Langsmith said: "The Galactics are used to seeing her with that cart. If we change now, they're liable to become suspicious."

"We'll set up some other plan, then," said Speidel. "As far as I'm concerned, we can write off any possibility of further cooperation from her."

"You're little boys playing a game," said Francine. "This isn't an exclusive American problem. This is a human problem that involves every nation on Earth."

"That ship is on United States soil," said Speidel.

"Which happens to be on the only planet controlled by the human species," she said. "We ought to be sharing everything with the other teams, pooling information and ideas to get at every scrap of knowledge."

"We'd all like to be idealists," said Speidel. "But there's no room for idealism where our survival is concerned. These *frogs* have full space travel, apparently between the stars—not just satellites and moon rockets. If we get their ship we can enforce peace on our own terms."

"National survival," she said. "But it's our survival as a species that's at stake!"

Speidel turned to Langsmith. "This is one of your more spectacular failures, Smitty. We'll have to put her under close surveillance."

Langsmith puffed furiously on his pipe. A cloud of pale blue smoke screened his head. "I'm ashamed of you, Dr. Millar," he said.

She jumped to her feet, allowing her anger full scope at last.

"You must think I'm a rotten psychologist!" she snapped. "You've been lying to me since I set foot in here!" She shot a bitter glance at Speidel. "Your gestures gave you away! The non-communicative emotional gestures, General!"

"What's she talking about?" demanded Speidel.

"You said different things with your mouths than you said with your bodies," she explained. "That means you were lying to me—concealing something vital you didn't want me to know about."

"She's insane!" barked Speidel.

"There wasn't any survivor of a plane crash in Ceylon," she said. "There probably wasn't even the plane crash you described."

Speidel froze to sudden stillness, spoke through thin lips: "Has there been a security leak? Good Lord!"

"Look at Dr. Langsmith there!" she said. "Hiding behind that pipe! And you, General: moving your mouth no more than absolutely necessary to speak—trying to hide your real feelings! Oozing betrayal!"

"Get her out of here!" barked Speidel.

"You're all logic and no intuition!" she shouted. "No understanding of feeling and art! Well, General: go back to your computers, but remember this—You can't build a machine that thinks like a man! You can't feed emotion into an electronic computer and get back anything except numbers! Logic, to you, General!"

"I said get her out of here!" shouted Speidel. He rose half out of his chair, turned to Langsmith who sat in pale silence. "And I want a thorough investigation! I want to know where the security leak was that put her wise to our plans."

"Watch yourself!" snapped Langsmith.

Speidel took two deep breaths, sank back.

They're insane, thought Francine. *Insane and pushed into a corner. With that kind of fragmentation they could slip into catatonia or violence.* She felt weak and afraid.

Others around the table had arisen. Two civilians moved up beside Francine. "Shall we lock her up, General?" asked one.

Speidel hesitated.

Langsmith spoke first: "No. Just keep her under very close surveillance. If we locked her up, it would arouse questions that we don't want to answer."

Speidel glowered at Francine. "If you give us away, I'll have you shot!" He motioned to have her taken out of the room.

When she emerged from the headquarters building, Francine's mind still whirled. *Lies!* she thought. *All lies!*

She felt the omnipresent sand grate under her feet. Dust hazed the concourse between her position on the steps and the spaceship a hundred yards away. The morning sun already had burned off the night chill of the desert. Heat devils danced over the dun surface of the ship.

Francine ignored the security agent loitering a few steps behind her, glanced at her wristwatch: nine-twenty. *Hiko will be wondering what's happened to me,* she thought. *We were supposed to get started by eight.* Hopelessness gripped her mind. The spaceship looming over the end of the concourse appeared like a malignant growth—an evil thing crouched ready to envelop and smother her.

Could that fool general be right? The thought came to her mind unbidden. She shook her head. *No! He was lying! But why did he want me to. . . .* Delayed realization broke off the thought. *They wanted me to take a small bomb inside the ship, but there was no mention of my escaping! I'd have had to stay with the cart and the bomb to allay suspicions. My God! Those beasts expected me to commit suicide for them! They wanted me to blame the Galactics for Bob's death! They tried to build a lie in my mind until I'd fall in with their plan. It's hard enough to die for an ideal, but to give up your life for a lie. . . .*

Anger coursed through her. She stopped on the steps, stood there shivering. A new feeling of futility replaced the anger. Tears blurred her vision. *What can one lone woman do against such ruthless schemers?*

Through her tears, she saw movement on the concourse: a man in civilian clothes crossing from right to left. Her mind registered the movement with only partial awareness: *man stops, points.* She was suddenly alert, tears gone, following the direction of the civilian's extended right arm, hearing his voice shout:

"Hey! Look at that!"

A thin needle of an aircraft stitched a hurtling line across the watery desert sky. It banked, arrowed toward the spaceship. Behind it roared an airforce jet—delta wings vibrating, sun flashing off polished metal. Tracers laced out toward the airship.

Someone's attacking the spaceship! she thought. *It's a Russian ICBM!*

But the needle braked abruptly, impossibly, over the spaceship. Behind it, the airforce jet's engine died, and there was only the eerie whistling of air burning across its wings.

Gently, the needle lowered itself into a fold of the spaceship.

It's one of theirs—the Galactics' she realized. *Why is it coming here now? Do they suspect attack? Is that some kind of reinforcement?*

Deprived of its power, the jet staggered, skimmed out to a dust-geyser, belly-landing in the alkali flats. Sirens screamed as emergency vehicles raced toward it.

The confused sounds gave Francine a sudden feeling of nausea. She took a deep breath, and stepped down to the concourse, moving without conscious determination, her thoughts in a turmoil. The grating sand beneath her feet was like an emery surface rubbing her nerves. She was acutely conscious of an acrid, burning odor, and she realized with a sudden stab of alarm that her security guard still waited behind her on the steps of the administration building.

Vaguely, she heard voices babbling in the building doorways on both sides of the concourse—people coming out to stare at the spaceship and off across the flats where red trucks clustered around the jet.

A pebble had worked its way into her right shoe. Her mind registered it, rejected an urge to stop and remove the irritant. An idea was trying to surface in her mind. Momentarily, she was distracted by a bee humming across her path. Quite inanely her mind dwelt on the thought that the insect was too commonplace for this moment. A mental drunkenness made her giddy. She felt both elated and terrified. *Danger! Yes: terrible danger,* she thought. *Obliteration for the entire human race. But something had to be done. She started to run. . . .*

An explosion rocked the concourse, threw her stumbling to her hands and knees. Sand burned against her palms. Dumb instinct brought her back to her feet. Another explosion—farther away to the right, behind the buildings. Bitter smoke swept across the concourse. Abruptly, men lurched from behind the buildings on the right, slogging through the sand toward the spaceship.

Civilians! Possibly—and yet they moved with the purposeful unity of soldiers.

It was like a dream scene to Francine. The men carried weapons. She stopped, saw the gleam of sunlight on metal, heard the peculiar crunch-crunch of men running in sand. Through a dreamy haze she recognized one of the runners: Zakheim. He carried a large black box on his shoulders. His red hair flamed out in the group like a target.

The Russians! she thought. *They've started their attack! If our people join them now, it's the end!*

A machine gun stuttered somewhere to her right. Dust puffs walked across the concourse, swept into the running figures. Men collapsed, but others still slogged toward the spaceship. An explosion lifted the leaders, sent them sprawling. Again, the machine gun chattered. Dark figures lay on the sand like thrown dominoes. But still a few continued their mad charge.

MP's in American uniforms ran out from between the buildings on the right. The leaders carried submachine guns.

We're stopping the attack, thought Francine. But she knew the change of tactics did not mean a rejection of violence by Speidel and the others. It was only a move to keep the Russians from taking the lead. She clenched her fists, ignored the fact that she stood exposed—a lone figure in the middle of the concourse. Her senses registered an eerie feeling of unreality.

Machine guns renewed their chatter and then—abrupt silence.

But now the last of the Russians had fallen. Pursuing MP's staggered. Several stopped, wrenched at their guns.

Francine's shock gave way to cold rage. She moved forward, slowly at first and then striding. Off to the left someone shouted: "Hey! Lady! Get down!" She ignored the voice.

There on the sand ahead was Zakheim's pitiful crumpled figure. A gritty redness spread around his chest.

Someone ran from between the buildings on her left, waved at her to go back. *Hiko!* But she continued her purposeful stride, compelled beyond any conscious willing to stop. She saw the red-headed figure on the sand as though she peered down a tunnel.

Part of her mind registered the fact that Hiko stumbled, slowing his running charge to intercept her. He looked like a man clawing his way through water.

Dear Hiko, she thought. *I have to get to Zak. Poor foolish Zak. That's what was wrong with him the other day at the conference. He knew about this attack and was afraid.*

Something congealed around her feet, spread upward over her ankles, quickly surged over her knees. She could see nothing unusual, but it was as though she had plowed into a pool of molasses. Every step took terrible effort. The molasses pool moved above her hips, her waist.

So that's why Hiko and the MP's are moving so slowly, she thought. *It's a defensive weapon from the ship. Must be.*

Zakheim's sprawled figure was only three steps away from her now. She wrenched her way through the congealed air, panting with the exertion. Her muscles ached from the effort. She knelt beside Zakheim. Ignoring the blood that stained her skirt she took up one of his outstretched hands, felt for a pulse. Nothing. Now, she recognized the marks on his jacket. They were bullet holes. A machine gun burst had caught him across the chest. He was dead. She thought of the big garrulous red-head, so full of blooming life only minutes before. *Poor foolish Zak.* She put his hand down gently, shook the tears from her eyes. A terrible rage swelled in her.

She sensed Ohashi nearby, struggling toward her, heard him gasp: "Is Zak dead?"

Tears dripped unheeded from her eyes. She nodded. "Yes, he is." And she thought: *I'm not crying for Zak. I'm crying for myself . . . for all of us . . . so foolish, so determined, so blind. . . .*

"EARTH PEOPLE!" The voice roared from the spaceship, cutting across all thought, stilling all emotion into a waiting fear. "WE HAD HOPED YOU COULD LEARN TO COMMUNICATE!" roared the voice. "YOU HAVE FAILED!"

Vibrant silence.

Thoughts that had been struggling for recognition began surging to the surface of Francine's mind. She felt herself caught in the throes of a mental earthquake, her soul brought to a crisis as sharp as that of giving birth. The crashing words had broken through a last barrier in her mind. "COMMUNICATE!" At last she understood the meaning of the ultimatum.

But was it too late?

"No!" she screamed. She surged to her feet, shook a fist at the ship. "Here's one who didn't fail! I know what you meant!" She shook both fists at the ship. "See my hate!"

Against the almost tangible congealing of air she forced her way toward the now silent ship, thrust out her left hand toward the dead figures on the sand all around her. "You killed these poor fools! What did you expect from them? You did this! You forced them into a corner!"

The doors of the spaceship opened. Five green-skinned figures emerged. They stopped, stood staring at her, their shoulders slumped. Simultaneously, Francine felt the thickened air relax its hold upon her. She strode forward, tears coursing down her cheeks.

"You made them afraid!" she shouted. "What else could they do? The fearful can't think."

Sobs overcame her. She felt violence shivering in her muscles. There was a terrible desire in her—a need to get her hands on those green figures, to shake them, hurt them. "I hope you're proud of what you've done."

"QUIET!" boomed the voice from the ship.

"I will not!" she screamed. She shook her head, feeling the wildness that smothered her inhibitions. "Oh, I know you were right about communicating . . . but you were wrong, too. You didn't have to resort to violence."

The voice from the ship intruded on a softer tone, all the more compelling for the change: "Please?" There was a delicate sense of pleading to the word.

Francine broke off. She felt that she had just awakened from a lifelong daze, but that this clarity of thought-cum-action was a delicate thing she could lose in the wink of an eye.

"We did what we had to do," said the voice. "You see our five representatives there?"

Francine focused on the slump-shouldered Galactics. They looked defeated, radiating sadness. The gaping door of the ship a few paces behind was like a mouth ready to swallow them.

"Those five are among the eight hundred survivors of a race that once numbered six billion," said the voice.

Francine felt Ohashi move up beside her, glanced sidelong at him, then back to the Galactics. Behind her, she heard a low mumbling murmur of many voices. The slow beginning of reaction to her emotional outburst made her sway. A sob caught in her throat.

The voice from the ship rolled on: "This once great race did not realize the importance of unmistakable communication. They entered space in that sick condition—hating, fearing, fighting. There was appalling bloodshed on their side and—ours— before we could subdue them."

A scuffing sound intruded as the five green-skinned figures shuffled forward. They were trembling, and Francine saw glistening drops of wetness below their crests. Their eyes blinked. She sensed the aura of sadness about them, and new tears welled in her eyes.

"The eight hundred survivors—to atone for the errors of their race and to earn the right of further survival—developed a new language," said the voice from the ship. "It is, perhaps, the ultimate language. They have made themselves the masters of all languages to serve as our interpreters." There was a long pause, then: "Think very carefully, Mrs. Millar. Do you know why they are our interpreters?"

The held breath of silence hung over them. Francine swallowed past the thick tightness in her throat. This was the moment that could spell the end of the human race, or could open new doors for them—and she knew it.

"Because they cannot lie," she husked.

"Then you have truly learned," said the voice. "My original purpose in coming down here just now was to direct the sterilization of your planet. We thought that your military preparations were a final evidence of your failure. We see now that this was merely the abortive desperation of a minority. We have acted in haste. Our apologies."

The green-skinned Galactics shuffled forward, stopped two paces from Francine. Their ridged crests drooped, shoulders sagged.

"Slay us," croaked one. His eyes turned toward the dead men on the sand around them.

Francine took a deep, shuddering breath, wiped at her damp eyes. Again she felt the bottomless sense of futility. "Did it have to be this way?" she whispered.

The voice from the ship answered: "Better this than a sterile planet—the complete destruction of your race. Do not blame our interpreters. If a race can learn to communicate, it can be saved. Your race can be saved. First we had to make certain you held the potential. There will be pain in the new ways, no doubt. Many still will try to fight us, but you have not yet erupted fully into space where it would be more difficult to control your course."

"Why couldn't you have just picked some of us, tested a few of us?" she demanded. "Why did you put this terrible pressure on the entire world?"

"What if we had picked the wrong ones?" asked the voice.

"How could we be certain with a strange race such as yours that we had a fair sampling of your highest potential? No. All of you had to have the opportunity to learn of our problem. The pressure was to be certain that your own people chose their best representatives."

Francine thought of the unimaginative rule-book followers who had led the teams. She felt hysteria close to the surface. *So close. So hellishly close!*

Ohashi spoke softly beside her: "Francine?"

It was a calming voice that subdued the hysteria. She nodded. A feeling of relief struggled for recognition within her, but it had not penetrated all nerve channels. She felt her hands twitching.

Ohashi said: "They are speaking English with you. What of their language that we were supposed to solve?"

"We leaped to a wrong conclusion, Hiko," she said. "We were asked to communicate. We were supposed to remember our own language—the language we knew in childhood, and that was slowly lost to us through the elevation of reason."

"Ahhhhh," sighed Ohashi.

All anger drained from her now, and she spoke with sadness. "We raised the power of reason, the power of manipulating words, above all other faculties. The written word became our god. We forgot that before words there were actions—that there have always been things beyond words. We forgot that the spoken word preceded the written one. We forgot that the written forms of our letters came from ideographic pictures— that standing behind every letter is an image like an ancient ghost. The image stands for natural movements of the body or of other living things."

"The dances," whispered Ohashi.

"Yes, the dances," she said. "The primitive dances did not forget. And the body did not forget—not really." She lifted her hands, looked at them. "I am my own past. Every incident that ever happened to every ancestor of mine is accumulated within me." She turned, faced Ohashi.

He frowned. "Memory stops at the beginning of your. . . ."

"And the body remembers beyond," she said. "It's a different kind of memory: encysted in an overlay of trained responses like the thing we call language. We have to look back to our childhood because all children are primitives. Every cell of a child knows the language of emotional movements—the clutching reflexes, the wails and contortions, the sensuous twistings, the gentle reassurances."

"And you say these people cannot lie," murmured Ohashi.

Francine felt the upsurge of happiness. It was still tainted by the death around her and the pain she knew was yet to come for her people, but the glow was there expanding. "The body," she said, and shook her head at the scowl of puzzlement on Ohashi's face. "The intellect . . ." She broke off, aware that Ohashi had not yet made the complete transition to the new way of communicating, that she was still most likely the only member of her race even aware of the vision on this high plateau of being.

Ohashi shook his head, and sunlight flashed on his glasses. "I'm trying to understand," he said.

"I know you are," she said. "Hiko, all of our Earth languages have a bias toward insanity because they split off the concept of intellect from the concept of body. That's an oversimplification, but it will do for now. You get fragmentation this way, you see? Schizophrenia. These people now—" She gestured toward the silent Galactics. "—they have reunited body and intellect in their communication. A gestalten thing that requires the total being's participation. They cannot lie because that would be to lie to themselves—and this would completely inhibit speech." She shook her head. "Speech is not the word, but it is the only word we have now."

"A paradox," said Ohashi.

She nodded. "The self that is one cannot lie to the self. When body and intellect say the same thing . . . that is truth. When words and wordlessness agree . . . that is truth. You see?"

Ohashi stood frozen before her, eyes glistening behind the thick lenses. He opened his mouth, closed it, then bowed his head. In that moment he was the complete Oriental, and Francine felt that she could look through him at all of his ancestry, seeing and understanding every culture and every person that had built to the point of the pyramid here in one person: Hiko Ohashi.

"I see it," he murmured. "It was example they showed. Not words to decipher. Only example for recognition, to touch our memories and call them forth. What great teachers! What great masters of being!"

One of the Galactics stepped closer, gestured toward the area behind Francine. His movements and the intent were clear to her, interpreted through her new understanding.

The Galactic's wide lips moved. "You are being recorded," he said. "It would be an opportune moment to begin the education of your people—since all new things must have a point of birth."

She nodded, steeling herself before turning. *Even with the pain of birth*, she thought. This was the moment that would precipitate the avalanche of change. Without knowing precisely how she would set off this chain reaction, she had no doubt that she would do it. Slowly, she turned, saw the movie cameras, the television lenses, the cone microphones all directed at her. People were pressed up against an invisible wall that drew an arc around the ship's entrance and this charmed circle where she stood. *Part of the ship's defense*, she thought. *A force field to stop intruders.*

A muted murmuring came from the wall of people.

Francine stepped toward them, saw the lenses and microphones adjust. She focused on angry faces beyond the force field—and faces with fear—and faces with nothing but a terrible awe. In the foreground, well within the field, lay Zakheim's body, one hand outstretched and almost pointing at her. Silently, she dedicated this moment to him.

"Listen to me very carefully," she said. "But more important, see beyond my words to the place where words cannot penetrate." She felt her body begin to tingle with a sudden release of energy. Briefly, she raised herself onto her toes. "If you see the truth of my message, if you see through to this place that I show you, then you will enter a higher order of existence: happier, sadder. Everything will take on more depth. You will feel more of all the things there are in this universe for us to feel."

Her new-found knowledge was like a shoring up within, a bottomless well of strength.

"All the window widows of all the lonely homes of Earth am I," she said. And she bent forward. It was suddenly not Dr. Francine Millar, psychologist, there on the sand. By the power of mimesis, she projected the figure of a woman in a housedress leaning on a windowsill, staring hopelessly into an empty future.

"And all the happy innocence seeking pain."

Again, she moved: the years peeled away from her. And now, she picked up a subtle rhythm of words and movements that made experienced actors cry with envy when they saw the films.

"Nature building Nature's thunder am I," she chanted, her body swaying.

"Red roses budding

"And the trout thudding water

"And the moon pounding out stars

"On an ocean wake—

"All these am I!

"A fast hurling motion am I!

"What you think I am—that I am not!

"Dreams tell your senses all my names:

"Not harshly loud or suddenly neglectful, sarcastic, preoccupied or rebukeful—

"But murmuring.

"You abandoned a twelve-hour day for a twelve-hour night

"To meddle carefully with eternity!

"Then you realize the cutting hesitancy

"That prepares a star for wishing. . . .

"When you see my proper image—

"A candle flickering am I.

"Then you will feel the lonely intercourse of the stars.

"Remember! Remember! Remember!"